AS IF I WERE A RIVER

AMANDA SAINT

URBANE
Publications

urbanepublications.com

First published in Great Britain in 2016 by Urbane Publications Ltd
Suite 3, Brown Europe House, 33/34 Gleamingwood Drive, Chatham, Kent ME5 8RZ
Copyright © Amanda Saint, 2016

The moral right of Amanda Saint to be identified as the author of this work has been
asserted in accordance with the Copyright, Designs and Patents Act of 1988.

ISBN 978-1-910692-63-9
EPUB 978-1-910692-64-6
KINDLE 978-1-910692-65-3

Design and Typeset by Julie Martin
Cover by Julie Martin
Printed in Great Britain by CPI Group (UK) Ltd, Croydon, CR0 4YY

urbanepublications.com

For John

KATE

*H*ello Ani, we're all very excited today as your mum and dad have found out that you are a baby girl. I'm going to be your aunt when you get here and even though I live on the other side of the world, I'm going to make sure that we see each other as much as we can. Finding out that there is going to be another girl in the family has made me realise how important it is that you know about the women that came before you.

For a very long time, your mum and I didn't know the truth about our family, and if there's one thing that I've learnt in my life it's that if you don't know where you come from then you can never really know who you are, and where and what you should be. So to give you a head start, I want to tell you the story of our family and how your mum and I found out the truth. It all started on the night the man I was married to, Jimmy, disappeared...

•••

The hands on the clock above the cooker didn't seem to move, unlike mine as my fingers drummed and fidgeted on the table. I clenched them together in my lap. The only sound in the room was the clock ticking. Occasionally a siren wailed in the distance and once a police helicopter buzzed overhead. My eyes were as fidgety as my fingers and I couldn't keep them still. They bounced around, lighting on the wooden bread bin, the smoothie maker, the chalkboard by the door that had 'bin day' written on it, the red cardigan I'd left on the back of the chair. And back around again in the same sequence. Another half-an-hour passed. I started to feel a bit sick and shaky but strangely removed. Like I was watching myself wait. My other senses felt heightened and I could smell the food rotting in the compost bucket, hear a drip from the gutter outside that the landlord had been promising to fix for months.

'Nothing's wrong. He'll be back in a minute, of course he will,' I said aloud.

The sound of my voice in the silent kitchen unnerved me, spurred me into action. I picked up Jimmy's mobile from the kitchen table where he'd left it, and then slammed it straight back down again in frustration. Ten minutes later I knew I had to go and look for him. I grabbed my coat from the hook in the hallway and stuffed my keys and phone in the pocket as I shrugged it on. As soon as I opened the front door the wind blew it out of my hand and flung stinging needles of rain in my face.

There was a lone fox walking away from me in the middle of the road, his fur glowing orange in the streetlights. Otherwise the street was deserted. Have you seen him, I wanted to ask the fox. He stopped and looked back at me. Our eyes met then he ran off into someone's garden, disappeared down the alley at the side of the house. Another gust of wind got me moving and I turned left to go next door. I needed to tell someone, anyone, what was happening. I rang Gloria's bell. The intercom buzzed and she said a wary sounding hello.

'Glor, it's Kate. Jimmy's gone out and not come back. I'm really worried,' I blurted out.

The door release buzzed.

'Oh Kate, come on in then.' Her voice was tinny and crackly through the intercom.

She opened the door into her flat wearing her pyjamas, an aroma of recently devoured pizza lingered around her.

'So, tell me then,' she said as she walked down the hallway to the kitchen.

'Jimmy popped out to the shop for some cigarettes an hour ago and he hasn't come back. I think something's wrong. There must be something wrong.' I took a deep breath, placed my hand on my chest to try and calm my racing heart.

'Maybe he's bumped into someone he knows and stopped to have a chat, or gone for a pint with them. Or the shop was shut and he went to a different one.'

'But it's almost midnight. The pubs are all closed by now and Eddie's shop never shuts this early. Something must have happened.'

I knew I sounded crazy but the shop was only a five minute walk away, he should have been back ages ago.

Gloria gave a loud, exaggerated sigh. 'Do you want me to come and look for him with you?'

...

As we approached the row of shops the two boys that always hang out there were in their usual spot outside the fried chicken shop. They had a tan Staffie puppy with them. Jimmy and I were saving to buy our own house, so we'd rented in this area just a few months before as it was cheaper. Although our street was nice enough we were surrounded by high-rise estates and I often felt scared when I was out alone at night. I'd bought into the media hysteria about dangerous teenagers in hoodies just like everyone else. Gloria and I both looked down at the ground as we approached, but as we drew level with them I plucked up the courage to ask them whether they'd seen Jimmy.

'The bloke you is always with, yeah?' The one holding the puppy's lead asked.

The puppy, excited by new arrivals, jumped up against Gloria's legs. She gave it a quick stroke on the head then pushed it away. I felt weird that they'd noticed us before. But why wouldn't they have? We'd seen them nearly every day since we'd moved in, and we'd noticed them.

I nodded and quickly met his eyes before looking back down at my shoes again. He had glaring red acne scars all over his face.

'Nah, we ain't seen him, 'ave we Jinks. Not today anyway.'

Jinks shook his head slowly before staring off into the distance with a look of complete indifference.

'Why, lost him 'ave ya?' Acne face laughed.

I turned quickly away to go into the shop, Gloria following close behind me. The noise from the TV hit me as I pushed the door open. The sound of motor racing droned around the shop, the excited shouting of the commentator bouncing off the tins of baked beans and cans of Strongbow. Eddie the owner looked up at us from his seat behind the counter, tearing his eyes from the TV perched on a three-legged wooden stool just a couple of feet in front of him.

'Hello,' he said with a smile as he recognised us both.

'Hi Eddie.' I tried to smile back at him but it felt more like a grimace. It must have looked bad as Eddie's smile faltered before disappearing completely.

'Is something wrong?' He said.

My mouth was suddenly dry and I couldn't answer, just made a clicking noise in the back of my throat, so Gloria told him we were looking for Jimmy.

'Ah, your young man,' he nodded his head towards me, 'no I haven't seen him today.'

As what he said sank into my numb brain I found my voice again. 'Are you sure? He left home over an hour ago to come here.'

Eddie shook his head slowly. A piece of his shiny black hair fell down over his eyes. He pushed it back unconsciously.

'I'm sure. He hasn't been in today.'

'Ok, thanks.' Gloria took my arm and led me away.

The confusion I was feeling was mirrored on her face. What on earth was going on? We stood on the pavement outside trying to make sense of it. Jimmy hadn't been to the shop.

Gloria recovered first and linked her arm through mine. 'Come on, let's go home. I bet he's there now and is wondering where you've got to.'

I knew this wasn't true though. If he'd been at home he'd be ringing me to find out where I'd gone. The boys were sitting at the bus stop opposite the shop now, drinking cans of Stella and pouring some on the floor for the puppy to drink.

'Maybe he's doing the dirty on ya. Shacked up with someone else,' Acne Face called across to us.

Gloria and I hurried off without looking at them, heads down to keep the rain out of our eyes. When we got closer to our flats I could see our cat Cheddar waiting on the doorstep to be let in. Much as I love him my heart sank when I saw him there.

'Jimmy's not back then or he would have let Cheddar in.'

Gloria looked up. 'I bet he's indoors.'

I shook my head. I don't know how but I just knew he wasn't. As I pushed open the door, I could sense the emptiness of the flat before we went in. There was that stillness that lets you know no-one's home.

'Jimmy?' Glor called.

Silence.

We sat down at the kitchen table. Jimmy's phone was lying there between us and we both watched it as if any minute now it was going to tell us what was going on.

'He must have seen someone he knows,' Gloria said.

'But who? None of his friends live round here. And where would they have gone? He was tired. It's late. He wouldn't have just gone off with someone.'

Gloria put the kettle on. It was her answer for everything – a nice cup of tea. Still is.

'There'll be a simple explanation, you'll see.' She got clean cups out of the dishwasher. 'He'll be back any minute now.'

By the time we'd drunk our tea there was still no sign of him. I checked the street again from the front window. Deserted.

'He's been gone almost two hours now. Something must have happened.' I stood up then sat straight back down again. Twisted my wedding ring round and round on my finger. What the hell was going on?

Gloria and I stared at each other in silence. Neither of us knew what to do next. The hands on the clock above the cooker seemed to be whirring round now and before we knew it, it was almost three o'clock in the morning.

'Where could he be, Glor?'

She shrugged but I could see she was starting to worry too. 'Maybe you should ring the hospitals. Maybe he's had an accident.'

So I called the A&E departments at our nearest hospitals but Jimmy wasn't there.

'There's nothing we can do now, Glor. Go home and I'll see you tomorrow. Today, I mean.'

'Are you sure? I can stay if you want.'

'No, it's OK. I'll be alright.'

I went and lay down on the sofa knowing that I wouldn't be able to sleep but that if I didn't at least pretend to rest then Gloria wouldn't go home. And I really wanted her to.

She hovered. 'Ring me if he comes back. When he comes back.'

As soon as I heard the front door shut behind her I got up and went back into the kitchen. Where the hell was he? I picked up Jimmy's mobile again, scrolled through his recent calls and texts. Me, Alan, Baz, Martin. The usual suspects.

I didn't know what to do with myself so went into the bedroom and lay down on the bed thinking I should probably try to sleep. I rolled over on to my side, wrapping myself in the duvet as I went, then lay watching the rain run down the window. Cheddar padded into the room and jumped up onto the bed. He curled up in the bend of my knees and went back to sleep. The weight of him was comforting, helped me to feel a bit calmer.

I hugged Jimmy's pillow and tried to swallow the panic bubbling up inside me. Where had he gone? My phone rang on the bedside table. I sat bolt upright. It had to be Jimmy.

'Hello? Hello? Jimmy is that you?'

Noises in the background: cars, voices, a siren. But nobody said anything and then the line went dead.

LAURA

The bell above the door jangled loudly. I'd been dancing to the Bee Gees on the radio, so I quickly turned it down. When I looked up it was him again. He blushed and I felt my own cheeks burn. How silly. What was I blushing for?

'Hello again. Forget something?' I said.

He shut the door behind him and then walked towards me purposefully and that's when I knew. He was going to ask me out. Bloody hell. What would I say?

'Um, yes. I...' His voice tailed off in a croak.

I swallowed a giggle. Surely I wasn't that scary. He cleared his throat and was about to speak again when Dad came through from the back.

'Can I help you, sir?' Dad said loudly, as if he was serving up fancy food in a posh restaurant rather than running a corner shop. God he could be so bloody pompous sometimes. I willed him to shut up and go back out.

'Err, yes. I'll have a packet of Golden Virginia please. A small one.'

Dad handed it over and he scurried out the door, keeping his eyes on the floor.

'Dad! What did you have to come out then for?' I glared at him.

'What? What have I done now?' he said, poking me in the side. Then he realised.

'Surely not, Laur. He's a bit old, isn't he?'

'I don't know how old he is but he seems nice and I think he likes me, and you ruined it.'

With that I flounced off to the stockroom, got my coat and went out the back door. If he was so keen to be in the bloody shop let him look after it for a while. I slammed the door behind me pretending I couldn't hear Mum calling after me. She got on my nerves sometimes as well. They both did. When were they going to realise I wasn't a little girl anymore? I stomped up the alley and as I rounded the corner I crashed straight into him. He was standing there smoking a cigarette and I knocked it clean out of his hand.

'Oh God, I'm so sorry!' I said as he put a hand up against the wall to steady himself.

'That's OK. Not to worry, I've got plenty more.' He waved the packet of tobacco he'd just bought in the shop at me.

I smiled. 'You have. You bought two packets already today so you either smoke an awful lot or you're stocking up in case of an emergency.'

He laughed and when he did he threw his head right back. I liked that. He didn't seem so self-conscious now we were away from the shop.

'Yes, well. I think we both know that I kept coming in for something else, don't we?'

I looked down at the ground, not sure what to say, but the smile on my face was making my cheeks ache.

'Would you like to go for a walk with me?'

A walk? Not really what I had been expecting. 'Um, where do you want to walk to?'

He obviously hadn't thought about that as he didn't answer for a few seconds.

'How about along the canal to the pub down there, the Water Witch? We can have a drink. Have you got time?'

I didn't. Dad would go mad at me for buggering off for so long. But I didn't care. I also didn't mention that I wasn't old enough to drink. After all, I would be in a couple of weeks.

'That sounds lovely.' I linked my arm through his as we moved off down the street. 'I'm Laura by the way.'

'And I'm Ken. It's very nice to meet you Laura.'

•••

At the pub I didn't know what to drink. Apart from going with Mum and Dad a few times and sitting in the garden with a straw stuck in a bottle of coke, I'd never been to a pub before.

'What are you having?' I asked.

'A pint of bitter.'

'OK, I'll have the same.' It was clear I should have gone for something more ladylike as Ken looked a bit shocked. What was that fizzy wine type stuff? Babycham, that's it. I should have asked for that.

'Actually I'll have a Babycham,' I blurted out.

He smiled and I felt like he knew but he didn't say anything.

'OK, a Babycham it is. Would you like some crisps?'

'Um, salt and vinegar.'

I sat down on a bench table overlooking the canal while he went to the bar. There was only one other person out there, a man on his own who smiled and said hello as I sat down.

'Nice spot, isn't it?' He nodded towards the canal.

'It is, very nice.' I agreed. I felt so grown up having a real drink in a pub and no-one spotting that I wasn't old enough to be there.

Ken came back with the drinks and crisps and for an awful moment I thought we weren't going to know what to say to each other. But even though there was a little silence it didn't feel too awkward.

'So are you from Lancaster then, Ken?' He didn't have an accent like mine so I doubted it.

'I am. Born and bred. How about you?'

'Yes the same, I was born in the flat above the shop and have lived there all my life. Where do you live?'

'Grasmere Road. So just round the corner from the shop. I bought the house a couple of months ago.'

Owns his own house already – maybe he really is old. Or is he rich?

'So this is nice, isn't it?' He gestured at the pub and the canal.

'Yes, it's lovely. I've not been here before, have you?'

'No. It only just opened last week. When the canal was first built, this building was stables for the horses that pulled the boats. The pub's named after the boat that used to take passengers up and down the canal before the railways came along.'

'Oh, right. How come you know so much about it?'

'I've just completed a PhD in History. My thesis was on the Lancaster canal and the social and economic impacts it had on the city.'

My God, what on earth was I going to talk to him about

now? My life consisted of selling crisps, chocolates and newspapers and I'd left school at 16 with just a few 'O'Levels, although I had got A's in them all. I gulped a huge mouthful of the Babycham. The bubbles went up my nose and I started to choke. I'd never been so embarrassed in my life. He'd definitely think I was a daft cow now.

'Oh dear, are you OK?'

I managed to get control of myself but my eyes were watering and knew I probably looked a right state.

'Yes, I'm fine.' I wiped my eyes and hoped I didn't have mascara smudged across my face. 'Just went down the wrong way.'

'Pretty fizzy stuff as well, that. Don't know how you can drink it.'

'Well, actually it's the first time I've had it. It's not very nice.'

'Why didn't you stick to your first choice of a pint then?' He asked.

And before my brain knew what my mouth was doing I found myself telling him I'd never been to the pub for a drink before so I didn't know what I wanted but thought Babycham was more ladylike than beer.

He flung his head back and laughed at that and even though I was really embarrassed by how things were turning out I found myself joining in.

Ken pushed his pint over towards me, 'Why don't you try that and see if you like it any better. If you do, I'll get you one.'

I took a small sip and it was delicious, smooth and a bit toffee-like.

'Much better.' I said.

'I'll get you a half.'

...

When Ken passed over the new drink he pulled it back from my hand before I could take it from him.

'Actually, are you going to get me in trouble,' he whispered, 'are you old enough to drink this?'

I shook my head and grinned at him as he passed it over. 'Not quite, no. But I will be in a couple of weeks, so if you don't tell anyone I won't either.'

After that everything was really easy and we sat and chatted about music, films, his research, all sorts. We had two more drinks and I was quite tipsy. In fact, when I stood up I felt giddy and I had to hold onto Ken as we walked off down the tow path.

'Oops. I think I might have had a bit much,' I giggled.

'I think you might have too. Will I be in trouble with your dad?'

'Let's not tell him. Then you can't be.'

We wandered slowly back along the canal and when we went past the derelict old mill buildings Ken said what a shame it was that they'd been left to rot, especially as they were so beautiful. I'd never met anybody like him before that cared about things like that and knew so much about them. The only real date I'd ever been on was with Michael Williamson, who was in the year above me at school, and we'd gone to the pictures one night a few months ago. He was dull and obviously thought I was some kind of gullible idiot as he told me Williamson Park was named after his family and that his dad owned it. As if everybody that lived in Lancaster didn't know about the history of the park; and as if I didn't know that his dad owned the hardware shop in town.

When we got to St Peter's Road and headed back down towards the shop I didn't want the afternoon to end. I wondered if he thought I was too young and unsophisticated for him, or if he was going to ask me out again. My head was so full of wondering that I forgot to speak or listen.

'Hello, where have you gone?' Ken nudged my arm.

'Sorry, I was miles away.' As if I needed to tell him that. Sometimes I just wished my brain would engage before my mouth. 'What were you saying?'

My belly did a little somersault. I could tell by the way he was looking at me that he hadn't been put off.

We'd almost reached the end of the road so I pulled him to a stop. I didn't want to get right outside the shop and have Dad come charging out to ruin it again.

'I was wondering if you'd like to come out with me again some time?' Ken said.

'I'd love to. When?' I bit my lip, Angie was always telling me the best way to get boys interested was to play hard to get. Not that Ken was a boy, he was definitely a man.

He looked chuffed to bits though, as if he hadn't been sure I'd say yes.

'How about Friday night? We could go for a meal.'

I just stared at him. It was like he'd been beamed into my life from another planet. We never went out for meals. I'd never been to a restaurant, unless you counted the chippy that had a few tables out the back.

'That would be lovely, Ken.' My voice had gone a bit posh and it made me giggle.

He laughed too and then he leaned forward and kissed me gently on the mouth. I couldn't breath and didn't know what to do with my lips. Before I had a chance to respond he'd pulled back from me.

'Great. I'll pick you up at seven then.'

I nodded. My words had gone.

We crossed over onto Moor Lane and then we were at the shop and he stopped outside the door.

'I'll see you on Friday then,' he said.

'Yes. Thanks for this afternoon. I had a really nice time.'

'Me too. Bye.' He gave a little wave and then turned and walked away. I waited to see if he'd look back and he did, and we both grinned and waved again.

...

'Where the bloody hell have you been?' Dad said as soon as he saw me.

'None of your business.' I went straight past him out the back and up the stairs to my bedroom. The look on his face was priceless. Then I lay on my bed and thought about Ken's face, his greeny-grey eyes and wavy hair that made me think of cornflakes. He liked me. This smart and funny man with a house and qualifications liked me, and was going to take me out for a meal in two days' time.

KATE

The daylight coming through the bedroom window woke me. I must have slept in the same position all night. My arm was dead and there was dribble on Jimmy's pillow that I was hugging tightly.

'Jimmy?' I don't know why I called his name. I could tell by the quiet that I was the only person in the flat.

Cheddar was at the bottom of the bed looking at me with his big ginger eyes. Jimmy had been gone all night but I just felt numb. What was wrong with me?

I couldn't really face talking to my boss Lionel so I texted him with a small lie about a migraine. Then I made tea. As the kettle roared and rattled its way to boiling point it was if the panic inside me rose with it. I stumbled to the kitchen sink and threw up. My legs were shaking and I clung to the side of the sink to stop myself from falling; then great hacking sobs rose up and I let go and sank to the floor. Oh God, what's happened? Where is he?

I checked mine and Jimmy's phone for calls and texts, but there was nothing on either. I wanted to call Jules but it seemed too soon. I rang Jimmy's brother, Alan, instead.

'Hello Alan. It's Kate.'

After a short, shocked silence he asked what I wanted and when I told him what had happened, unbelievably he started laughing. When he managed to stop he didn't seem concerned.

'Well, I'm glad he finally had the balls to do it. We've been telling him he should leave you for years, looks like he finally took our advice.'

Then he hung up. Even though there's never been any love lost between us, I couldn't believe his reaction. I rang Baz next – he'd been friends with Jimmy since secondary school and was the best man at our wedding. If Jimmy had been planning anything he would definitely have told him. I got Baz's voice mail so left a message telling him that Jimmy had been out all night and I was worried.

Then I rang Martin, Jimmy's friend from work, and got his voicemail too. Baz sent a text a few minutes later: 'Just going in a meeting. Not seen or heard from him since the wknd. Sure he's fine & will B home soon x'

•••

I spent the day wandering round the flat going over the night before in my mind. Looking for clues. Even if Jimmy hadn't disappeared at the end of it, the night would have stuck in my mind anyway because of what happened in the restaurant. We'd been for dinner at Toni's, our local Italian. We always go when we can't be bothered to cook. It's actually called Antonio's but we like to call it Toni's, as we always do that – call places and people by pet names to pretend we knew them well. We'd never met Toni, who knows if there even was one, but it always made us laugh when we did it.

Jimmy had the chorizo and bean stew as always and I had the fish, which made me feel like I was being good even though it was cooked in garlic butter. But what made the night so memorable was that the man at the table next to us caused a scene. I first noticed him because he was so hairy. He had these massive forearms resting on the table that were covered in thick, coarse black hair, which crept down to his hands and fingers, with more sprouting from the neck of his shirt. Like the American Werewolf in London, I thought as we sat down.

You could feel the tension emanating from their table, their voices becoming louder even as they tried to control them. I tried not to listen but couldn't help myself. She just kept apologising, which made me wish I'd started listening earlier as I'd missed what she was sorry about. I kept glancing over to see what the hairy man was doing as he wasn't saying anything. He looked stunned, bewildered then hurt before he finally descended into a cold rage. At the point the rage set in he stood up from the table and tipped the food from his plate into the woman's lap and then walked out without saying a word. Despite what had happened I felt the hairy man had real dignity – as the door to the street swung closed behind him, his back was straight and he never once glanced back.

A stunned silence enveloped the restaurant. Then one of the waiters rushed over to help the woman, who sat there without moving and looking strangely serene even though the food must have been burning her legs. The buzz of conversation started to revive around the room. Everyone pretended that they hadn't seen or heard a thing. Jimmy raised his eyebrows at me from across the table:

'You better watch what you say, or that will be me doing that next,' he joked.

We laughed, and I kicked his leg gently under the table.

'As if,' I said and we tucked back into our dinner. Everything seemed so normal.

Had Jimmy meant something by that comment? It seems portentous now he's disappeared but surely he had been joking? I played this scene over and over in my mind and asked myself the same questions all day long as I haunted the flat, floating from room to room. Driving myself mad. Cheddar got dizzy as he trailed behind me and in the end left me to it. He looked at me sadly from the chair in the kitchen each time I passed, as if he could tell that something was wrong.

My phone rang three times throughout the day and each time my whole body tingled with adrenaline. It had to be Jimmy. It never was. Gloria twice, Lionel once. I couldn't face speaking to either of them. Lionel left a pissed off sounding message that I'd called in sick so close to print deadline. I felt bad about not speaking to Gloria though. I could hear the genuine concern in her voice for me and knew I should speak to her to put her mind at rest but I just couldn't.

I sent her a text instead, telling her that Jimmy wasn't home and I hadn't heard from him, but that she shouldn't worry about me. I knew she'd be knocking on the door when she got home from work.

Jimmy's phone also rang three times. I listened to the voicemails and it was his work twice, wondering where he was, why he hadn't let anyone know he wasn't going to be in. Jimmy worked for an insurance company call centre, teaching people how to answer the calls. He hated it and from the things he told me about it I'm not surprised. He basically sat and listened to his colleagues taking calls, made notes on what they did well and what they did badly and then had reviews with them to discuss it. Mind numbing doesn't even come close to describing it. He wouldn't do anything to change it though, which drove me mad. Said it's all he knows how to do and it's too late to change it – at thirty-six. It made me want to shake him sometimes.

The third time Jimmy's phone rang, at about half-past-five in the afternoon, it was Alan.

'Why are you answering Jimmy's phone? He's back then.'

'No, he's not. He left it behind when he went to the shop.'

He didn't say anything but I could tell that he was taken aback by that then he hung up on me again. He's such a rude and nasty little man, if he was my brother I wouldn't have anything to do with him but Jimmy always idolised him.

I thought I should probably eat so made a ham sandwich, but when I took a bite it was like glue in my mouth. I could barely swallow it so left the rest on the plate and just sat there. The same questions were running through my mind. What's going on? Where has Jimmy gone?

When I looked up at the clock I was surprised to see that it was seven o'clock. I'd been sat at the table for an hour and a half. I didn't really know what I'd been doing all day. I needed to do something to distract myself so I lay down on the sofa and switched the TV on. Jon Snow told me about the latest deaths of young boys masquerading as soldiers in Afghanistan; the government's austerity measures to pull the country back from the brink of bankruptcy; how they would not be swayed by the students rioting; and a whole ream of other terrible news. I switched it off and stared at the blank screen instead as

I thought about Jimmy.

We'd met at a wedding ten years before. I was a friend of Tom the groom – I went to university with him – and Jimmy was a work colleague of the bride, Jenny. We'd been sat next to each other at the meal. The only young people at a table filled with elderly, forgotten relatives. Obviously neither of us ranked very highly in the important guest stakes. Unusually for me, I'd had quite a lot to drink to get over my embarrassment at being on my own at a wedding. Couldn't even get a date let alone a husband is what all those old university friends would be thinking, or at least that's what I'd been telling myself for the past two weeks as the big day approached.

I soon forgot these thoughts though as Jimmy chatted to me and made me laugh. We talked all the way through the three courses, both of us not really bothering to turn and speak to others on the table. I noticed his long dark eyelashes and how when he laughed you could see that one of his molars was twisted in a mouth of otherwise perfectly straight, white teeth. He was tactile and kept gently touching my hand, elbow, knee, as we got to know each other. After the speeches were done and the announcement came asking us to move outside while they prepared the room for the evening, I felt a pang of disappointment. Surely he'd go off and find his friends from work now. Instead he took me by the hand, grabbed a bottle of red from the table and pulled me to my feet.

'Come on, let's get out there quickly while there's still somewhere to sit shall we?'

I laughed a yes, picked up our empty glasses and my bag and followed him out on to the sunny terrace, where he weaved round groups of people to an empty table at the back overlooking the garden. We sat there all night apart from the occasional trip to the dance floor. Some of my old university friends had stopped by the table for a chat, as had some of his colleagues, but it was as if we'd come to an unspoken agreement that we were going to stick together until the reception was over and we went back to our expensive hotel rooms to sleep it off.

The ring of the doorbell brought me back and I knew that it would be Gloria come to check on me. As I swung my feet down from the sofa, I wiped the tears from my cheeks. Gloria looked questioningly at me and I shook my head as she stepped into the hall.

'Oh Kate, you must be going out of your mind. Where could he have gone?'

I shook my head again as there really wasn't anything to say, I didn't know.

'Have you called the police?'

'No, not yet. They won't even take a report until it's been twenty-four hours.'

'How do you know that?'

'I Googled it.'

'It's almost eight o'clock now so you're not far off the twenty-four are you? Ring them now. You have to do something. What have you been doing all day? Have you tried ringing any of his friends? Or his family?'

She made my head spin with her urgency and questions, but she also made me realise that I'd been in a daze all day. She was right. I should have been doing something more instead of making a couple of phone calls and lying around reminiscing.

'I rang Alan. He thinks he's left me.'

'What? Just like that? No way.'

'Who should I call anyway? Do I ring 999?'

Gloria shrugged. 'I don't know. I haven't had to report anyone missing before.' Her face went bright red. 'God, sorry Kate. I shouldn't have said that.'

Google told us that we had to contact the local station. My hands shook as I dialled the number and I swallowed repeatedly trying to get words past the huge burning lump in my throat. Gloria gave me a reassuring squeeze on the shoulder.

'Hello. My husband is missing.'

LAURA

I couldn't think of anything else. Where would he take me? What should I wear? Even Angie, usually the font of all knowledge, hadn't been much help the previous evening.

'I wouldn't know, Laur, not having been taken to a restaurant before. Is he proper posh then?'

'Not really. Not posh, just a bit different. And nice. He's lovely.'

'Oh shut up! You going all daft on me? Remember, we don't have to be wives and mothers anymore – we've got options. We can be anything we want to be.'

'You shut up! I'm not saying I'm marrying him and having bloody babies, am I? I just asked what I should wear.' I heard her take a breath to speak but carried on talking before she got the chance. 'And anyway, what are you doing with your life that's so different? Working in the bakers and chasing after the boys that were in the year above us at school – hardly the feminist dream is it?'

Mum called me for tea then and I was glad as I didn't want to row with Angie but sometimes she could get on my nerves.

So I still hadn't decided what to wear by three o'clock and

he'd be picking me up in four hours. I thought he wouldn't take me anywhere too posh – probably the Berni Inn that had opened up in town. I wore my favourite red dress in the end. I'd made it myself, basing it on the one the woman wore in Saturday Night Fever. I loved that film. My dress was silky and floaty and I always felt so glamorous in it, and a bit daring as it was off the shoulder. Ange and I had gone all the way to Manchester on the train to get a strapless bra to go with it; there was no way I was going to wear nothing like she'd suggested, and I'd been so excited about buying sexy lingerie with my own money for the first time. I was turning into a woman.

But when I'd gone into the kitchen and shown Mum and Dad how I looked in the dress, they'd made me feel ashamed and a bit dirty. Mum called me a floozy and Dad said 'There's no way you're going out of the house dressed like that'. Sometimes he's so old fashioned. There was no way I was going to let them make me feel bad about it though. I was being taken out to a restaurant by a man with a PhD and a house, and I wasn't a child who could be told how to dress any more.

So I stayed in my room until just before Ken was due to pick me up, watching out the window for him. When I saw him round the corner I rushed out, popping my head around the door and saying bye to Mum and Dad. They were engrossed in the television and barely looked up.

'Make sure you're back before midnight,' Dad said.

I didn't even bother to reply. I was so sick of being babied. Ken was at the head of the alley when I let myself out the back door. He stopped dead when he saw me and I could tell by the expression on his face he thought I looked great.

'Hello.' I felt shy even though we'd had such a nice time the other day.

'Hello. You look lovely.' He stepped forwards and kissed me on the cheek then held up his arm for me to take. 'Shall we?'

We went to the Water Witch again. It was different this time though. Lots of people talking loudly to be heard over the jukebox. As I watched Ken pushing his way into the bar to get us some drinks my tummy felt all tight and funny. He didn't even ask me what I wanted to drink this time, just got me a half of the same beer he had. Even though Angie would have been horrified and would probably have called him a patriarchal sexist pig, or something like that, I liked it. It made me feel like we were a couple already.

We spotted a small table in the corner that was free and Ken put his hand in the small of my back as we walked over to it. It was as if every nerve in my whole body were alive in that one spot. Even though I wanted to make the most of my first date with a proper man, part of me wanted the night to be over so he'd be kissing me again.

When we finished our drinks he said we'd better go. No Berni Inn for Ken though, he'd only gone and booked a table at the posh French restaurant down on St George's Quay. When he told me, my first reaction was I didn't want to go. I wouldn't fit in. But as if he could tell, Ken grabbed my hand and laced his fingers through mine. 'Unless you'd prefer something else?'

The sun was still lighting up the sky and it was a beautiful summer evening. I really didn't want to be cooped up inside feeling uncomfortable in what I imagined was going to be a stuffy restaurant, but I also didn't want Ken to think I was an unsophisticated shop girl.

'No, that sounds lovely.'

And it was. It wasn't stuffy at all and I ate the most delicious fish I'd ever had, in a butter and wine sauce. I'd only ever had fish in batter from the chippy before, as we never had it at home. Unless you counted fish fingers and I don't think you really could.

Afterwards we walked along the quay holding hands and the moonlight was shining on the water and I thought I was going to burst. It was so romantic. Ken walked me home and outside the shop he stopped and pulled me into his arms and looked down at me.

'I had a great time tonight, Laura.' He smiled and pushed my hair back behind my ear.

'Me too.' Then he was kissing me. Not a gentle brush on the lips like last time but properly kissing me. My arms tightened around him and his hand tangled up in my hair. My breath was catching in my throat. Then the light came on in the shop and I pulled back quickly. Please don't let Dad come out here.

'I better go in,' I said but still holding onto Ken's hands. I didn't want the night to end.

'OK. Do you want to come out with me for the day on Sunday? I could drive us to the beach.'

'I'd love to.'

•••

'But we always go out for a drive to the country together on Sundays,' Mum whined.

'Well everything can't stay the same forever can it, Mum? I keep telling you I'm not a kid anymore and it's true. I've got my own life now.'

'Don't talk to your mother like that. I don't know what's got into you lately, Laura, I really don't,' Dad chimed in.

'Nothing's got into me. I'm just not a little girl anymore. I'm a grown woman and I can do what I like, and I will.' I slammed my bedroom door behind me.

Ten minutes later I was ready to go and they were still sat at the kitchen table looking all mournful. Anyone would think I was moving to the other side of the world rather than going out for the day. Really, I couldn't believe what a stupid fuss they were making.

'See ya later, then.' I smiled, hoping they'd got over it.

'Yes, OK,' Mum said. Dad didn't even look at me. Neither of them told me to have a nice time.

I sat on the wall opposite the shop to wait for Ken. The sun was lovely and warm and I was glad I'd worn my new summer dress that I'd finished the week before. It was white with deep red cherries all over it. I loved that dress when I was making it but after what happened that day I never wore it again.

Ken pulled up in a burgundy Austin Allegro, which was the car that I'd always wanted! Not that I could drive. But I planned to learn. I jumped in the passenger seat and he leaned straight over and gave me a kiss, then pulled back and stroked my cheek gently.

He drove quite fast but I felt really safe and he took me to Silverdale, a lovely little village about half an hour away from Lancaster. We wandered down through a meadow to a deserted beach that was sandy and pebbly with a sheltered spot at the base of the cliffs surrounded by rocks, where he laid out the blanket. He'd brought a picnic too and while I sat rubbing sun lotion into my arms and shoulders he got out cheeses, ham, lemonade, bread and apples. I hadn't ever met anyone remotely like him before.

After we'd eaten he packed it all away then we wandered along the shore line, our feet in the water, holding hands and not really saying much. He just kept looking at me and smiling and every time he did, that tight feeling in my tummy pulled a little tighter.

We wandered back to the blanket and lay down side by side on our backs still holding hands. Ken was quiet and seemed distant.

'Are you OK, Ken? You've gone all quiet.'

'Sorry. Just keep thinking about the new job tomorrow.'

He'd told me about it the other night over dinner. An assistant lecturer in History for undergraduate students. He must be so brainy.

'Are you nervous?'

'A bit. But not about the job itself, but that I'm doing the wrong thing. What I've always wanted to do is write.'

'Write what?'

'History books about Lancaster. But ones that aren't all dry and stuffy. Books that are true but that read like novels, capture the imagination.'

'Well, can't you still do that?'

He rolled over onto his side then and looped his arm over my waist.

'I suppose I can.' He dropped his face to mine and started kissing me. We kissed for ages and things were starting to get a bit hot and heavy, which made me really nervous and completely excited all at the same time, when a massive Alsatian dog appeared out of nowhere and stuck his snout in between us.

Ken leapt back and pushed the dog away.

'Oi, get out of it,' he said but the dog came straight back, tail wagging like mad, and started licking Ken's hand. Then a woman appeared from around the cliff, the dog's lead trailing from her hand.

'Rufus. Get back here.' The dog looked at her but didn't go. 'I'm so sorry. He's just very friendly, and nosy!'

'That's OK,' I said stroking Rufus's head.

She called him again then picked up a stick and threw it into the water. And he was off. Ken and I lay back down again. This time I rolled onto my side and put my arm over him. It felt like I was being really forward but he looked up at me and smiled.

'What about you? What do you want to do?'

'Me? Oh, I don't know. I wasn't brought up to think like that. I was always going to work in the shop when I finished school.'

'But there must be something you want to do.'

I shook my head. He really did come from a completely different world. Why did there have to be something? Not everybody could be something, some people did just work in shops. He could tell I was feeling uncomfortable and changed the subject. Not long after that the sun went in and it started to feel chilly so we packed up and went back to the car. Then we went in the pub in the village for a drink. Ken really liked to go for drinks, I'd noticed. When we got back, we pulled up opposite the shop and there was a policeman waiting outside.

I looked over at Ken, fear making my tummy tight this time. 'What's he doing there?'

'I'm sure it's nothing. Come on, let's go find out.' He walked round and opened my door, helping me out. He kept hold of my hand as we walked over to the policeman.

'Are you Miss Beasley? Laura Beasley?' He sounded so official and I couldn't figure out what on earth I'd done wrong. Unless it was about drinking in pubs before I was eighteen.

'Yes, yes I am. What's the matter?'

'I'm afraid there's been an accident, Miss. You need to come to the infirmary. Your parents are there; they've been involved in a car accident.'

I stumbled into Ken. 'Oh my God, are they OK?' Saliva gushed into my mouth and I was sure I was going to be sick but I managed to swallow it. Ken put his arm around me.

'Come on, I'll drive you there.'

'Are they OK?' I almost shouted at the policeman.

'Best if you get to the infirmary as quick as you can, Miss.' And that was when I knew. They weren't OK.

KATE

The ringing tone droned endlessly in my ear and I was about to hang up when she answered breathlessly.

'Hello?'

'Hi Jules.'

'Hiya, are you OK?'

'Oh Jules, something's happened to Jimmy.'

I told her about the meal out, the trip to the shop and his vanishing into thin air. The fact that Gloria and I went to the shop only to discover that Jimmy hadn't been there. That he'd left his phone behind. That I'd checked our online banking and he hadn't used his card. She listened in silence until my voice trailed off.

'God, Kate. You must be going out of your mind. What's he playing at? Make sure you give him hell when he gets back.'

'But where could he have been? Why wouldn't he have come back from the shop if he was coming back? Something must have happened to him. Can you come home?'

She didn't answer straight away.

'Please Jules. I'm scared. What if he doesn't come back?'

'Of course he will. And I can't just come rushing back can I. It's not like I live round the corner.'

'I'll pay for your flight. Please.'

'What about my job? And you're overreacting – he's an inconsiderate shit for doing this but there's no need to panic. He'll come back soon.'

'Laura didn't come back. Lots of people don't. Please.'

'Laura? Laura who?

'Our mum, Laura.'

'God, what are you bringing her up for now? What's she got to do with anything?'

'She disappeared.'

'No she didn't, she ran off with another man. Anyway, that was years ago and has nothing to do with this. Have you rung Alan or Baz?'

'Yes, neither of them know where he is. And I've reported him missing to the police.'

I could tell that changed her mind. That's when she realised it was serious. That Jimmy had genuinely gone missing.

'OK, I'll try and get some time off and book a flight. I'll let you know when I'll be getting there but if anything happens ring me.'

•••

When Jules arrived the next evening, Jimmy had been gone for almost forty-eight hours and I wasn't sure what was going on, how I felt, or whether any of it was real. Most of the time it was if I was watching everything going on around me, like I wasn't really a part of it. One of the first things Jules asked once she'd established that Jimmy hadn't returned since she called from the airport is whether I'd told Ken. She'd come over all Zen since moving to Japan and was badgering me into getting back in touch with him. The importance of family, future regrets, you name it she'd been saying it almost every time I spoke to her.

Considering the situation, I would have thought she'd give it a miss this time though.

'No I haven't and I have no intention of doing so, so leave it.'

'Oh Kate, you have to stop punishing him you know.'

'Jules, I mean it. Just leave it.'

In the kitchen, Gloria was sat at the table. They looked curiously at each other. They'd never met before as Jules had been in Japan for almost two years without a visit home. Jimmy and I visited her about three months before we moved to Battersea and I'd loved it but Jimmy had acted all weird. It was the furthest from home he'd ever been, the first time he'd ever been outside of Europe, and it seemed like his sense of self had been left at Heathrow waiting to be picked up again on the way home, with all its Englishness intact, unsullied by the weird foreignness.

After a cup of tea, made by Gloria of course, and a curious skirting around the issue that had brought Jules rushing back from Japan, she went off to have a shower and Gloria went home. While I waited for Jules, I thought about Ken. I hadn't seen him since I left home to go to university twelve years before. We'd spoken on the phone intermittently for the first couple of years after I left but we had nothing to say really. The years of resentment that had built up inside me made it harder and harder to be civil until in the end I stopped calling. After Laura left it was like he couldn't be bothered with us. If he wasn't at work, or at the functions that go along with being a university professor, then he was drinking whiskey in the chair by the fire. Brooding and angry all the time. He basically abandoned us to Granny, let her bring us up, and I don't remember him ever showing any interest. So I lost interest in him. I stopped trying to get him to notice us.

After I left university I didn't give him my new number or

address and told Jules or Granny not to give it to him either so the only news he ever got of me was second hand, through them; if he even asked, which to be honest I think is doubtful. I didn't invite him to the wedding. Jules was upset and kept insisting that I should; Granny said the same thing but I was adamant. It was my wedding and I didn't want him there pretending that he cared.

Jules appeared. Pink, warm and steamy from the shower. She always has it so hot I don't know how she can bear it scalding her skin. When I got a waft of the minty shower gel that Jimmy always used, it set me off crying again. The panic was never far away and I could see Jules was scared, thought I might be hysterical and didn't know how to handle it. I'd always been the strong one, the one in charge, making the decisions, looking after the pair of us, so despite how scared I was about Jimmy that motherly instinct kicked in when I saw her frightened face and I forced myself to get control.

Once I'd calmed down we sat and talked quietly, going over events again. I'd told this story so many times already, to Jules, to Alan, to myself over and over, then to the police. The police were the least concerned. They took the details but basically said that as Jimmy was a grown man he was entitled to leave without telling anyone and they would have a chat with his family, friends, work colleagues, and see if they could find anything out. But that would be about it. Gave me a reference number and told me to send in information of who Jimmy knew and they'd contact them. That I should contact the Missing People charity too, as they would be able to offer some assistance.

Jules stared at me with her mouth hanging slightly open. 'They can't mean that. They have to do something. Obviously something's wrong. Jimmy wouldn't leave like that without saying anything.'

'What do you mean leave without saying anything? He wasn't leaving me. Why does everyone keep saying he's left me? Something must have happened when he went to the shop.'

Even as I said this my mind questioned it. Alan said he was glad Jimmy had left me. Now Jules was saying he could have left too.

The doorbell rang. My stomach lurched. It must be the police. It was almost midnight and apart from Gloria, who'd just gone home to bed, no-one else would be coming round at that time of night. Maybe they'd found him. I rushed to the front door but I didn't want to open it, not sure I could face whoever was there. But then I realised it could be Jimmy, he'd left his keys behind so he'd have to ring the doorbell to get back in. I somehow convinced myself in a matter of seconds that it really was Jimmy so pulled the door open with hope rising like the sun in my heart.

What I saw was so different from what I'd been expecting that I couldn't quite take it in. Not Jimmy. Not the police. An old man. Shoulders hunched against the wind and the rain that had been relentless for days. His straggly grey hair plastered against his head, rain carving its way down the furrows and wrinkles in his face. Neither Jules nor I said a word. We just stared. He stared at us and it was as if we were frozen, no-one knowing what to do. He broke the silence.

'Please, can you help? Sorry to knock on your door but I saw the light on. I need money for the bus to get to the shelter.'

What is he talking about? Money, shelter, my brain couldn't make sense of it. But then I took in his clothes. Old, dirt-encrusted, ragged. He was homeless and knocking on the door asking for money. In all the years I had lived in London that had never happened before. Why was he here now? Was it something to do with Jimmy?

'I just need two pounds. I wouldn't normally do this but the rain, it's too much, I need to get inside for the night.'

His voice was gravelly with a bronchial undertone. He looked pathetic and I wondered if Jimmy was somewhere needing help too.

'Wait here, I'll get you some money.'

I went back into the house to find my purse and Jules followed me after pulling the door shut.

'What are you doing Kate? You shouldn't give him money. He'll keep coming back asking for more.'

I ignored her and opened the front door. He was still there in the same position, with the same sad look on his face. I gave him ten pounds but he tried to give it back.

'No that's too much, I just need two.'

I pushed it back into his hands. 'Take it.'

He looked me in the eye and screwed it up in his grubby hand. 'Thank you, bless you, thank you.'

Then he scurried away, head bent down so the rain didn't go in his eyes. I stared after him, not caring that the rain was soaking me. When he got to the corner and waited to cross the road he stood there, his head rocking from side to side constantly as if he couldn't quite believe that there was nothing coming in either direction even though he'd looked just a second ago. That's when I realised I'd seen him before. I'd seen him standing on the kerb for up to ten minutes before doing this. Jimmy noticed him first when we were having brunch one morning in the pub up by the bridge. He laughed at him and I'd told him off, said I couldn't believe he could be so cruel. He looked ashamed then and apologised but another time I was going past the same pub on the bus and Jimmy and Alan were sat outside having a drink and the homeless man was on the kerb in front of them. They were laughing at him, calling things out.

I shut the door and went back into the living room where Jules was curled up on the sofa. 'I feel so helpless, Jules. What's going on? Where can he be?'

It didn't make sense. He wasn't in any of the local hospitals, nobody saw him when he left the house, so where had he gone?

'Have you checked his phone?'

'Of course I have. Nothing out of the ordinary.'

'What about his email?'

'No, I haven't looked. I'm not sure what the password is to get into his laptop.'

'Well, let's try.'

We sat on the sofa with Jimmy's laptop waiting for the login screen to appear. What would he use as a password?

'Try Manchester United.' I said.

'Nope, that's not it. What's the team he plays with called?'

'God, I don't know. It's all blokes from his work though so maybe something to do with the company name?'

'Which is?'

'Platinum Insurance. Actually, I don't think they'd use that. We'll never guess it. We'll have to take it somewhere and get them to reset the password for us.'

'OK, so let's make a list of people to speak to tomorrow who might have some idea of where he could be.'

'But I don't get it, Jules. Why would he just pretend to go to the shop and go off? Something must have happened to him.'

'Oh, Kate. People do the strangest things sometimes. Especially men.'

'I emailed the police a list of people to contact so maybe we should start with them.'

'OK, and they are?'

'Shirley and Alan.'

Jules wrinkled her nose. Neither of us were very enamoured

of Jimmy's mum and brother.

'Baz. You remember him – he was best man at the wedding.'

Jules nodded.

'Martin – a friend from work who he plays football with – and Linda, his boss.'

'OK, so we have a plan. Let's go to bed. And you never know we might not even need it as Jimmy might get home any moment.'

Once Jules was settled in the spare room I lay in bed thinking back over the last few weeks. Did Jimmy seem like something was wrong? I didn't think so. We'd had a bit of a row about money but we had that quite regularly, he thought I worried too much about the future and I didn't think he worried enough, but we'd been fine since. Well, at least I'd thought we were. Maybe he was a bit quiet but I'd been really busy at work so pretty tired and quiet myself. Actually, he made that special meal for me the night after the money row.

I'd been to a spinning class on the way home and came in all sweaty and red faced and he'd bounded through from the kitchen and hustled me into the bedroom.

'I have a surprise for you and you're not allowed to come into the kitchen or the living room until I say so.' He was excited and even though I'd been looking forward to a shower and then curling up on the sofa with some trashy TV it was infectious.

'Ooh, what kind of surprise?'

'I couldn't possibly say. But you need to shower and then get dressed up as if we were going out for a fancy meal.'

'Are we?'

'No more questions. Get ready then wait here until I come to get you!'

Then he hurried off. I knew it was his way of apologising for the argument and that he would be cooking something nice for dinner. Well, heating something nice up. His cooking skills didn't stretch far and I had an inkling it would be M&S Gastropub food. It usually was. But still, it was the thought that counts.

After a long hot shower, I dried my hair and put make-up on then went to the wardrobe to choose a dress to wear. He was going to so much effort to make things right again I knew I should do the same. I chose a silky kimono-style dress that I knew he loved me in. With big bold blocks of blue, black and white he said it made my eyes stand out and showed my curves to perfection. The V at the front was cut so low, almost down to my waist, that I always wore a lacy vest top underneath it when we went out but seeing as we were staying in I decided to leave it, and my bra, off. I slipped it off the hanger and as the silk slid down over my body I started to feel excited at the prospect of the make-up sex I knew the evening would culminate in. I didn't put on any underwear at all but slipped my feet into my black, patent Kurt Geiger heels.

When Jimmy came to collect me from the bedroom he whistled, slipped his hand inside the kimono and cupped my left breast as he kissed me hard. We nearly didn't eat the dinner but in the end he pulled back and led me into the living room where he'd laid the table with candles, lit the open fire and draped fairy lights along the top of the fireplace. After the food – Moussaka and salad as usual – we had chocolate fondants then make-up sex on the rug in front of the fire.

It was all lovely. Nothing was wrong. There was no way that Jimmy would have pretended to go to the shop and just leave me. Definitely not. Something must have happened to him. It must have.

LAURA

I couldn't believe they were gone. Mum was dead by the time they got her to the Infirmary and Dad died the next day. I sat by his bedside holding his hand until he went. But he didn't wake up. I didn't get to speak to him again. The last time I spoke to either of them was to have a stupid row about me going out with Ken. It was a lorry that did it. The driver had a heart attack at the wheel and ploughed straight into them.

I rang Granny and Granddad from the payphone in the Casualty department and their next-door neighbour drove them over from Clitheroe. I didn't tell them until they got there though. Granny crumpled when she found out her only daughter, her only child, was dead, and Granddad had to grab her and hold her up. Then they both sat grey-faced in the corner of the waiting room. Granny kept saying 'But she was only forty-two.' Over and over again. Dad's parents were both dead as he was older than Mum, eleven years older. And I didn't even think to ring Uncle Ray, his younger brother, until a couple of days later. We'd seen quite a lot of him and Auntie Jean when I was little but then they'd moved away, somewhere down South, and we hardly ever saw them after that.

Granny wanted me to go back with her and Granddad

and stay with them but I wanted to go home. Ken wanted to stay with me and ring his new job to say he couldn't go in but I wouldn't let him. Imagine how that would have looked. But he came straight round after work every night and stayed with me all weekend. He stayed over and slept in my single bed with me but we didn't even really kiss. He just cuddled me while I sobbed and stroked my hair until I cried myself to sleep.

Granddad sorted out all the arrangements and a couple of weeks after they died, on a sunny Friday morning, they had a joint funeral. They were cremated, that was what they'd wanted apparently. All of the neighbours were there, Uncle Ray and Auntie Jean came too and apologised that their kids, Gary and Karen, weren't there, but I couldn't even think who they were. Angie didn't come. She'd run off to Manchester with Terry Daniels, who was one of the boys we went to school with. They were fed up with small town life she told me on the phone. She also said now that Mum and Dad were dead I was free so I should come and join them. I put the phone down on her and I've never seen or heard from her again.

After the service we all went back to the Brittania pub, which was just up the road from the shop. Dad went there a lot and Mum used to go with him occasionally. Dave ran the pub and came in the shop every morning for his paper. His wife, Sheila I think her name was, put on a buffet spread and they'd closed the pub for us. It was the first time I'd been to a funeral.

Ken had taken the day off work and he stayed by my side the whole time. I don't know what I would have done without him. After everyone had gone and we were walking back down the road towards the shop I pulled him to a stop.

'Take me somewhere else, Ken. I don't want to go back there.'

So he took me to the Water Witch and we sat outside by the canal and it seemed such a long time since we'd sat there together that first time.

'You don't have to go back there, Laura. You can come home with me. Stay at mine for a bit until you feel up to going home.'

'But what about the shop? I need to open up again soon as we're not making any money.' It was then that it really hit me that it wasn't 'we' anymore but 'I'. I wasn't making any money. What was I going to do? I couldn't manage the shop and live there all by myself.

'Don't worry about that now. You can leave it for a few more days.' Ken rubbed my thumb with his and I stared down at his hands. Without Ken I wouldn't really have anyone, apart from Granny and Granddad, and they were miles away.

'It's my birthday the day after tomorrow,' I said without looking up. 'My eighteenth.'

'Well that settles it then. You are coming home with me, and despite everything we are going to celebrate your birthday this weekend.'

•••

The next morning I woke in Ken's double bed and he wasn't there. When I got up and went downstairs he wasn't there either and I was shocked to see that it was nearly midday. His house was quite big, well anything seemed big to me after spending my whole life cooped up in the poky flat above the shop, and it needed decorating. I wandered out into the garden, which was wild and overgrown. It was terraced and the first level, which was the smallest, had a patio and seats built into the wall. The next level was wider with long grass and wildflowers everywhere, and the level after that was about fifty feet long and had a couple of apple trees, a pear tree and a plum tree. There was an old shed right at the end with a mouldy armchair in front of it.

I wandered back into the kitchen and made a cup of tea and some toast then went back out to the patio and sat there enjoying the sun and the sound of the birds. It was as if the funeral had lifted something from me. Obviously I was still upset but I didn't feel as if my life was ending anymore. A knock on the window upstairs startled me and when I looked up Ken was standing in the bedroom waving at me. I waved back and waited where I was, I knew he'd come and join me.

He kissed me on the lips as he sat down next to me and for the first time since the accident I felt my body coming back to life. That tight feeling that I had in my tummy every time I'd seen Ken on those first few dates was there again and I leaned over and kissed him again. He pulled away and laughed at me.

'Maybe we shouldn't get too carried away out here where the neighbours can see.' He nodded up towards the windows next door where anyone could look straight down onto us.

'Let's go inside then.' I stood and pulled him to his feet and led him into the house. I felt a bit shy and embarrassed but at the same time I could tell that he liked it so I felt powerful too. I'd never felt like it before. I led him right up to the bedroom and we lay down on the bed together. He rolled on top of me and started kissing me really hard, his breathing was heavy and his hand slid up under the t-shirt and he stroked my breast. I gasped. Nobody had ever touched me there before. Ken pulled back.

'Are you OK?'

'Yes.' I buried my face in his neck, 'It's just that I've never done this before.'

'I know you haven't. And we don't have to do it now either, if you don't want to.'

That's when I knew that I loved him. He was so kind and thoughtful, and smart and sexy, and I felt so lucky that he had chosen me.

'I want to.' I said and pulled his mouth back down onto mine.

•••

On the morning of my birthday Ken woke me with breakfast in bed. He'd made real coffee, which I'd never had before and was delicious, as well as bacon, eggs and toast. He wasn't the greatest cook and it was all a bit overdone but it was so sweet of him. He'd also put some of the wildflowers from the garden in a glass on the tray. I felt like I really was a woman now.

Everything I'd ever been told about sex wasn't true. Although it had hurt a tiny bit to start with, there wasn't blood everywhere after. I didn't think I'd had an orgasm but I'd definitely had a sort of warm feeling down there and it was all really lovely.

'Happy birthday, gorgeous,' Ken said as he placed the tray on my lap. Then he leaned in and kissed my neck. My body reacted instantly and my erect nipples pushed against the t-shirt I was wearing. Ken laughed and brushed my left nipple with his thumb and kissed me on the mouth before backing off.

'Breakfast first,' he said then disappeared from the room.

He was back a couple of minutes later with his own tray and we sat together in bed munching away and drinking our coffee. When we'd finished he took the trays away and I leaned back and watched the birds playing in the apple trees while I waited. He soon reappeared with an armful of presents, which he dropped on the bed all around me. I giggled with excitement at the sight of all of them. I've always loved birthdays. The presents were all in shiny red paper with gold ribbons and bows – I couldn't believe he had made so much effort for me. Tears welled and I suddenly felt really guilty for being so happy when Mum and Dad were dead.

'Hey, come on,' Ken said, 'No sadness today. They would want you to have a nice birthday.'

He was right. Even though we'd been having silly arguments recently, we'd always got on well and had lots of fun together. They'd always made a big fuss of my birthday. Parties every year when I was little and for my sixteenth they'd hired a boat for the day and we'd gone up and down the Lune. When we were right out in the countryside and there was no-one around, Dad had gone really fast. Mum was pretending not to laugh and hitting him on the arm, saying 'Bill, you are awful. Slow down.' But we knew she loved it really.

I smiled up at Ken. 'Sorry, I know they would.'

He picked up a big squashy present and handed it to me. 'Open this one first.'

Tearing at the paper like an over-excited toddler, I gasped when I lifted it out. A beautiful jumper with an orange and brown zig-zag pattern, tight-fitting with a V-neck and big bat-wing sleeves. Really fashionable and completely gorgeous.

'Oh, Ken. I love it.'

He smiled shyly as if he hadn't been sure I would. 'Good. Go on, open the others.'

He'd really splashed out and as well as the jumper he'd bought me a long woolly crochet scarf in a rainbow pattern, a bottle of Anais Anais perfume, which had only just come out and smelt so fresh and flowery I sprayed it on straight away. Then there was a huge box of chocolates from that fancy shop that had been in the high street forever. Ange and I used to stand outside sometimes after school and gaze in the window wishing we could eat everything in there.

I flung my arms around Ken and kissed him all over his face.

'You shouldn't have got me all this!'

'Why not? You only turn eighteen once and you deserve it after everything that's happened. You deserve it anyway.'

'Thank you, thank you, thank you!' I kissed him again and this time he kissed me back. He whipped off my t-shirt, pushed me back on the bed and made love to me in the middle of all the wrapping paper, presents and bows. It was amazing.

Afterwards Ken drove us to Granny and Granddad's. They tried to be cheerful for my birthday, and Granny had baked a cake, but I could see that their hearts weren't in it. We stayed for a couple of hours then Ken said we had to go as he had planned a surprise for me. Him and Granddad walked out to the car together and I stayed behind and gave Granny a cuddle.

'He seems like a lovely fella, Laur. Make sure you hold onto him,' she said.

In the car I kept on at Ken to tell me where he was taking me but he wouldn't give anything away. We drove back to Lancaster but instead of going to his house he drove up to Williamson Park and got the blanket and picnic basket we'd taken to the beach out of the boot.

'When did you sort that out?' I asked. Amazed again at everything he was doing to make the day special.

He tapped the side of his nose with his index finger, 'I am a man of many talents, Laura. And I can't possibly tell you how I manage to be so great.' With that he grabbed hold of my hand and led me off to a secluded spot up behind the memorial where he laid the blanket out. We sat down on it and from the basket he pulled two glasses and a bottle of champagne! Well he said it was a cheap version of champagne but it was the poshest drink I'd ever had.

He poured us a glass each and then toasted me. I took a big sip and the bubbles tickled my nose but it was much nicer than that Babycham stuff. We sat there and looked out at the view across to the mountains in the Lake District. I loved summer in Lancaster when the relentless rain that we had for most of the year finally eased off for a bit but I really loved this view in the winter when the snow was on the mountains.

Before I'd finished my drink, Ken took the glass out of my hand and told me to shut my eyes. I couldn't believe that there was going to be more surprises.

'OK, now you can open them.'

Ken was on one knee in front of me holding open a small box. A box with a ring in it.

'Laura, I love you. Will you marry me?'

I didn't know what to say. I'd only known him for a few weeks. My eyes flicked from his face to the ring and back again. He looked so hopeful, and I did love him too. Definitely I did.

I giggled nervously. 'Yes. Yes, I will. I'd love to.'

He looked so relieved and he grabbed me and pulled me into a big hug then took the ring, a small pearl on a gold band, his grandmother's I later found out, and put it on my finger. I gazed at it in awe. I was getting married.

KATE

I called the police as soon as I got up in the morning but there was no news of Jimmy. I called the hospitals again too but he hadn't been admitted and they wouldn't tell me whether any men suffering from amnesia had. He could have been there but just not know who he is. Things like that happen all the time. Most of the people I spoke to were abrupt with me but one nice lady at St Thomas's said that as I had reported him missing if any men were brought into A&E suffering with amnesia the police would be informed and if he matched Jimmy's description then they would get in touch with me.

Jules was still sleeping so I sat in the kitchen with a cup of tea. Wondering if he'd had an accident and lost his memory. Did he leave me? Does Alan know where he is? What did I do wrong that he would want to leave me without even telling me? But I felt sure he wouldn't have done that, we were happy. Or were we? Had he run off with another woman? He could have been killed or kidnapped. I remembered the things Jules and I told ourselves about Laura after she'd left. We made up stories about how she'd been kidnapped by pirates, trapped in an enchanted forest, turned into a mermaid. Anything other than she'd just upped and left us, because mums that loved their little girls didn't do that, did they? And we had to make up something as all we'd been told was 'she had to go away'. No explanation as to why or where, she just had to. We hadn't been told what had happened for years.

Jules came into the kitchen, bleary eyed and still half asleep.

'Any news?'

'No.'

She sat down opposite me.

'Where can he be?'

'I don't know. I spoke to the police this morning and they said no news. They said again that I should speak to the Missing People charity, that they send out nationwide alerts.'

Jules didn't say anything and we just sat there blankly for a moment, both feeling bewildered and unsure of what you do in these situations.

'I don't want to go on TV.' I said.

Before she could answer my phone rang and I jumped up, ran to get it off the table in the living room. Jimmy! But it was Lionel. Again. He still thought I was sick so I had to tell him what was really going on.

'Lionel, hi.' I went into the bedroom, shut the door and got back in bed under the duvet, sat cross legged staring out into the garden. God, I didn't want to start telling people. It made it seem really real.

'Kate, hello. Are you OK?'

'Um, yes. No, er, something's happened Lionel.'

'What?'

'It's Jimmy. He's been missing for the past couple of days.'

'Missing? What do you mean?'

'Gone. He went to the shop and he didn't come back.' My voice cracked on the final word.

'What? When?

'Wednesday night. I met him after work and we went for drinks and dinner then it was after that.'

'Oh my God. Kate. Are you alright? Shall I come over?'

'No, no, it's OK. My sister is here; she came home from Japan.'

'Right, OK.'

'So, I don't know yet when I will be back at work.'

'No, of course you don't. Don't worry about that. What have the police said?'

'Not much really. I had to send them details of his friends and family and they will check with them but that's about it.'

'Really? Surely not. Shouldn't they be searching for him? Having press conferences to alert people?'

'Well that's what we thought but no. They said he's a grown man and he can do what he likes.'

'God, that's terrible. I can't believe that.'

I didn't know what to say. I couldn't really believe it either. After a few seconds of my silence, Lionel cleared his throat.

'OK, keep me posted Kate and I'm sure everything will be OK.

As I ended the call I wished I could be so sure. Jules came in straight away so she'd obviously been waiting outside the door for me to finish on the phone.

'Who was that?'

'My boss.'

'Have you told him?'

'Yes, just then. He thought I was sick until now.'

'I looked at the Missing People website. You should call them. You don't have to go on TV but they send out pictures and details of Jimmy and do other stuff.'

'Don't you think we should talk to Alan and Jimmy's mum first?'

Neither of us wanted to. They took against me, and by extension Jules, right from the start for some reason.

'Granny. Do you think I should tell her?'

'Yes. But maybe not yet. Let's see what we can find out from the Rude Family first.'

I gave a ghost of a smile at mine and Jules's nickname for Jimmy's family.

•••

The train pulled into the station and I searched for Jimmy among the faces of the Saturday shoppers and lunchers that flooded in. Was he wandering around confused, no idea of his name, address, his entire life? I bit my lip to stop myself from crying. As if Jules could tell I was struggling she held my hand and gave it a little squeeze, I squeezed back without looking at her. If I looked I'd definitely cry. I knew she'd be really worried too. Jimmy had been a part of her life for as long as he'd been in mine. And they got on well despite her initial disapproval, which was of me and the way things happened when Jimmy and I got together rather than of Jimmy himself.

As the tube train sped north I remembered her uncharacteristic primness about it all. After Jimmy and I had been out on a few dates together, I invited him over to my flat for dinner. I lived alone even though it was expensive. I wasn't suited to sharing with groups of people, I'd learnt that at university. Besides, most people of my age thought I was boring as I didn't go to clubs, get drunk or take drugs, so there weren't exactly flocks of friends wanting to live with me anyway. Nobody ever really came round. Of the friends I'd had at university the only ones I'd kept in touch with were Tom and Claire. I met Tom occasionally and we went out for drinks or dinner, but he never came to my place and I never went to his, and Claire didn't live in London so we had phone calls, emails and occasional weekend visits.

Jules came over whenever she was around but that wasn't often. She was always off somewhere doing something, yoga retreats, backpacking, bar work, living in a camper van. She couldn't seem to stay in one place for very long.

So as I prepared for Jimmy's first visit I knew that I would have to hide my teddy bears. At twenty-three I'd known for years that I was too old to have them out still anyway but they kept me company. They'd kept all the secrets that I'd whispered to them over the years. I'd had them all since I was little; I couldn't remember a time when they hadn't been there. I felt guilty as I put them on the back of the top shelf in the airing cupboard. Back where it was dusty and dark. I tried to tell myself I was being silly, they were just teddy bears, but their shiny round eyes looked at me with reproach as I shut the door. I think I knew even then that they weren't coming out again.

I felt a good kind of nervous as I prepared the food for the evening. I loved to cook and I was excited to have someone to cook for. I'd bought new sexy underwear too, just in case we ended up in the bedroom at the end of the night. Even though we'd slept with each other that first night at the wedding we hadn't done it again since. We both agreed we should wait, that we'd been drunk at the wedding and shouldn't rush into it but see how things go. We'd been out six times in the space of three weeks and although the sex hadn't been wonderful that first night I was keen to try again. I really liked Jimmy, and he seemed to really like me so I hoped that this might be the night that we got close again.

When he knocked on the door my stomach did a little somersault and I quickly checked in the mirror and put a slick of lip gloss on as I went to the door. The food was ready – I'd made it all in advance so that it could just be heated up when he arrived and I wouldn't have to spend too long in the kitchen. He looked nervous and excited when I opened the door and thrust flowers and wine at me before I'd had a chance to say hello. Then we both laughed and relaxed as he followed me through to the front room. I put the flowers in a vase and came back from the kitchen with two glasses of wine to find Jimmy perched on the edge of the sofa looking uncomfortable.

'What's wrong?' I asked as I sat down next to him and handed him one of the glasses.

'Look, Kate, I know we've only known each other a few weeks and been out just a few times but I've got to tell you something.'

I nodded, a feeling of dread rising in me. How could I have got it so wrong? He was going to dump me, like everyone else did. Not that there had really been anyone else. Just a few dates with people that either ended in feeble excuses at the end of the night or unreturned calls if they hadn't got the courage to tell me to my face that they weren't interested.

'Well, before I'd even met you at the wedding I'd had a date arranged with this woman, a friend set it up ages ago. And I went on it. And, um, I went out with her again last week as we'd said we'd see how things go.'

His voice faltered as he looked at me. I knew that what I was feeling would be showing on my face. I was gutted, my stomach clenching and lurching again but not with excited anticipation this time. I felt sick. I'd really thought I might finally have found someone who liked me, would care about me, want to spend time with me. I heard him swallow before he started to speak again.

'She phoned me this evening just before I left to come here. Wanting to arrange another date. And, I, I, sort of told her that I couldn't as I'd met someone else.'

This wasn't what I'd expected to hear and I didn't know what to say. So I didn't say anything. Jimmy's face had gone red and he kept looking down at the floor rather than at me.

'So, um, I suppose that what I'm trying to say is that, er, I think it's been going great and um, I was sort of hoping that you might think that too.'

He smiled then, his crooked molar poking out of the left side of his mouth. I stared at him, stunned by this announcement after expecting to be dumped.

'Well, do you?'

'Yes, yes, I do.'

He took my glass off me and put it down next to his, which he'd been taking huge gulps from, then leaned forward and started to kiss me. I knew it had been a good idea to buy that underwear and put the teddy bears away. He was a wet and slobbery kisser but I didn't mind. I found it quite exciting. When his mouth moved from mine down to my neck, his hand went up under my top and he pushed me back on the sofa. His knee pressed against my groin. I moaned softly. I was so sick of being alone, not having anyone's body touching mine. I didn't want to wait anymore and see how it went.

'Jimmy?'

'Mmm?'

'Let's not see how it goes any longer. Why don't you move in?'

He stopped kissing me and the pressure from his knee was removed. He leant back and looked at me. I thought I had gone too far that he was going to back off then. But he smiled slowly.

'Really?'

I nodded then pulled his mouth back down to mine.

Jules squeezed my hand again then and the past receded, and

I was back in the train. We were nearly at our stop. I had been lost in this memory for a long time.

•••

As we walked down the road to Shirley's house my hands were clammy and my stomach clenched up tighter with each step. I hated going there. Hadn't been for years. They were just so awful. They didn't treat Jimmy that nicely either but he didn't seem to mind. He'd been going there to visit them for the past five years or so without me. I refused to go in the end. What was the point of sitting there either being ignored or subtly, and sometimes blatantly, insulted? We weren't bonding, getting to know each other, becoming a family. So I stopped going. They never came to our house and Jimmy went to see his mum once a week and saw Alan for nights out. I suddenly wondered if any of this was true. Is that really where Jimmy had been going? Or had he been lying? Is that why Alan was so sure he'd left me?

I needed some Dutch courage to face them after all those years. I stopped.

'What?' Jules asked.

'I can't go there yet. I haven't seen them in years. Let's go and have a drink, steady my nerves.'

'It's a bit early isn't it?'

'No, it's almost midday. The pubs will be open. Let's walk back. There's one up near the station.'

Jules has never taken much convincing to have a drink so we retraced our steps and went into the pub. It was deserted, just a bar maid cleaning glasses who smiled and said hello.

'You're keen,' she said, 'I've only just opened the door!'

We both gave her tight little smiles and she could tell instantly that we weren't up for a laugh and her professionalism kicked in. 'What can I get you?'

I had a large white wine and Jules a bottle of lager. We sat down as far away from the bar as we could get then were mostly silent as we drank and geared ourselves up for the Rude Family visit.

•••

Shirley's face crumpled into its usual scowl when she opened the door and saw me and Jules there.

'Oh, it's you. I figured you'd turn up sooner or later.'

'Hello Shirley. Can we come in?'

'I suppose so.'

Jules pressed her hand into my back from behind me and I knew she'd be biting her tongue so as not to react to Shirley's rudeness.

Shirley finally opened the door wider and walked away back into the house. She didn't say anything but we took this as an invite and followed her in. She was like a pudding as she waddled down the hall in front of me. Soft and rolling, so deceptive. She looked like someone you see when they show old footage of women scrubbing their stoops. Salt of the earth, keeping this country great. But she wasn't. She was vicious and vindictive and as I remembered all the hateful things she'd said over the years I just wanted to turn and run. But I wanted to find out what had happened to Jimmy more, so I didn't.

In the dark and overcrowded room, I sat down on the sofa without being asked. Jules looked round in horror as she sat next to me. The already small room had been made minute by being stuffed to the gills with large, dark wooden furniture – cabinets mainly, which in turn were overflowing with dreadful china ornaments. Babies' faces with one tear on one cheek. Ladies with parasols and flowing gowns. Teddies, cats, bears, birds, elephants, plates, mugs, bells. It was overwhelming and the smell of dirt and dust caught in my throat.

'Well what do you want then?' Shirley said as she brought her pudding frame to rest in an oversized armchair that was just a slightly lighter shade of brown than the cabinets.

'Is Alan here?'

'He's in bed. He's on nights this week.'

Nights? I didn't even know he was a shift worker. I thought he worked in a phone shop. I suppose he could have changed jobs ten times though for all I knew. I never asked about Jimmy's family and he never told me.

'How can you not be worried that Jimmy's gone missing? Do you know where he is?' I hadn't meant to blurt it out like that and I could feel Jules's surprise next to me and Shirley's hackles rise opposite me.

'Like I told the police when they rang this morning, no we don't know where he is. But we're sure he's fine. And I don't know why you've got the police involved.'

She puffed herself up in indignation, she reminded me of one of those frogs whose throats swell when they get ready to croak, and I could tell she was going to start with the usual rant about how unsuitable I am for Jimmy.

'You wouldn't know Missy as you never come to visit, not that we want you to, but we have lots of talks round here. Our Jimmy should never have married you in the first place and we've been telling him that all along. Hopefully he's finally taken some notice.'

'So, what, he's left me? Is that what you're saying? Did he tell you he was going to?'

She was smug. Her eyes gleamed with malice. 'No, he didn't tell me that. But that's what I reckon he's done. Me and Alan'll be seeing him before long I'm sure. He's not a baby he can go wherever he likes without getting your permission.'

'How can you be so sure? He wouldn't be leaving me. We were happy. And even if he was, why would he do it like this, why wouldn't he just talk to me about it?' I was shouting by the end of this sentence and Shirley was just gearing up to start shouting back at me when Alan burst through the door in just his pants.

'Oi. What the hell's going on? What are you doing here shouting your mouth off?' He pushed my arm as he went to stand guard by his precious mother. As if she needed protecting from anything or anyone. 'Don't you think you can come here and talk to Mum like that.'

Jules jumped to her feet then, my guard dog it seemed.

'She didn't talk to her like anything. You two are the ones that are bloody rude. Kate's husband, your brother and son,' she jabbed her right index finger at them both, 'has been missing for three days and I think she's quite entitled to come here and find out why you two don't seem to be bothered.'

It was descending into a shouting match and I couldn't deal with it. I believed them that they didn't know where Jimmy was but I didn't believe he'd left me. I didn't believe he'd be in touch with them in a few days. The reason they didn't seem bothered is because they weren't. They didn't care about Jimmy, never had, and I could always see that even if Jimmy couldn't, or wouldn't. The only thing they cared about was themselves and each other. It was weird the two of them living there together, spending most of their time together. Alan was a grown man of thirty-five and had never left home.

'Come on Jules, let's go.' I grabbed her arm and pulled her with me.

Alan followed, his pasty white gut hanging over the waistband of his pink panther boxer shorts. I stared. Why was he so fat? Jimmy said they went to the gym together twice a week.

'And make sure you don't come back.'

Alan's voice was cut off as Jules slammed the door behind us and we hurried away from the madness that is the Rude Family house.

LAURA

The day after he proposed Ken took me to meet his mum, Una. If I thought Ken was different and like nobody I'd ever met before then Una was even more so. Her shock of long white hair was twisted into an untidy bun at the back and lots of it escaped and framed her ruddy face. She was gardening when we arrived at her front gate, wearing a long, white calico dress, and her feet were bare. I'd never seen anyone her age in a dress like that and definitely never gardening in it. There were muddy smudges all over it and on her face and hands. She pulled me into a hug as soon as Ken introduced us. Mum and Dad weren't cuddly people and I stiffened at first but then I relaxed and hugged her back fiercely.

'Laura, welcome. I'm so glad to meet you. Ken's not stopped talking about you for the past few weeks.'

He blushed and looked down at the ground. He seemed younger with his mum there.

'Thank you. It's good to meet you too.' I pulled back and smiled at her.

She dropped her arms from around me and took my hands. 'I'm so sorry about your parents.'

I blinked back the tears that were always ready to come. But

I wasn't going to cry today. We had happy news.

Una quickly changed the subject telling Ken to make us all a drink while she got cleaned up.

Ken and I took the tea tray to the back garden, which hadn't had nearly as much love and attention as the front, and we sat and waited for Una to reappear. My hands were slick with nervous sweat. She'd only just met me and we were going to tell her we were getting married.

'Is she going to be alright about this, Ken?'

He took my hands in his and I wished I'd had the chance to wipe them on my skirt.

'Of course she is. She'll be very happy for us.'

We waited in silence. I wished I'd had the chance to tell Mum and Dad. But would it even be happening so quickly if they hadn't died?

Una reappeared in a bright pink smock and matching trousers. She reminded me of the Indian women that Ange and I used to see on our shopping trips to Manchester. What would Mum and Dad have made of her?

As soon as she sat down Ken just blurted it out: 'We've got something to tell you. We're getting married!'

His happiness and excitement was bubbling away in his voice. My heart seemed to skip a couple of beats as I looked at him. Why had he chosen me?

Una jumped straight back up again and came round to fling her arms around both of us. She pulled us into her and laughed. 'I knew it! Congratulations!' She gave us both a squeeze. 'How lovely. What lovely, lovely news after such a sad time.'

•••

We got married four weeks later. I didn't want a big deal so soon after the funeral so it was just in the town hall. Granny and Granddad were my only family there and I had two friends, Shelley and Karen who I'd been at school with. They'd come into the shop to see me when they'd heard about the accident. We'd been quite pally at school but I hadn't seen them so much since leaving as Ange didn't like them. She didn't come, even though I'd popped round to see her mum and asked her to let Ange know. Ken had lots of people there. Una of course, and her brother, his Uncle Michael. His best man was Raymond, who he'd been at university with, and then he had colleagues and other friends. All of their names escape me now but there were about twenty of us in all.

The reception was in the function room at the Water Witch. I'd wanted it there as it felt like mine and Ken's place. Every now and then I was sad about Mum and Dad but on the whole it was a lovely, happy day. I wore a dress I made myself. It wasn't a proper wedding dress but an ivory version of the red one I'd made that I wore on my first date with Ken. I had daisies in my hair and carried a bunch of yellow chrysanthemums. Everyone said I looked beautiful, and for the first time in my life I really felt it.

The next day Ken bundled me into the car really early in the morning and wouldn't tell me where we were going no matter how many times I asked. We headed south and after driving for a few hours we came off the motorway at the Birmingham junction. I couldn't help feeling disappointed that we were going to Birmingham for our honeymoon. I'd never been there before but it didn't sound like a very romantic place to me. But we just stopped for lunch then we carried on further down south. All the way to Devon.

We finally stopped in a wooded valley with towering cliffs on both sides, at a hotel called The Hunters Inn. And that's where we stayed for the next five nights. It was so beautiful.

Like most honeymooners we spent a lot of time in bed but when we weren't making love we walked for miles and miles. A path led from the hotel to a rocky beach through ancient woodlands, past tumbling rivers and waterfalls. There were paths out along the cliffs where we watched the sea crash against the rocks hundreds of feet below us.

One afternoon we lay down on a grassy ledge in the sun and Ken fell asleep. I looked up at the sky, watching a gull float on the wind and I suddenly felt really panicked. Perhaps I had as little control over where I was going as that gull, only able to go where the wind took him. Or like the river we'd walked by so many times since arriving, which veered off in different directions depending on the obstacles it came across on its path to the sea. That was me. One moment I was Mum and Dad's little girl working in the shop, the next an orphan, but at the same time becoming a grown, married woman. Married to a university lecturer and just about to start living a life I had no idea how to live.

Tears rolled silently down my face and dropped into the grass beneath me. Ken snored slightly, the gull screeched and I wiped my eyes with my sleeve. No point lying around crying about it.

UNA

Dearest Kate,

It's been so long since I've seen you. I wish you would come to visit. But maybe it's easier this way. It's not so hard to tell you in writing as it would be to say it to your face. Or maybe it is. First I just have to say how sorry I am. I shouldn't have done it. I should have told you about it a long time ago. You and Jules. You're like my daughters rather than granddaughters. I think that's where the problem lay. I can see that now...

KATE

We looked through the info on the Missing People's website. Unbelievably it said that over two hundred and fifty thousand people go missing in the UK every year. I thought it would be impossible to vanish now, everyone was always going on about us being the most watched and tracked nation in Europe. Well, where were all these people then? Where was my husband?

There was a whole section dedicated to Missing Adults, which told us that many of the grown men who go missing don't want to be found. Was Jimmy one of them? Didn't he want to be found? How could he do that to me? Too cruel. I couldn't believe he would do that. Something must have happened to him. But what? Where did he go? He was going to the shop. That's all he was doing. That's definitely what he was doing.

'Oh God, Jules. Where is he?' I was hyperventilating. Seeing all of this information made it real again. Sometimes it seemed like I was floating along in a dream and I was calm then. But then something would pierce the bubble and suddenly I'd be panicking.

'We'll find him, Kate. We'll find him.' Jules crooned as she rocked me and I sobbed helplessly in her arms. When I managed to pull myself together Jules got a pad and pen out of her bag and started writing in it.

'What are you doing?'

'Writing down everything we know so far and trying to make some sense out of it.' She scribbled away and I just stared at her hand moving backwards and forwards across the paper. When she'd finished her notes said:

- Jimmy went to the shop on Thursday November 24 at about 11pm to get some cigarettes.
- Should have been back in 15 mins tops. Been gone 3 days.
- Didn't take his phone and hasn't used the bank a/c
- Alan and Shirley think he's left and will contact them soon
- He didn't contact his work to say he wouldn't be in
- He hasn't been admitted to any local hospitals
- The police are checking with Alan, Shirley, Baz, Martin and Linda

'So what good does this do?' I asked.

'It helps me to think things through to look at it like this. You should try and speak to Baz now.'

I dial Baz's mobile number. Voice mail.

'Baz, hi. It's Kate. Not sure if the police have called you yet but I've officially reported Jimmy missing now. Can you call me please?'

Jules watched me from the doorway. 'OK, Martin next.'

I got Martin's voicemail again too and I was about to leave him a message when my mobile started ringing in the kitchen. Jules ran to get it.

'It's a London number.' She thrust it as me as she ran back into the living room.

I froze as a tingling feeling rose from my feet and rushed up my body. Was it Jimmy calling from a phone box?

'Hello?'

'Hi, is that Kate?' A woman's voice said.

'Yes, speaking. Who's this?'

'Hi Kate, this is Linda from Platinum Insurance.'

'Oh, hi Linda.' Jimmy's boss. 'The police have called then?'

'Yes, I've just spoken to them. I'm very shocked by the news but I can't imagine how you must be feeling. How awful.'

Awful? A bit of an understatement. 'Yes,' I managed to reply eventually.

'I thought it strange he'd been absent for the past two days with no call from him.'

She said this as if she thought I should be apologising for not calling on his behalf. Maybe I should have but it didn't occur to me to tell her. Jimmy's work had not really been a high priority in my mind.

'So do you have any idea where he might be, or does anyone there?' I knew even as I said it that she wouldn't. Nobody did.

'No I'm afraid I don't. As for the rest of the team, I just don't know. But the police are coming in to see us on Monday and talk to everyone here that knows Jimmy.'

'Oh thank God. It seemed like they weren't even interested and weren't going to do anything at all.' The relief of something finally being done made my knees buckle and I collapsed onto the sofa, a half sob, half hysterical laugh escaping from me. Jules took the phone from me and went off into the kitchen with it. I lay back on the sofa wiping my eyes and swallowing the sobs down. Crying all the time really wasn't helping. I could hear the murmur of Jules speaking and suddenly I was completely exhausted. I wanted to curl up into a ball and sleep it all away. Wake up to find that Jimmy was there all along, sleeping soundly next to me. We'd have breakfast in bed then spend a lazy day with the papers and a movie, hiding from the wintry rain.

Jules appeared in the doorway. The dark smudges under her eyes making the rest of her face look even paler than usual. Neither of us had got much sleep since Jimmy had vanished and she'd also got jet lag to contend with. She lay down next to me on the sofa and put her head on my shoulder.

'She said the police are going in on Monday to speak to them all.' Jules said.

'I know.'

'So that's good. They are doing something then.'

'Hmm.'

We both lay there with our own thoughts for a while until Jules got up rubbing her arms.

'I'm cold. I'll make a fire, you ring Martin.'

In the kitchen I sat at the table and redialled Martin's number.

'Jimbo.'

'No, it's Kate.'

'Oh, hi Kate. You alright?'

I told him what had happened.

'Bloody hell. Bloody hell. Kate, oh God.'

I didn't believe he could be that good an actor so I was convinced Jimmy hadn't concocted a plan with him.

'Martin, I'm so scared. What could've happened to him? How did he seem at work this week?'

'I've been on holiday all week. The last time I saw him was at footy. I went to footy practice last Saturday morning and then we went on holiday. We've been in Scotland all week for Claire's sister's wedding.'

'Oh yes. I'd forgotten you were going there. Is Claire there?'

'No, she's at the gym. She'll ring you when she gets back though.'

'OK. Where do you think he could be?'

'God, I don't know. Let me ring some of the lads from the team and see if they can shed any light on this. But he wouldn't just disappear like that, would he? Something must've happened.'

'That's what I think. But everyone else seems to think he's left me.'

'Of course he hasn't. There'll be an explanation for this. Maybe he's had a bump on the head or something and is confused.'

Things didn't seem quite so bad when I got off the phone from Martin. He made me feel much better, more positive about how things were going to turn out.

Jules was lying in front of the fire gazing at the ceiling. 'What did he say?'

'He's been away all week so hasn't seen him. But he doesn't think Jimmy would walk out like that. He thinks he's probably confused somewhere.'

Jules sits up 'He could be. He could also have planned this and left you but not had the balls to tell you about it. He could have been attacked and be hurt somewhere. He could be dead.'

'Shut up Jules, don't say that.'

'What? I'm just saying there are many possible explanations for this. We can't rule any of them out.'

'Well Martin's going to speak to the others from the football team and see if anybody knows anything.'

'Is there anyone else you can think of that we can ring to see if they've seen him?' She jumped as the fire popped and crackled loudly and an ember flew out onto the hearth.

'Not really, no. I looked through his phone but there's nothing on it – no messages or calls from anyone apart from who we've spoken to.' I sat down next to her rubbing my arms, it really was freezing.

'Maybe he had another phone.'

'What? Of course he didn't. Why would he have two phones?' I shook my head violently as if I could shake her words out of my ears.

'If he was keeping secrets from you. Maybe he was having an affair and he's run off with the other woman.'

'Just shut up, Jules. Why are you saying things like this? He hasn't been doing anything like that. Something must have happened to him.' I ran into the bedroom, slamming the door behind me, and flung myself face down on the bed. Why was this happening? I couldn't believe that she was saying all of these things. Why did everyone seem to think he'd left me? Why wasn't she supporting me?

There was a knock on the bedroom door.

'Sorry, Kate.'

'Just leave me alone, Jules.'

As always she ignored me and came and sat on the bed. She put her arm around me. 'I'm sorry. I know it's hard to hear that. But we do have to think of all the things that could have happened.'

'He wouldn't do that. Everything's been fine. He's not having an affair.'

Jules nodded but I could tell she thought it was the most likely scenario. After all, if something had happened to him when he went to the shop then he'd have been found by now, surely.

'Let's contact that Missing People charity now. You need to let them help, Kate.'

It was as if everything was going along at breakneck speed around me. Jimmy went to the shop, he didn't come back then next thing he's a missing person and everyone's acting like he's never coming back.

'OK. Come on then.'

Jules stood up and pulled me up from the bed then we sat at the kitchen table with the laptop. The doorbell rang as we were reading through the information on the site about what they could do to help. We looked at each other with questions in our eyes. Jimmy?

I rushed to the front door and Jules stood in the kitchen doorway watching as I pulled it open. It was Gloria.

'Hiya. Any news?'

She walked past me into the hallway and I couldn't help scanning the street before I shut the door. Nothing. Not a soul around. I shook my head.

'We're about to contact the Missing People charity,' Jules said.

Gloria nodded. 'Right. Good idea.'

'We've been to see his mum and brother this morning and I've spoken to Martin. They don't know anything.'

We all sat down around the kitchen table and Jules pulled the laptop over in front of her to carry on reading. 'Right, there's a form to fill in. It says depending on whether they think he's vulnerable or at high risk it can take up to three days for them to get back to you.'

Gloria put the kettle on and Jules went through the questions filling them in. She knew most of what they asked herself but read them all out loud to us, along with the answers she was filling in.

'It says will you be willing to talk to the media?'

I shook my head. Images of distraught families sitting at tables while crowds of journalists fired questions at them filled my head. I couldn't handle that.

'I think you should. Or I could do it for you.'

'Do you really think they'd be interested?' Gloria said.

We both looked up at her but she busied herself squeezing

teabags into mugs.

'I mean from what the police have said it seems like lots of men disappear and you never see anything about it on the TV do you? Only kids.'

She was right. How could that be OK? Why was a man disappearing when he pops to the shop not as important? Now I wanted to speak to the press. How dare they not care?

'Put yes.'

'OK, and if they do want to come and speak to you then I'll be with you.' Jules scrolled down to the next question.

Gloria and I sipped our tea listening to Jules go through the questions as she filled in the answers. The hot mug in my hands was comforting and my eyes were heavy and gritty as I leaned up against the radiator.

'What's Shirley's maiden name?' Jules asked.

'Um. I'm not sure. Is it the same as Alan's surname?'

Gloria looked back and forth between us, confused. 'Is Jimmy's surname not the same as Alan's?'

I shook my head. 'No, different dads.'

I racked my brains trying to remember what Jimmy told me about his dad, who he didn't know and had never met. And Alan's, also long gone. Was Shirley married to Alan's dad?

'I don't know her name. Why do they need that?'

Jules shrugged. 'Let's leave that blank then. What was he wearing?'

'Um. He had on a pale blue shirt, a dark blue jumper and black trousers. And his coat. A black, woollen trench coat.'

I could see him again, walking out of the door after he'd kissed me on the forehead.

'They want a photo of Jimmy, Kate. What one do you want to give them?'

We searched through the pictures on the laptop and I chose

one of him taken at Christmas the year before when we'd gone out for a meal with Martin, Claire and another couple from Jimmy's work. Jimmy looked happy in the photo. Surely things hadn't changed so much since then that he'd have just walked out and left me without saying anything?

•••

About a week after that, Cheddar's paw patting the side of my face woke me. It was still quite early and there was a chainsaw grinding in my head. Jules was still in bed; I could hear the dainty snores she always does when she's had too much to drink. There were four empty wine bottles on the kitchen table and one in the recycling box. No wonder I felt so rough. But for the first time since Jimmy had gone I hadn't gone to bed and just lay there running through the million different scenarios I'd come up with to explain his absence. I didn't even remember going to bed.

While the kettle was boiling I took two painkillers, drank a pint of water, then fed Cheddar. On the Missing People website I checked the forum. We'd been looking through it last night but I hadn't been brave enough to speak to anyone. There were so many people out there looking for their friends and family that had vanished. Most of the missing were teenagers who had run away, or just lost touch with their families after leaving home. I hadn't seen anyone else yet whose husband, or wife, went to the shop and didn't come back. On Jimmy's profile page his happy face smiled out at me. Where are you Jimmy? What are you doing? He must be somewhere. Someone must know where he was.

Another day sitting in the flat waiting for some news to arrive and going through the same old questions was not going to help. For the first time in weeks the sun was shining through the window and I wanted to get outside. I was going to look for him. I knew he must be in London. He didn't have much money on him when he left and hadn't taken any from the bank so he couldn't have gone far. He'd never hitch a ride and, anyway, where would he be going?

While I waited for my toast, I printed off fifty of the Missing posters and went to wake Jules to see if she wanted to come with me. Grunting at me she rolled away and buried her head under the duvet so I ate my toast, got dressed and went alone. There were already plenty of posters up in our neighbourhood. I needed to go further afield. Where could he be? Where might someone have seen him?

The streets surrounding his work seemed to be a good place to start so I headed for the City. Jimmy's office was opposite Liverpool Street station so I put them up around there and spoke to shopkeepers, pub staff, street cleaners. Doing something and the weak winter sun shining from the pale blue sky helped me to feel more positive so I decided to walk. I'd go through the park and then along the river. Maybe I'd see him. Maybe he'd be wandering around lost and confused and I'd find him and could take him home.

The steady beat of my feet as I cut across the park distracted me from the hangover and the constant questions and I got a bit of a march on. I stopped to get a bottle of water in the cafe by the pond and handed the woman another poster as I couldn't see the one I'd given them the other day anywhere.

'Please can you put this up?'

After reading through it she looked up but didn't really meet my eye. 'He your fella is he?'

I nodded. Please don't let her start asking me loads of questions.

'Well, much as I'd like to help love we can't be putting stuff like this up around the caff. Depresses people, it does.'

I snatched it back out of her hand and stuffed it in my bag and as I walked away I could hear her mutter about my rudeness. My rudeness? On the way to the City I stopped in a couple of petrol stations to see if they would put posters up. No. Company policy. Sorry. When I got up near Westminster Bridge I decided to leave the river as it was getting packed with tourists, so I cut through Southwark and London Bridge instead. On Borough High Street I saw a man blatantly fly posting – I had thought they only did that at night – so asked him to stick Jimmy's poster up too.

'Sure. Quick give it here.'

As he plastered it up I could see his eyes scanning it and reading that Jimmy had been missing for almost two weeks now. He looked at me with sympathy in his bloodshot eyes.

'Hope you find him.'

He gave my arm a pat then he was gone, lost in the crowds heading into Borough Market. Jimmy and I used to walk to Borough Market sometimes, though he wasn't a big fan of walking. He wasn't a big fan of Borough either – just for tourists he always said – but even though I'd lived in London for a decade by then a big part of me still felt like a tourist and I loved to go and do things like that. The last time I'd talked Jimmy into going there it was a summer's day and we'd bought hot pork rolls with stuffing and apple sauce then sat in the garden of Southwark Cathedral and eaten them.

Walking over London Bridge the views always take my breath away but that day I wasn't impressed. It was lunchtime and hordes of city workers were streaming in both directions around me. I scanned their faces to see if Jimmy was among them. Maybe if he had lost his memory something in his subconscious would bring him to this area as he'd worked there so long. I couldn't see him though.

When I walked up through Gracechurch Street the crowds of office workers were even denser, I felt like I was being buffeted from all directions and my scanning of faces was becoming frantic. People were starting to look at me with alarm and give me a wide berth. I stopped at the entrance to Leadenhall Market. Took some deep breaths. But the laughing and loud voices from the men in suits smoking outside the pub clamoured inside my head. Stop! Stop! Stop shouting!

When the group of four men nearest to me looked at me in shock I realised I'd said it out loud, shouted it out loud.

'Alright, love. Calm down.' They all sniggered and I heard someone say 'Nutter alert.'

I spun round quickly to get away from them but banged into someone behind me.

'Watch where you're going!' The woman spat out as I grabbed her arm to stop us both from falling.

'I'm sorry. Sorry.' I said. But she didn't even look at me as she flung her shiny blonde hair in my face and flounced off into the market. I could feel the eyes of the men outside the pub on me, wondering what I was going to do next, so I pushed through the crowds, desperate to get away from them. It was a bit quieter on Bishopsgate so I stopped and leant up against a fence surrounding a building site, waiting for my heart to stop racing. What was I doing? Did I really expect to find Jimmy just wandering around in the City? But it was better than sitting at home doing nothing. But what was I doing? I still had most of the posters in my bag.

The crowds on the street made my mind race with questions even more than it did when I sat at home so I decided to go in a cafe and have a drink and wait out the lunchtime rush before trying some of the shops back in Leadenhall Market. Jimmy used to talk about going there in his lunch break all the time.

Surely someone there would recognise him when I showed them the poster. I headed for the Pret-A-Manger opposite Liverpool Street station but it was packed when I got there. I just needed somewhere quiet to sit down for five minutes, where could I go?

'Kate?'

The voice was vaguely familiar but I couldn't quite place it. When I turned it was a woman with a short black bob and very red lipstick. I knew her face too. But I still couldn't place her.

'I thought it was you,' she said, 'what are you doing here? Is there any news?'

Linda. Jimmy's boss.

We moved out of the doorway and she put her Pret paper bag inside her massive purple leather one then looked back at me with a question on her face. I didn't know what to say. She'd think I was mad if I told her I was looking for Jimmy. So I grabbed the posters out of my bag and waved them at her, much less mad obviously.

'Hi Linda. No, there's no news. I have these posters and I thought I'd come and put them up around here near to some of the places that Jimmy used to go.'

'Oh, I see.' She looked like she thought it was a stupid idea. It probably was but I had to do something. But she held her hand out and gestured for me to give her some.

'I'll take some for you and get them put up in my gym and the pub we always go to for work dos.'

She was the first person that'd been nice to me all day and it was too much, so the ever-imminent tears welled up again and spilled down my face.

'Thank you.' I managed to croak at her as I wiped the tears away with my coat sleeve.

'Oh, Kate. You poor thing. Look come with me, you look frozen. Let's go and sit down somewhere quiet for a bit so you can warm up and tell me what's been going on.'

She pulled me away from the wall by my elbow and led me down past the station to a cafe on Brushfield Street. It was busy but not overwhelmingly so and we were taken straight to a window table looking out across the square.

'My treat. What are you having?' Linda said as we sat down. Then looked a bit flustered as if she thought she shouldn't have said treat under the circumstances.

In need of comfort I opted for a hot chocolate and Linda joined me. I excused myself once our order had been taken and in the ladies ran my hands under the hot tap to warm them then wiped the mascara smudges from under my eyes. Back at the table the hot chocolates were there and Linda had her hands cupped around hers.

'So?' She said as I sat down. 'Tell me everything that's happened in the past two weeks.'

It poured out of me and I talked without stopping for at least five minutes while she nodded encouragingly and seemed like she really cared. And Jimmy always said she was such a hard-faced bitch. When I'd finished she handed me a napkin and I wiped my tears then blew my nose.

'His family certainly sound charming. Have they always been like that?'

'Right from the very first time I met them.'

'And the police are not going to do anything else at all?'

'No. He's not considered vulnerable or at risk so that's it.'

'But surely the fact that he disappeared like that points to foul play?'

Hearing it put like that frightened me. Even though I'd been saying all along that something must have happened to him, actually calling it foul play out loud put a completely different light on it. Maybe it would be better if he had left me. But if he'd left me then where had he gone and why had he walked out of his job too?

'They seem to think not. Apparently lots of men just go like that. Have enough of the life they've got so leave it all behind.'

Linda was visibly shocked by this. She was obviously a woman whose life was ordered, planned and on a certain trajectory. People in Linda's world didn't walk away like that. But did they in mine? Is that what he'd done? I gulped down the panic as, for the first time, I faced up to the fact that I might never find out what had happened to him. I might never see Jimmy again.

'I find that astounding,' she said as she started to put her coat on. 'I'm afraid I have to get back now, Kate, but if there's anything at all that I can do to help let me know.'

'Um, there is something, actually. Do you know what's going to happen with Jimmy's salary? Will it just stop?'

Embarrassed to be so crass as to bring up money, I looked down at the table. But without Jimmy's salary I couldn't meet all of our outgoings. I'd have to break into our savings to pay the rent. Linda busied herself doing up her coat.

'Er, I'm not sure what will happen. I'll get someone from HR to get in touch with you, OK?'

I nodded and thanked her for listening. After paying the bill at the counter she gave me a wave and I watched her walk off down the street until she turned the corner.

Something had deflated in me and I no longer felt like it was worth putting the posters up. Everyone was so consumed with their own busy City lives that they probably wouldn't even see them, and if they did they wouldn't care. I ordered another hot chocolate and wished I had something stronger to put in it. The hangover was kicking in again and I could really do with a hair of the dog. I thought maybe some food would help so ordered a cheese and ham croissant but it was cloying and stuck to the roof of my mouth so after two bites I pushed it to one side.

Outside the streets were getting quieter as everyone headed back to their desks and I went into the pub further down the road towards Spitalfields Market, The Gun. It was still quite busy but there were plenty of seats and I ordered a large house white and sat in a corner near the fire. At the first sip my stomach retracted as if it was going to reject it but by the third I was feeling decidedly more human.

The wine brought back some of my earlier determination and by the time I'd finished I'd decided to go back to Leadenhall and see if any of the market traders or shop staff did know Jimmy and would put up my posters. What harm could it do?

Before I left I went to the bar again.

'Hi,' I said as the barmaid stepped forwards, 'could you do me a favour and put this up somewhere?' I held up a poster for her to see.

As she read it I could see recognition dawning on her face.

'You know him?' I leaned over the bar towards her.

Her eyes moved from the poster to meet mine as she took it from my hand.

'Yes, he comes in here quite a lot. Usually at lunchtimes. But I haven't seen him for a while.' She looked down to the other end of the bar and called to the barman there. 'Aaron, you know this guy too don't you?'

He took the poster. 'Yeah, I know Jimmy.' He looked at me. 'Who are you?'

'I'm his wife. When was the last time you saw him?'

'A couple of weeks ago I reckon. He was in at lunchtime.' He looked at the barmaid and their eyes met briefly before they both looked down.

'Who was he with?' I thought maybe if it was someone from his work I could go and speak to them.

'On his own. He often came in on his own at lunch and just chatted with us. I think Bronwyn was on that day with me.'

I looked back to the barmaid who was now pulling a pint for the man standing at the bar next to me. 'Are you Bronwyn?'

She shook her head. 'Nah, Bronwyn doesn't work here anymore. She left last week.'

It was if someone had popped my bubble of hope with a pin. I stuffed the rest of the posters back in my bag. 'Well, please can you put that up? Someone might be able to help.'

•••

The sun had disappeared behind a blanket of grey and white cloud when I got outside and it was much colder than earlier. I buried my face in my scarf as I walked back along Bishopsgate. Up ahead I could see a girl wearing a sandwich board walking backwards and forwards outside an office building. An 'end-of-the-worlder' as Jimmy and I always called them. But as I got closer I could see that she wasn't religious. She was working for the Missing People charity, wearing a sandwich board with missing posters on it. By the time I got to the crossing I could see Jimmy's face smiling out at me and for a moment it filled me with hope again that someone would recognise him.

I crossed and ran up behind her, grabbed her shoulders and spun her round. Her startled face pulled back from mine as she tried to get away from me.

'What are you doing?'

Up close I could see she was more girl than woman and her small white face was pinched with cold and fear.

'He's my husband. Jimmy.' I pointed at her board. 'Have you seen him? Has anyone seen him?'

The girl stepped back from me, blinking fast. 'What? What are you talking about?'

'The man on your board. He's my husband and I don't know where he is.'

I shouted this as if volume could make her understand. I could feel heads turning in our direction but nobody came to her assistance. Tears were running down my face and I wanted to shake her – surely she must know something about Jimmy. She was walking around with his face plastered across a sandwich board – how could she not know anything? She was looking around frantically now.

'Look leave me alone. You need to speak to the people on the call centre. Not me.'

A man in an expensive blue and white pinstripe suit appeared behind her. 'Is everything OK?' He asked, looking first at her then at me.

She nodded but still looked warily at me. I knew I must look mad and I was about to explain to him about the board and Jimmy when I realised there was no point. None of these people gave a shit. So I simply turned and ran. I slowed down to a walk once I could no longer feel their eyes boring into the back of my head but went straight past Leadenhall market and into Monument tube station. What was the point of trying to get anyone in the market to help me? Nobody cared that Jimmy was missing. I would have been better off staying at home and waiting for news for all the good that going into the City had achieved.

LAURA

When I threw up for the third morning in a row I knew I was pregnant. Ken had already left for work, and for the past week I had been sleeping straight through him getting up. Exhausted and not knowing why. But now it all made sense. Everything was happening so fast. Could I be a mum at just eighteen? Did I even want to be? I really wanted to speak to Ken but he didn't like me phoning him at work. I wanted my mum. I wanted her brisk no nonsense way of dealing things. I wanted her to tell me that everything was going to be OK. As I had no idea if it was.

I needed to speak to someone about it so I rang and booked a doctor's appointment for later that afternoon. But I was very confused all day while I waited – one minute frightened and feeling very alone, the next excited and overwhelmed.

When Ken finally arrived home from work he was full of chat about the new lecture he'd delivered for the first time that day and how well it had gone. I was glad he was feeling happy as even in the few months we'd been living together he'd often been mopey and sulky about work, as if he'd rather be sweeping floors or something rather than go to the university ever again. I was finding him harder and harder to figure out rather than feeling I was getting to know him better.

When he finally wound down I snuggled up next to him on the sofa. 'I have something to tell you.'

His eyes widened as if to say what could have happened in my day seeing as I was just a housewife; the shop sold to a stranger and me left wondering what to do with my time, and my life.

'I went to the doctors today and I'm pregnant.'

The shock on his face made my stomach somersault. Oh God, he didn't want it. What would we do now? But then he jumped up, pulling me with him then spinning me round. He whooped. It was my turn to look shocked. Ken had never seemed the whooping sort before.

'We're having a baby!' He shouted, then laughed, then pulled me back down onto the sofa with him, onto his lap.

'You're happy then?' I asked.

'Of course I am. Aren't you?'

'Yes. No. I don't know. I feel scared. Everything is happening so fast. I didn't even know you a few months ago and now we're married and having a baby.'

'It's love, Laura. That's what this is.'

So I pushed my doubts down deep and got on with the business of being pregnant and preparing the house for a baby.

•••

When Kate was born, I was excited, elated, scared and overwhelmed. She was so tiny and helpless and I didn't feel like I knew what to do with her. I needed my mum to tell me. To show me how to hold her head right, burp her, bathe her, feed her. How could I learn to be a mum without my own to teach me? Una was in Africa doing her charity work and Gran hadn't ever really got over Mum and Dad's death. Whenever I rang her to ask questions, or to get some support and feel like I wasn't alone in all this, she was short with me and told me to get on with it. That I'd figure out what to do, women had been doing it for centuries and there was nothing to it. It was as if she couldn't wait to get off the phone. I couldn't understand why she was being like that with me.

Ken was back at work just a few days after we came home from hospital and I was alone with the baby all day. All she seemed to do was cry, eat and sleep. In that order. Most of her time awake she cried until I fed her then she'd sleep for a short while then the cycle would start again. I started to feel like a machine. When Ken came home from work he'd look around at the mess and I could see in his eyes that he thought I wasn't a good enough wife and mother. That I should keep on top of things better. But there didn't seem to be enough time in the day to do all the things that Kate needed me to do and then tidy the house, make a nice meal and make myself look pretty for Ken.

But then when she was about four months old, it was if a switch was flicked and it suddenly got a lot easier. Kate was fun. The crying eased off and we started to have a nice time together. One day, after we'd been playing together on the living room floor and she was sleeping in the afternoon, I decided that it was high time Ken and I had some time together, just the two of us. I arranged for Shelley to come over and babysit and got dressed up in the top Ken had given me on my eighteenth birthday and my jeans, which I could just about fit into again. I did my hair and put make-up on and saw me reappear in the mirror.

'Hello Laura.' I said to myself as I finished putting my lipstick on.

I'd booked a table at the restaurant Ken and I went to on our first date. We had a great time and after what seemed months of not really talking to each other, neither of us could shut up. Ken told funny stories about some of the things his students wrote in their essays and I told him all the things he missed about Kate while he was at work. When we got home and Shelley had left we sat on the sofa holding hands and it felt like it did before we'd become parents.

'Let's go up to bed,' Ken said.

'But I'm not tired yet, this is the first night out I've had in ages and I don't want it to end yet.'

'I'm not tired either.'

Ken pulled me to my feet and kissed me, hard. We hadn't had sex for a long time. A couple of months before Kate was born, and suddenly I wanted it more than I ever had before.

'Let's stay down here.' I tugged at his shirt, pulling it free from his trousers then pushed him back down on the sofa and straddled him, kissing his neck.

'Wow, Laura, where's this come from?'

I didn't answer but kissed him on the mouth while pushing myself against him. He stopped talking then and that's the night that Julia was conceived. I didn't even think you could become pregnant again so soon after having a baby.

So nine months later, before I had even turned twenty, I was a mother to two girls – one a newborn and the other just a year old. I felt like I didn't have time to even think about anything but them for years after that.

UNA

My Dearest Kate,

I've got something to tell you that I should have told you a long time ago. You and Jules. And Ken. But I didn't know how to tell any of you. So many times I've thought I'd do it the next time I saw you and then when you came to visit it never seemed like the right time. But now I'm getting old. I can feel that real, proper old age is settling on me. So I have to tell you now. I thought that putting it in a letter would be easier, for me at least. What I'm going to tell you is not going to be easy for you to hear.

It's about Laura.

KATE

Everyone stopped what they were doing as I walked in. No-one knew what to say or do so I tried to make things easier for us all by being breezy and normal, as if I was over it already.

'Morning everyone.'

There was a coffee cup still on my desk where I'd left it last time I was in. Mould growing in the bottom, a rancid smell permeating the air around me. I sighed heavily and my stomach churned. Surely they could have put the cup in the dishwasher at least.

I switched my computer on and sat down in front of it. Lionel had rung me the night before wanting to make sure I understood how much work needed to be done if we were to get the next edition out on time. He was at a meeting when I arrived but would be back at lunchtime, Alison said. He'd emailed me an update of where he'd got to and what my priorities needed to be. But instead of getting on with it all I found myself staring at the plant, which had looked forlorn even before my time off and was now at death's door. It seemed more important for me to save the plant than to plough through the hundreds of emails in my inbox, to edit the features from our freelancers and go through the editorial list with Alison.

So I took the mouldy cup into the kitchen and threw it in the bin, then filled a glass with water. As I poured it slowly into the parched plant Mark appeared at my desk.

'Hello Kate. How are you doing?'

I smiled politely but wished he'd go away. His tone was too consoling. I needed people to treat me normally or I'd never be able to do this.

'I'm fine, Mark, thanks. Yourself?' I wiped the dust from the plant leaves with my fingers so that I didn't have to look at him.

'Are you sure? I wanted to get in touch but Lionel said we should leave you to deal with things in your own way.'

'It's fine, Mark, honestly. Anyway, I need to get on.' Somehow I smiled at him as I sat down. But inside every part of me was screaming. As if any of it was fine, as if I could just sit here and pretend that I could carry on as before. My computer was still chugging and whirring away as it attempted to get going, like an emphysema sufferer trying to drag some oxygen inside those wasted lungs. As I sat there listening to it, feeling everyone's unspoken questions clogging up the air in the office I knew I had to get out of there. I couldn't catch my breath. I could hear myself panting. There was no point to any of it and I couldn't bear to sit there pretending there was. I stood up so suddenly that my chair shot back and hit the drawers behind my desk with a loud bang. Everyone looked up. I grabbed my bag and walked fast towards the door.

'Kate, wait.' Mark called as the door swung shut behind me.

But I quickened my step and started to run down the stairs instead of waiting for the lift. I ran all the way down the full five flights convinced that Mark was chasing me so that he could drag me back to my desk. I burst through the door into the reception startling Tony, the security guard, who watched me dash past him into the street with a slack-jawed look of astonishment. Outside I hurried down the steps and turned left away from the tube station. It was raining and cold so the street was quiet and I sprinted faster and faster not knowing where I was going. Hoping I could run fast enough, or far enough, to get away from this nightmare.

Startled faces in the cafe windows followed my progress down Charlotte Street. When my lungs felt like they were going to burst I stopped. I was at the corner with Percy Street and Rathbone Place. I stood with my hands on my knees catching my breath then went into the coffee shop on the corner. I took my black coffee to the sofa upstairs and tried to pull myself together. What was I doing running away like that?

A woman with a baby in a buggy sat on the other side of the room and I watched as she fed him; if I concentrated on that then maybe I wouldn't think about Jimmy. I thought I'd start to question it less the longer he was gone, somehow find a way to live with it, but it was getting worse. I noticed the woman with the baby was giving me funny looks. She probably thought I was a mad baby snatcher.

So I left. But when I came out of the coffee shop I didn't want to go home. I went in the pub opposite instead. It was dark and quiet inside and a bit cold; a Christmas tree twinkled next to the fireplace, which was still full of old ashes. I got a double gin and tonic and sat in a gloomy corner. My phone had been ringing virtually non-stop for the past half an hour, Lionel every time. I couldn't speak to him yet. I'd ring him when I got home.

Instead I started churning the same old questions around in my mind. Where has Jimmy gone? What has happened to him? Has he left me deliberately? Has he been killed? Do his family know what's happened but aren't telling me? They seemed genuinely frightened now and like they didn't know the truth, but maybe they were good liars. I was so sick of it. My mind racing all the time. It made me want to run again but instead I got another drink and the gin was starting to penetrate the whirling thoughts, slow them down a bit, when the door swung violently open and bashed against the wall. A big man came crashing in. Jogging bottoms, bum bag and a cap. Definitely American.

I looked away. American tourists in London pubs love to speak to the 'locals', get a real genuine English vibe going on. There were only a couple of other people in there, men by themselves nursing pints of bitter, probably gearing themselves up for a bit of Christmas shopping, and I hoped they would be the focus of the fat man's attentions. I rummaged in my bag as I saw him looking around. Then he sat down at the table next to me.

'Hi,' he boomed at me.

I smiled quickly before burying my head back in my bag. Surely I must have something in there that I could do so that I didn't have to talk to him. Normally there would have been a book, a magazine, but I hadn't been reading. Couldn't take anything in. I turned the pages but it was just words with no connections, I never knew what was going on.

My phone rang again and even though there was no way I was going to answer it I realised I could cancel the call and pretend to be talking to someone.

'Hello?'

I didn't look at the American. I was about to start a fake conversation when the phone rang again.

'Shit,' I muttered.

I could tell he was looking at me, desperate to start a conversation, so I threw the phone in my bag. I'd tell him to leave me alone if he started talking. I knocked back the rest of my drink then headed to the bar to get another. Why couldn't he tell I didn't want to talk? I sat back down without looking in his direction. I thought I'd grab my stuff and move somewhere else but he was talking to me before I got the chance

'Hey, are you English? Do you live in London?'

It was getting busier now with the start of the lunchtime crowd but there was still a muted feel to the atmosphere and he was too big, too loud.

I gave a curt little nod. I would not be dragged into an inane conversation with him. How dare he? He didn't even stop to think about what might be going on in my life and whether I would want to talk to him or not.

'I've just arrived here. I'm on holiday. I've come from Connecticut to visit my daughter for Christmas. She lives here now. I thought I'd come out today and see the lights in Oxford Street and visit these quaint little pubs that you've got here.'

The drivel was falling from his mouth and he barely stopped to take a breath. He didn't want a conversation with me, he just wanted to talk at me. Well I didn't want to be talked at and I was going to get my stuff and move when he said: 'Say, do you know where Elton John lives? I'd really like to see him while I'm here and I thought if I went by his house I might be able to see him.'

I was stopped in my tracks by this. It was so clichéd it was surreal. People always tell you stories about American tourists saying mad things but I'd always assumed they were exaggerated. But here he was asking me if I could direct him to Elton John's house. I left my coat and bag where they were, put my drink down and stared at him. His doughy face with the wet hole in the middle endlessly moving, either spewing out rubbish or stuffing it in. He smiled at me and I don't know what came over me as usually I would have smiled politely back and said no, but I was seething.

'Are you fucking mental?' I spat out.

That stopped him in his tracks. Only momentarily though. He chose to brush my obvious rudeness aside and steamroller on with his attempt to bond with a local. I started to talk over him.

'I said are you fucking mental? Do you know where Elton John lives, ha!' I laughed manically, the gin coursing through me, feeding the anger, which was thrilled to have found an outlet. 'You come and start rabbiting on at me when I clearly don't want to talk to you, or listen to you,' heads all around the pub were turning in our direction now, 'but you carry on regardless, and then you ask me if I know where Elton fucking John lives. Well just fuck off, fuck off, fuck off.'

The final fuck off was bellowed in his face at a phenomenal level that I'm not sure my voice had ever achieved before. I could feel the blood pounding in my temples, hear myself panting and it was the only sound in the pub now apart from Elvis singing Blue Christmas quietly in the background.

The American tourist was finally silent. His face was a mottled red and the wet hole in the middle was now pursed in shock and disapproval. People sniggered behind me then conversations resumed. The barman was looking at me warily, wondering if he'd have to come and throw me out. I was already gathering my things, putting my coat on and draining my drink. Momentarily I was triumphant that I'd got him to be quiet and I gave him one final glare as I flounced out of the pub. But once I got outside, I was drained, shivering, crying, and I wanted to go back in and apologise. It wasn't his fault that my life was in ruins. I shouldn't have taken it out on him. But I couldn't face him so I got on the tube and went home.

•••

When I woke the next morning my body ached all over from the running, my head from the bottle of red wine I drank by myself in my room when I got home. The phone ringing had woken me. I ignored it, it was never Jimmy and he was the only person I wanted to speak to. We used to lay in bed for hours on winter weekends, sometimes not getting dressed at all.

When he moved in with me, we'd spent the whole weekend in bed taking it in turns to get up and get food and drink. We'd had sex about four times every day, talked for hours and hours and barely slept. But that was years ago and I couldn't actually remember the last time we'd had a weekend like that. He was always out and I'd been spending more and more time with friends, but most often alone. If he came back, I'd make sure that we had more time together at the weekends again.

I lay completely still, hoping that this would stop the waves of nausea that were washing over me with increasing force and frequency. It didn't, the room span and darkened, and I rushed to the bathroom where I vomited large amounts of dark red liquid. I hadn't eaten a thing the day before and I was still in the clothes I'd worn to go to work.

Cheddar was on the bottom of the bed and he looked at me with disgust when I stumbled back in. I felt slightly better though and the intensity of the sawing in my head had dropped from chainsaw level to a much more manageable handsaw. I dozed again but the phone woke me forty-five minutes later. I didn't even know where it was but it was definitely in the room somewhere. I left it ringing from its secret location until it went to voicemail. Once the room was silent again I felt able to get up.

My phone was in my coat, which was screwed up in a ball in the corner of the bedroom. I couldn't believe it was almost midday. There were nine missed calls, all from Lionel. I climbed back into bed, my head pounding, knowing that I should go and get some water and some tablets but unable to make myself do it. Where was Jules and why hadn't she tried to wake me for work seeing as she'd been so keen for me to go back? Had I seen her last night? I couldn't remember. I started on the red wine as soon as I got home. But that's about all I can remember.

Next thing I knew someone was pounding on the front door, ringing the doorbell repeatedly. I looked at my phone and it was gone two o'clock. The sleep had got rid of my headache but my mouth was like a dirty carpet so I went to get some water, having no intention of answering the front door. But as I walked past it the letter box opened and Lionel peered through the gap into the hallway.

'Kate, thank God. I've been so worried. Let me in.'

I opened the door and walked away from him into the kitchen. By the time he came in I was greedily guzzling water straight from the tap.

'For fuck's sake, Kate. What's going on? Why haven't you answered any of my calls? I've been worried sick!'

'Lionel, please. Don't shout.' I sat at the table and dropped my head into my hands. 'I didn't mean to worry you. Sorry.'

'You look terrible. I'll make us a cuppa shall I?' He crossed to the kettle, giving my shoulder a squeeze on the way.

'Yes please. Can you put some toast on for me too? I'll be back in a second.'

After changing into leggings and a jumper dress I washed my face and cleaned my teeth. When I got back to the kitchen the tea was ready and Lionel had made enough toast for five people.

We sat munching it and sipping tea in silence for a while, then Lionel put his mug down. 'I know things didn't go well yesterday. We should have planned it better. Not got you back in when I wasn't there to support you. Why don't you get ready and we go in together now?'

But I was shaking my head before he'd even finished the sentence. 'No, I can't Lionel.'

He reached over the table and took my hands in both of his. 'I know it's a terrible thing that's happened, Kate, but you can't mope about in here for ever. It's not good for you.'

Mope about! My husband, the person I'd shared the last ten years of my life with, and who I thought I was going to spend the rest of it with, disappeared without a trace and he thought I was moping about. All he cared about was getting me back to work. To sort out his crappy little magazine with its adverts for microscopes and third-rate articles from self-important lab assistants, who wished their work was good enough to get in the New Scientist but settled for Euro Science News.

He started to move round the table towards me but I put up my hand to stop him. 'Just go Lionel. I want you to go now. I'm not moping about. I can't pretend that nothing has happened, that I can carry on like before.'

'Kate come on. You have to. You can't give up. You've been off for a month now. You need some structure back in your life. Just come back for three days a week until you get used to it again.'

Even though I tried to hold them back the tears started. 'I can't. You don't know what it's like. I can't go back to work and get on with life as if this hasn't happened. As if Jimmy is just a memory I can put behind me.' I dropped my head onto my arms on the table and sobbed.

Lionel was silent for ages, just rubbing my back.

'Oh, Kate,' he said eventually, 'I wish I could make it better for you.' Then he left.

UNA

Darling Kate,

I keep starting this letter over and over again as I just can't seem to find the words. It's about Laura and I should have told you long ago. I should never have done what I did in the first place, but there's no changing that now.

I'm getting old and I feel like if I don't tell you now then it will be too late. I just wanted you and Jules to be happy and settled, that's why I did it. I want you to know that and always keep it in mind, if you can. Because you are going to be angry with me and you have every right to be. So I just wanted to start by saying how sorry I am, and I hope that you'll be able to forgive me.

LAURA

When Kate was five and Jules almost four, Una came home for good from her charity work in Africa. Too old now, she said. At the start of the summer we went for a holiday to the caravan at Silverdale while Ken stayed behind for the last few weeks of term. When we arrived the rain was lashing down and the wind roaring so we huddled up around the Calor gas heater playing snap with the girls until we went to bed.

The next day we woke to endless blue skies and there was a real warmth to the sun for the first time in weeks, so we packed up a picnic and headed to the beach for the day, laden down with bags, buckets, blankets and a wind break.

Kate and Jules were playing in a rock pool, gathering bits of seaweed and shells to decorate their sandcastles. Me and Una were reading, both of us propped up against the cliff like bookends, keeping the stuff lying on the blanket in its place.

After a while, Una put her book down and turned to face me. 'So what are you going to do now, Laura?'

'What do you mean?'

'Well, Kate's starting school and Jules is going to be at playschool four mornings a week so you're going to have time for you. What do you think you might do with it?'

My mind went blank. I'd never done anything apart from going to school, working in the shop and being a wife and mother.

'I haven't even thought about it, Una. Why, do you think I should get a job?' I couldn't imagine what I would do. Perhaps I could get a job in Woolworths, or somewhere like that, after all shop work was the only experience I had.

'Well, no that wasn't what I was thinking. Do you want to get a job?'

I pictured myself standing behind a counter punching things into the till as people bought sweets and my heart sank.

'Not really, no. I'd hate to work in a shop again.'

'Why do you think you'd have to do that?'

'Well, it's all I know, all I've ever done.' I looked over at the girls who were still absorbed in the sandcastle town they were creating. It was hard to believe that I wasn't going to have them with me all the time anymore.

'That doesn't mean you can't do something different, does it?' Una gave my arm a little push. 'You're a bright girl, Laura, you could do anything you want.'

Unexpectedly, tears welled up at this and my throat was so choked I couldn't speak. No-one had ever said anything like that to me before. Actually, that's a lie. Mr Cooper my English teacher at school had said I was a natural when it came to writing essays. He used to read them out occasionally and I always wished the fire alarm would go off or something so that he'd have to stop.

'What about becoming a student again? Learning about something you love.' Una added when it became obvious I wasn't going to speak.

I laughed at that. 'What go to school again? No way, Una. I'd hate it and I'm too old!'

'Not school as such. You could study at home. Do a degree with the Open University. I think it would be really good for you.'

I stood up, the conversation was scaring me. Making me feel insecure and as if the life that I'd got used to was going to be taken away from me again. 'Well, it's certainly something to think about.'

'Mummy, Mummy, look at our castle.'

Jules's voice rang out across the beach, which was empty apart from us and a man sitting in a deckchair with his feet buried in the sand. He looked up from the newspaper he was reading and smiled at Jules and Kate.

'But in the meantime, I have a castle to view.' I smiled in Una's direction but didn't really meet her eyes then wandered over and sat on the sand while Jules and Kate showed me around the enchanted castle they'd built for their dolls to live in.

But Una had planted a seed in my mind that was determined to grow, despite my best attempts to kill it off. Whenever I found myself with a quiet moment over the next few weeks my mind started throwing all these different possibilities at me. I'd always been an avid reader, sometimes getting through two novels a week before the girls were born. I loved to find out what made people who they were. Perhaps I should do psychology. Or sociology. Or English Literature. But what for? What would I do with all that learning anyway? It was a stupid idea.

•••

After two weeks at the caravan, which were mainly filled with sunshine and days at the beach, Una went home and Ken took her place. After their initial excitement that Daddy was there, the girls were a bit shy around him. As he was around them. Sometimes it seemed like he didn't know what to say to them, or how to say it. One time I'd come into the kitchen and they were sitting at the table opposite him looking completely baffled while he told them about the history of the Lancaster canal as if he was delivering a lecture to his students. He did it to me sometimes too and it seemed like the fun, thoughtful Ken that I'd first fallen in love with, the one who was so impulsive he asked me to marry him just a few weeks after we'd met, was turning into a stuffy Professor before my eyes.

I really didn't want him to be like that on this holiday though and was going to make sure that we all had fun together, that he got to know his daughters properly. And it worked. After a few days he did seem to forget about work as he played in the sand with the girls, threw them around in the waves and showed them all the secret rock pools that he'd discovered when he was their age.

On the last day of the holiday he got up really early and went off in the car but wouldn't tell us where he was going. He was back within a couple of hours with a blow-up boat. He pumped it up down on the beach and we all got in and he rowed us around the headland and back. Then he took the girls for a walk out along the cliff tops and I floated around in the boat reading my book.

That night after the girls were in bed, Ken and I sat outside the caravan watching the sun set over the hills. He was relaxed and tanned and looked more like himself than he had in ages.

'Una said to me that I should start thinking about what to do with myself now the girls are growing up and will be off at school.'

'Did she?' For some reason this annoyed him. He dropped my hand and didn't look at me as he spoke. 'And what did she tell you to do?'

'She didn't tell me to do anything. She just said I should think about it. She said I could do a degree with the Open University. That I'm bright and can do anything I want.'

'You are very bright, Laura. But isn't this what you want to do? Be a mum and be there for the girls.'

'Of course it is. But I'm going to be at home on my own after the summer and what will I do then? There's only so many hours a day I can fill with cleaning and cooking.'

'So, what? You want to turn into the sort of mother that Una was? Always off somewhere doing something else. Hardly ever seeing your children?'

The anger in his voice was a shock. He'd always been so proud of Una and all the things she'd done to help women less fortunate than she was.

'Now she's back from saving the women of Africa she's turning you into her project. Probably wants you to take over where she's left off.' He shouted this at me and I just sat there. I couldn't figure out where it had all come from.

'But, Ken...'

He stood up so abruptly that his chair fell over. 'I'm going for a walk.'

And he was gone before I could even think what to say to him. He didn't come back for hours and when he did I was lying in bed hoping that my eyes weren't red from crying anymore.

'Ken, I'm sorry. I didn't mean to upset you.'

He sat down on the edge of the bed with his back to me. I could smell beer and cigarette smoke on him so he'd obviously walked to the pub in the village.

'No, I'm the one who's sorry, Laura. I shouldn't have shouted at you like that.' His voice was flat. 'Let's go to sleep and we can talk about what you might like to do with your life when we get home. OK?'

Then he stripped off, got into bed beside me and was asleep

within minutes. I lay there for hours, hating myself for ruining the holiday when we'd been having such a great time.

But the next morning it was as if nothing had happened and Ken was cheery again, although if you looked closely you could see he was feeling a bit worse for wear after his night in the pub.

'Come on girls, one last trip to the beach while your Mum packs up everything to go home.'

Jules wailed. 'No, don't want to go home. I want to live here.'

Kate put her arms around her sister. 'I want to live here too.' And then she was crying as well.

I wanted to join in and wail along with them. No, I don't want to stay here and do the packing. I want to go to the beach too. But after how Ken had reacted last night I thought I should probably keep my thoughts to myself and just get on with it. After they'd gone I sat on the step watching them getting smaller and smaller as they walked down the path to the beach, until they disappeared completely. Then I went in and did the packing.

•••

The next few weeks at home were filled with getting Kate ready for her first day at primary school. Shopping for her uniform was hard work as Jules couldn't, or wouldn't, understand why Kate was going without her.

'We always do the same,' she said.

'I know. But Kate's a bit older than you so now she has to go to school by herself. You'll go next year.' I picked up the skirt she'd just added to the basket and hung it back on the rack.

'No! No!' Jules screamed so loudly that I could feel everyone in the shop turning to look at us.

'Come on, Jules. You'll be going to playschool and having

lots of fun there. Making lots of new friends.'

'Don't want to. Want Kate.'

I dropped the basket on the floor and grabbed both of them by the hand. 'We're going home.'

Then Kate started too. 'But Mummy I haven't got my uniform. I need it.'

'We'll get it another day.' It was all I could say. If I didn't get out of there I was going to have a tantrum too. For the first time, I looked forward to those mornings when they'd both be out of the house.

The next day I dropped the girls at Una's and went into town to get Kate's uniform. I got Jules one too so she could try it on later when Kate tried hers, even though she wasn't going to need it for another year.

When I went to pick them up, Una took one look at me and bundled them into the garden to play.

'What's wrong?' She asked as we sat down at the kitchen table with a cup of tea.

'Nothing. It's just been hard this week. Jules won't accept that Kate's going to school and she isn't.' I dunked a Rich Tea into my cup and held it there too long so when I lifted it out half of it fell back in. I burst into tears.

'Oh, Laura. There's no need to cry. Jules will get over it and once she's in playschool and made lots of friends she'll forget that she even wanted to go to school with Kate.'

I nodded. I couldn't tell her that the real reason I was crying was because ever since she'd brought it up, I suddenly wanted to do something with my life but because of how Ken had reacted I couldn't. How could I tell her that he was angry at her and thought she was trying to turn me into the sort of mother that she'd been? One that goes off and does her own thing.

'I know. I'm being silly. I better get off anyway.'

I could tell she wanted me to stay but I got the girls from the garden and left before I told her everything.

KATE

The whole flat echoed with the sound of the door slamming. Jules had stormed off again. She wanted me to go to Lancaster with her for Christmas to spend it with Granny and Ken. She wouldn't take no for an answer but I was definitely not going. This was the latest bee in her bonnet; first it was go back to work, then the family reunion at Christmas. But she'd just have to get over it as I didn't want a family reunion. I'd have liked to see Granny but wanted nothing to do with Ken.

I was spending Christmas with Gloria. She didn't tell me what to do. She just drank with me and listened to me, and told me her own tales of woe. We wallowed together. While I had a disappearing husband she had a violent ex-boyfriend to complain about. I decided to go and see her before Jules came back and started again. As I got my stuff together, I heard the door open. Jules was back already, so she must've only been sat outside on the step. She appeared in the living room doorway, all downturned mouth and red eyes.

'Kate, please. I'm worried about you. All you seem to do now is sit in here and drink or go out with Gloria and drink. What's happening with you?'

'What do you think is happening? My husband has vanished.

What am I supposed to do, just forget about it? And I don't just sit in here, I go for a walk every day.'

'Yes, but looking for Jimmy. You're not going to find him by walking the streets, Kate.'

'Shut up Jules. You think you know everything all the time.'

I picked up my bag and as I walked past her to the front door, she tried again. 'Kate, please come to Granny's, she'd love to see you, she said it's been ages. You have to talk to Ken sometime.'

I didn't reply, just shut the door behind me and enjoyed the silence. I couldn't hear her anymore.

Gloria was tired and not really up for going out but I convinced her to come to the pub by the bridge.

'Please Glor, I've had a really shit day with Jules going on and on at me. I had to go out to get away from her.'

'Can't we just stay here?' She stretched her legs out on the sofa in front of her.

'No. I need to be distracted. Try and have some fun.'

•••

Twenty-five minutes later, Gloria and I were sitting down at a table by the window in the Draft House, with an expensive and strong Belgian beer each. We also had a bowl of dry roasted peanuts and another of cashew nuts in place of dinner. It was quite busy and for the first time I felt a little festive twinge as the Christmas cheer in the air and the fairy lights draped all around the pub worked their twinkly magic. I wanted a night off from thinking about it all, Jimmy and Ken. And bloody Laura who, after being banished from memory many years ago, kept popping up too. As if I didn't have enough to deal with. So, that night the plan was to drink, to forget, to dance and pretend everything was normal for the night. When I told this to Gloria she shrugged off the slightly sullen mood she'd been in since I made her come out, and lifted her glass to me.

'Down the hatch then,' she said.

We clinked glasses then drained almost the whole bottle of Leffe Blond that we each had. The effect was instantaneous and I knew my eyes were developing the same glaze that was taking over Gloria's. We smiled, both of us feeling a little fizz of excitement. Feeling naughty. We were having a night out and I for one was determined to have fun.

I went to the bar and got two more beers, and two shots of espresso vodka, and when I got back to the table Gloria was looking even naughtier. We downed the shots then she rummaged in her bag and pulled out a joint and shook it at me.

'Fancy it, Kate? It'll get you where you want to go much quicker.'

I hesitated. I didn't do drugs. Never had. The hesitation was momentary though. In for a penny in for a pound, I thought. I felt like an adventurous teenager, not a thirty-two-year-old woman with a shit life, as we giggled and gathered all our stuff together. In the garden we huddled under the brazier. Freezing despite it. We smoked the joint really quickly so we could go back inside to the warm and my head was completely buzzing and spinning slightly as we went back through the door. Everything seemed much louder inside than before even though it all looked further away. I giggled, and giggled. Gloria started too when she sat down and we sat there giggling like schoolgirls. This was more like it. No doom or gloom. Just feeling nice, and happy, and giggly. No wonder Gloria smoked it every day. Time started to fly by and before I knew it I'd had another two vodka shots and two more beers and we were on our way to the brazier again. The pub was really busy by then, everyone was cheery and the festive fun was going on full-throttle all around us. Considering I didn't normally drink that much, although I had been indulging more and more recently, and never smoked, I was managing to stay upright really well. We'd been eating a lot of nuts though.

Outside, people were smoking all around us and the air was thick with it. It started to catch in my throat then Gloria passed me the joint and with the first drag I knew. I'd gone too far. As I blew the smoke out my head reeled and the ground rocked beneath me. Even though it was freezing, beads of sweat were forming on my top lip and my forehead. Saliva gushed into my mouth and before I even realised what was happening, I threw up. Then I collapsed onto the chair behind me and did it again. Gloria jumped back, laughing, but I could sense everyone else's shock and disgust as the space around us cleared. People would much rather be cold than have to deal with my puke.

Gloria was laughing hysterically even though I could see that there was sick on her boots.

'You pulled a whitey, Kate!'

She thought this was hilarious but I had no idea what she was talking about. I was mortified and even though my vision was blurred and everything was zooming in really close then whooshing away from me again, I managed to stumble out into the street.

Gloria hailed a cab even though it was only a ten-minute walk and we sat in the back with the freezing cold wind blowing in our faces from the windows I made her open. My head was reeling and spinning all over the place. The cabby's eyes kept flicking my way in his mirror. He knew how close I was to vomiting in his cab, he'd seen it all before. We pulled up outside our flats and Gloria told me to go to bed, that she'd pay the cab driver. As I stumbled through the front door, Jules was there waiting, hovering in the hallway like an anxious parent.

'Kate, you look awful. Are you alright?'

I rushed into the bathroom and threw up again and she waited in the hallway behind me. When I was done I rinsed my mouth in the sink. The waves of disapproval coming from Jules were almost strong enough to knock me down.

'What have you been doing?'

'Nothing. I think it was the prawns.'

I don't know why I lied to her but I don't think she believed me anyway.

My phone rang in my bag and as I got it out, I didn't recognise the number.

'Hello?'

'Kate?'

'Yes.'

'Oh, hi. It's Jenny.'

'Jenny?'

'Tom's wife.'

Tom, university friend. Jenny, wife.

'Oh yes, hello.' I couldn't think why she'd be ringing me? 'Is there something wrong with Tom?'

'No, no. God I feel a bit silly now. I mean, we hardly know each other but I saw your Facebook post earlier and I wanted to say how sorry I was. How awful it is. And see if there's anything I…we…can do.'

Facebook? I had no idea what she was talking about.

'Well, thanks Jenny. Thanks for calling.'

I threw the phone down on the sofa and turned to Jules.

'Have you been putting things on my Facebook?'

She looked guilty straight away. 'I thought it might help. I thought someone might know something and if they knew what you were going through they might tell you.'

'What did you put?'

She crossed her arms over her chest as she stepped back

from me. 'Just that Jimmy was still missing and you were really worried and if anybody knew anything they should call you.'

'How dare you. Did I ask you to do that? If I wanted everyone to know I'd tell them.'

'Sorry, Kate, sorry. They know anyway. I was just trying to help.' She held her hands out to me but I pushed them away.

'Well, you're not. You're not helping at all with your constant going on at me about making up with Ken and now this, poking your nose in. I don't want it. I don't want you here. Get out. Go to Granny's for Christmas and don't come back.'

I slammed my bedroom door with all my might then flung myself down on the bed. She'd ruined all the hard work of the evening to have fun, forget, to get in bed and go to sleep with happy thoughts instead of all this, all the time. Six weeks since Jimmy had vanished and nothing, no news, nobody had seen him or heard from him. It was driving me insane.

•••

The next morning, Christmas Eve, my head was thick and I woke on top of the bed in my clothes and boots. It was eleven o'clock and Jules had gone. The note on the kitchen table told me she'd gone to Granny's, she'd call later, she was sorry. Well, wasn't everyone but it didn't make any difference, didn't make it any better. A voice message from Gloria told me she'd gone food shopping and I should come round about three o'clock to get Christmas started. The festive feelings I'd managed to get going the night before were long gone and I didn't want to go. I knew she wouldn't accept that though. I had to spend Christmas with Gloria.

The phone rang as soon as I'd hung up from listening to Gloria's message. It was the police. My stomach lurched and I didn't know if it was in fear or anticipation. But the next minute it was sinking in disappointment, they had rung to tell me that there was nothing more they could do for me. They'd spoken to Jimmy's colleagues at work, to his friends and family. That no-one knew anything but that Shirley and Alan were convinced that he'd left me and would be in touch with them soon. They didn't say so but I knew they thought I should just face up to it, that Jimmy had walked out on me but didn't have the guts to tell me. I couldn't believe that he would do that. He loved me, we'd been together for years. I mean, it was no grand passion but we'd been happy, hadn't we? I'd been happy enough anyway.

I sat down on the floor with my back against the radiator. Where had he gone? As I stretched out my legs my feet kicked a box under the bed and knocked the one on top of it onto the floor. Its contents spilled out and as an array of colourful erasers fell around my feet, I remembered the last time I'd seen this box and my collection properly. When we got home from Granny's at the end of that scary and confusing day when Laura left, I ran straight upstairs to my room and slammed the door shut to get away from Jules. Why won't they tell us where Mummy's gone? I didn't know the answer to her question and I wanted her to stop asking me. I wanted Laura to be there like she always was, giving us hot milk and one biscuit each before reading us a story. Then coming with me into my room to tuck me in and kiss me goodnight when Jules had fallen asleep. But she hadn't done that for ages, and now she'd gone somewhere without saying goodbye.

In the car on the way home I was really scared. I could sense that Ken was angry and even though he'd never been much of a talker, he was completely silent, didn't say a word after he bundled us in the car. Granny tried to make him leave us there for the night after they'd been talking quietly in the kitchen. Ken was always a bit distant and remote, only occasionally playing with me and Jules, but I'd never been scared of him before; well only a couple of times when I found him shouting at Laura. One time he was gripping her and shaking her. He'd flung her away from him when I'd come in and she had red finger marks on her arms. She'd hugged me and told me it was nothing to worry about, that grown-ups had fights sometimes. But in the car on the way home from Granny's a creeping sensation of dread spread all over me and by the time we got home I was so scared of Ken I had to get away from him.

Jules came running up the stairs behind me and tried to get into my room but I was sat against the door so that she couldn't push it all the way open. She screamed and banged on it for ages but I wouldn't let her in. I kept expecting Ken to come up and take her to bed but he didn't. After a while she stopped screaming but I could hear her out there whimpering. The whole time she was out there I sat and sorted through my eraser collection. I'd pulled it out of my bag as I leant against the door and it calmed me down as I looked through it. I always took it to school with me. Lots of girls had eraser collections and we compared and traded at break times.

My best friend at school was a girl called Stacey Worthing and we spent lots of our pocket money on erasers. We were both so proud of our collections and never got bored of looking at them. Even though Stacey's was good, I thought mine was better. I had a fruit section that had six different types of fruit in it, which was more than anyone else had. The banana was my favourite, it looked and smelled just like the real thing, just in miniature. And the best thing was it didn't bruise like real bananas. It always made me feel sick when Laura gave me a banana and it had those sludgy brown bruised bits on it. I couldn't eat it then.

As Jules cried and whimpered outside my bedroom door and

I tried not to think about what was happening and where Laura might have gone, I sat and sniffed my banana eraser, while I turned my second favourite, the strawberry one, over and over in my left hand.

'Kitty Kat, please let me in.'

Jules started banging on the door again. I felt a bit better so I packed the collection away and opened the door to let her in. Her sad little face was grubby from the tears as we climbed into my bed with our clothes and shoes on and wrapped our arms around each other, wondering what Ken might be doing downstairs.

I never played with my eraser collection again after that night but I kept it in the metal box with pictures of biscuits on it, which Laura gave me specially to keep them in for all those years. It went everywhere with me: to university, to my own flat, then to the homes I'd lived in as a married woman. I pushed the memories away. I couldn't think about Laura leaving us now. I had enough to deal with wondering what had happened to my husband. I couldn't drag up old forgotten memories of the woman who didn't care enough about me to stick around and be my mother.

I scooped the erasers back into the box and made sure the little clip was properly shut before shoving it right under the bed where I couldn't see it. Then I crawled into my unmade bed and pulled the duvet over my head as I hugged Jimmy's pillow and the tears rolled down my face.

•••

After a shower I felt a bit better and knew I should make an effort. I couldn't wallow in self-pity alone in the flat at Christmas. What good would that do? I went into the kitchen and got a drink – a large glass of the white wine that I found in the fridge. It didn't really taste of anything and I drank it fast. The little buzz started after about the fourth large gulp and as I emptied the bottle into the glass I could feel the whirl of thoughts slowing, only fractionally, but they were slowing.

Last Christmas, Jimmy and I had gone away with Martin and Claire to a cottage on a little island off the west coast of Scotland. We'd all been convinced we were going to have a white Christmas – I mean Scotland was practically in the Arctic Circle. We'd flown to Glasgow and hired a car and as we'd come out of the airport we thought it would only be a matter of minutes before we started to hit the snowy roads.

'Do you think we should have asked about snow chains for the tires?' Martin said as he overtook a lorry.

Claire laughed. 'Bloody hell, Martin, we're not in Iceland!'

It was about a three-hour drive to get there, and even though it was an island it was joined to the mainland with a bridge. As we went further north and the road cut through the Loch Lomond National Park, the mountains in the distance were snow-capped but still there was none on the ground.

'I'm going to complain,' Claire said, 'How dare there not be snow on our Christmas holiday in Scotland.'

'But at least we'll be able to get out walking, it'd be hard in the snow.' Jimmy said from the front seat where he was holding the satnav on his lap and telling Martin the directions rather than just letting him see the map for himself.

I nudged Claire and winked: 'But you hate going out walking, Jimmy. Bet you spend the whole holiday on the sofa watching films and eating cake.'

'Well, that's where you're wrong. I'm getting fit next year and I'm joining the gym with Alan and joining the football team at work. So I thought I could walk up some of the big hills while we're here and get started.'

Claire and I had really laughed, there was no way Jimmy would do that. He was a right couch potato. But he did, he joined the football team and went to the gym two nights a week, sometimes more, with Alan. But I was beginning to wonder if he had been lying to me about the gym, after almost a year of exercising his body hadn't really changed that much and when I'd seen Alan, he was paunchy. I pushed this thought away. Why would he lie?

I realised I'd better go and get Gloria a present. I couldn't just sit around brooding on questions I had no answers to.

I couldn't face going into town so I headed to Eddie's. Acne-Face was outside with the puppy. He smiled at me as I approached; he'd got all familiar since I asked him if he'd seen Jimmy the night he disappeared, always saying hello, asking me if I'm alright and if I'd found him yet. When Eddie put the poster of Jimmy up in the shop he asked me if the number on it was mine. He made me feel uneasy.

'No, I haven't found him yet, and yes I'm fine,' I said before he had a chance to say anything.

He sniggered. 'Well I'm glad you're fine and I'm sorry you haven't found him yet. You know, I don't have a girlfriend at the moment if you're looking for a replacement.'

He laughed loudly and stepped towards me. I ignored him and went into the shop. For once it was silent and Eddie was putting stuff out on the shelves, his little TV blank and mute on its stool.

'Hi Eddie.'

'Hello Kate. Any news?'

I shook my head. He asked every time. I knew he meant well but I wished everyone could treat me more normally. Everyone was always telling me that I had to start moving on, getting back to normal, but nobody treated me like I was. 'Have you got any boxes of chocolates?'

He pointed over to the other side of the aisle from where he was stacking.

'Yes, down there on the bottom shelf.'

I got Gloria a large box of Celebrations, as that's all he had, and a large bottle of Vodka too. Eddie laughed when I took it up to the counter. 'Happy Christmas!' He held the vodka bottle up in the air as if we were doing cheers.

'Happy Christmas to you too, Eddie. These are for Gloria. Have you got any wrapping paper?'

What he handed me was awful, faded and almost see through with lots of teddy bears, big and small, dressed up in Santa outfits. I bought it anyway, Gloria wouldn't mind. She'd only rip it off so we could get stuck in to the vodka before our Marks and Spencer's Christmas dinner for two. Maybe I could give the smoking another try too, see if I couldn't revive the festive feelings at least for the next few days.

UNA

Dear Kate,

I wish you had come here for Christmas. Jules arrived today and told me about the horrible and silly argument you had. I know you must be going through hell but she really did think she was helping. Please forgive her.

I've been trying to write to you for ages now. Every attempt so far has ended up in the bin. I thought you might come here and I could tell you what I need to say in person, no matter how hard that would be. But now Jules has told me how badly you're coping with Jimmy's disappearance, and I can't believe you hadn't told me about that. I'm not sure now is the right time.

But perhaps there is never going to be a right time. I'm so sad for you that this has happened with Jimmy. How dreadful that you are just left with all those questions in your mind about where he could be. But you have to find a way to move on. You can't let this ruin your life.

I know because I let things that happened in mine change me, make me the kind of person I would never have imagined I could be. Do things I wouldn't have thought I was capable of. And that's what I need to talk to you about. You and Jules. But I see that it's you that has suffered the most because of my decisions. I'm so sorry, Kate, I did it all because I love you.

I hope that if I tell you this now, rather than adding to your burdens, once you have got over the shock that it might actually help you.

It's about Laura. We didn't tell you the truth.

LAURA

After Christmas, once Kate had gone back to school, which she loved, and Jules was back at playschool, which she also loved, Ken and I had a week together before he had to go back to work. Things between us had been strange since the row on holiday and despite what he'd said that night when he came back from the pub, we'd never talked about it again. The time I had to myself when the girls were at school was filled with cleaning, cooking and reading. I was bored and, as the time when Jules would be at school all day got closer and closer, I was thinking more and more about what Una had said.

On their first day back when I got home from dropping the girls off, Ken had his coat on.

'Come on. We're going to Williamson Park for a walk.'

It was quiet in the park but the winter sunshine had some warmth in it, although the trees were stark and tinged with frost where the sun hadn't reached yet. Ken held my hand as we strode along and I watched the sparrows hopping around in the bushes we passed. I was building up to saying something to Ken about when Jules would be at school too when I felt his arm go round my shoulder.

'Penny for them.' He touched his head gently against mine.

I couldn't think how to start. I didn't want him to fly off the handle again.

'Look, Laura. I know we need to talk about it.'

I turned to face him. 'It?'

'It. You. And what you want to do once Jules is at school too.'

I was so happy that he'd brought it up. That he'd known I was thinking about it. That we were still close despite the strange few months we'd had. 'I will need to do something, Ken. I've been a bit bored to be honest.'

'I know you have. And I wasn't being fair. I should never have said those things about Una. I know you won't be like that.'

'No, I won't. I don't want to go off and leave you all. That's not what this is about. I just want to have something to do. Una was right. I am bright and I could do an Open University course. I want to look into it.'

He pulled me to a stop and took me in his arms. 'Well, do it then. Now's the right time. You can get some information and if you decide it's what you want to do then you can start in the autumn when the girls are back at school.'

'Really?' I clapped excitedly.

'Really. And I can help you over the summer holidays. Get you used to studying again.'

•••

A few weeks later, the information pack I'd sent off for arrived in the post. For some reason I couldn't open it. Since I'd decided that it was what I wanted to do I'd started to doubt myself. I probably wouldn't even be able to do the work. And if I could manage to scrape through it, what was I doing it for? What was the point in any of it? I was hardly going to have a career, was

I? So the envelope sat on the side in the kitchen while I avoided looking at it and tried to pretend it wasn't there.

By the weekend it had been there for four days. Una came for lunch before taking the girls to the pictures to see the Care Bear film. They'd both gone Care Bear mad after being given one each for Christmas. After they left I was in the kitchen washing up when Ken pulled me away from the sink and handed me a tea towel.

'Come on. Leave that. It's about time you opened it.'

He steered me over to the table and pushed me down onto a chair then handed me the envelope.

'Go on. It's just an information pack. Nothing bad will happen.' He winked and I loved him so much right then. Sometimes he knew exactly what to say and what I needed to hear.

I ripped it open. There was a letter and a brochure and all sorts of other pieces of paper in it. I sat and read through the whole lot and tried to push away that voice in my head that was telling me I couldn't do it. I'd never know unless I tried, would I? And it didn't seem that daunting after all. I was breathless and had a floaty feeling in my chest, excited that the only thing left for me to do was to decide what to study.

Ken reappeared at my side. 'Well?'

'Well, what?' I laughed and flung my arms around him.

'Did it bite you?'

'No, it didn't. I'm going to do it. I just have to decide which course.'

'What do you think you might like to do?'

'English Literature, Psychology or Sociology.'

'OK, well let me know when you've decided. Now, enough of all this academic talk. It's time for sexy talk and I'm taking you upstairs before the girls get back.'

•••

I couldn't decide. One day I wanted to do Literature, the next Psychology but Sociology got struck off the list pretty early on. In the end, I went for Psychology thinking that maybe, one day, I might be able to be a counsellor or a psychologist. I mean what would I do with a literature degree? Yes, I loved reading novels but I was never going to write one, and I didn't want to be an English teacher or work in a publisher's. But the thought that I could end up helping people one day was a good one. I wish I'd had someone to talk to about Mum and Dad dying when I was so young, and then being a mother of two before I was twenty. So I wanted to learn how to be that person for someone else that needed it.

•••

I sent off my application and waited for a response. My O-Level results were pretty good so I hoped they'd let me in even though I'd left school at sixteen. I was snappy and irritable with everyone while I waited to hear. Months went by before finally the envelope dropped onto the mat one Friday near the end of June. I was in! I'd be starting in October and they'd send more details about the course soon. Ken was at work already so I rang Una. I had to tell someone.

'Una. Guess what?'

'I can't. I hate it when people say that.'

'I've been accepted into the Open University! I'm going to study for a degree in Psychology!'

'Oh Laura, that's fantastic. How exciting. I'm taking you out to lunch to celebrate. Meet me at the Water Witch at half past twelve.'

We got a bit tipsy as by the time I arrived Una had already

ordered a bottle of champagne and we'd drunk half of it before the food turned up. It felt like the world was turning into a different place again, like when I'd first met Ken. Only now I was making the changes happen, they weren't out of my control.

Una insisted on picking the girls up and taking them back to hers for the night so Ken and I could celebrate together.

Before Ken had managed to get his key in the lock I'd flung the door open. 'I got in. I got in!' I jumped up and down. I'd been dying to tell him all day. Then I noticed that he was pale and haggard. 'What's the matter?'

'Nothing. That's brilliant, Laura. I better watch out though or you'll be psychoanalysing me every day over breakfast.' His words were right and I could see that he was really trying to make them sound bright and breezy for my sake, but something was definitely wrong.

He sat down on the sofa. 'Where are the girls?'

'Una's got them. She said they could stay over so we can have a night out to celebrate. But what's wrong? And don't say nothing because I can tell that there is.'

I couldn't have been more shocked when he burst into tears. I'd never seen him cry before.

I sat down next to him and put my arm around his shoulders, which were shuddering and shaking as he sobbed with his face in his hands. What was going on? Every hair on my body was standing on end as I prepared myself for what I was about to hear.

'Ken, what is it? Tell me.'

'It's George. He's dead.'

For a moment I had no idea who George was. How could Ken be so upset about someone I didn't even know? Then I remembered. It was his boss. Not only his boss but his mentor, the person who'd supervised him in his PhD.

'How? What happened?'

Ken's sobs had tapered off but his voice was still hiccupping and broken. 'He had a heart attack. In his office this morning. When Pam went in with a cup of tea and his papers he was on the floor. He died in the hospital, they couldn't revive him.'

'Oh Ken. I'm so sorry.' I dropped my head onto his shoulder.

'He was so young, still. Not even sixty yet.'

I squeezed him tight. There was nothing I could say. We sat there quietly for a while then he got up. 'I'll go for a shower, we'll get ready and go out. We need to celebrate your brilliant news and raise a toast to George. He definitely wouldn't want us to sit around moping.'

I'd only met George a handful of times at various faculty functions but from the impression I'd got then, Ken was right, moping was not an activity that George would approve of. 'Are you sure?'

Ken nodded and after he'd gone, even though I felt a bit bad on behalf of George, I couldn't help having a little dance of excitement again about my news.

•••

We ended up getting absolutely plastered. We went for drinks before dinner, had wine with it, then went back to the pub for more drinks afterwards. That on top of the champagne I'd had at lunchtime meant that the last hour or so in the pub, and the walk home, were very hazy. I couldn't really remember what we'd been talking about or how we'd got home but suddenly we were there.

As soon as we got inside the front door, Ken started peeling my clothes off. He had an urgency about him I'd never seen before. It was so exciting. He pressed me up against the front door and tugged my skirt down, pulling my shirt open and burying his face in my cleavage. His groin pressed really hard against mine and I thought I was going to come before we'd even really got started.

He bit my nipples in turn as he removed my bra and it was like an electric jolt went straight from them to my groin. I was desperate for him to be inside me. I fumbled with his fly but he pushed my hands away and opened his trousers, then, just moving my knickers to the side, he was thrusting inside me, fast, and we both came almost immediately. He bit into my shoulder as he collapsed against me. It had never been like that between us before.

We stumbled up the stairs with our clothes hanging off of us and collapsed into bed. I woke a few hours later with a desperate need for water and as I was standing at the kitchen sink filling my glass, it was then that I realised. I hadn't put my diaphragm in.

KATE

A new year. I hadn't seen or heard from Jimmy in over eight weeks. That doesn't sound that long but believe me it felt like I'd lived a year in that time. He wasn't coming back. Just like Laura didn't. We never heard from her again and I wasn't going to hear from Jimmy again. I'd been doing some research into men that go missing and sometimes if life gets too much they just go. Feel incapable of admitting that something's wrong and that they can't cope so they don't say anything to anyone. Sometimes they come back, sometimes they don't. There's no way I could accept that he would walk out and leave me not knowing though. That would just be too cruel.

There was one story of a man from Leeds who had a wife and teenage son, and he went out as if he was going to work one day and ended up living on the streets in Brighton for two years. His family never gave up and they found him in the end and he went home. Had Jimmy suffered a similar kind of mental breakdown? I just couldn't figure out what he would have been feeling so pressured about.

Reaching my arm out from under the duvet I pulled my phone from my bag. God, only 5am. Gloria and I had stayed in the night before and watched a movie for our New Year's Eve celebrations. The Hangover, which was stupid and funny and made me forget about things for a while. Gloria said it was apt but strangely enough I didn't have a hangover. Probably because I hadn't had enough sleep yet. I was probably still drunk, and stoned. Should I get up and go and look for Jimmy in some of the places that he loved to go to? Maybe he'd be there on the streets like that man was. If Jimmy had a breakdown perhaps he'd go somewhere that means something to him. We went to Bournemouth once, maybe he's there? Or Bristol? Jimmy always wanted to go to other cities, he didn't really like the countryside or the beach. Where was our first holiday together? Yorkshire. We went for a long weekend to York. I should go to York.

Pushing the duvet back I stood up too quickly and the room disappeared as my vision blurred. Maybe I was more hungover than I thought. So I got back in bed and lay down. There was nowhere I could go at that time on New Year's Day anyway. The trains wouldn't be running until later. I snuggled back in and hugged Jimmy's pillow to me. I hadn't changed the bed sheets since he went. I thought I could still smell him on his pillow, that mix of his own muskiness and the minty shower gel he used. He never wore aftershave. My eyes drooped. It was definitely too early to get up.

The next time I woke, it had just gone midday and I realised how futile it would be to go to York and wander around looking for Jimmy. He wouldn't be there. I was beginning to think that I would never find out what had happened to him. But how could that be? How could something like that happen? It's the sort of thing you read about in novels, or see in a film, it's not real life.

Instead of going to York I called Gloria and we went to the pub. I was so drunk when I got home I went to bed with my coat and boots on again. The next day I woke up determined to be more positive, to get a grip, be healthier. I rang the Sanctuary Spa to see if they could fit me in for the treatments that Gloria and Jules clubbed together to buy me for Christmas. I'd always wanted to go there but it's so expensive that I could never afford it. I was embarrassed about what I brought them. I'd have to get them something else, make up for it.

When I got to the spa there were hardly any other women there so I had my choice of luxurious loungers and plenty of pools, steam rooms and saunas all to myself. My first treatment was a full body massage and by the time I got to the allotted treatment room I was already feeling much more relaxed. I had a large glass of wine with my lunch so felt glowy and warm.

The massage therapist was good, firm but not too hard. When she turned me over to do the front I found myself getting turned on as she massaged the tops of my thighs and her fingers brushed ever so slightly against my groin. Then she moved on to my chest and her fingers were so gentle as they moved over the tops of my boobs, as if she really was caressing me. It'd been so long since someone touched me like that. I was so embarrassed. Could she tell?

I squirmed and fidgeted. I wanted her to stop but I didn't at the same time. I cleared my throat.

'Is everything, OK?'

'Yes, fine. But perhaps you could leave my chest now.' I wasn't sure if I could take anymore without making a complete fool of myself.

'OK, no problem.' Her voice was neutral. She hadn't noticed. Or was professional enough not to let it show if she had. I didn't think too deeply about which one was true.

LAURA

Before I knew it the summer holidays came around again and Kate had finished her first year of school. She could read and the teacher was thrilled with how quickly she'd picked it up. We went to the library and got her some books to take away to the caravan with us. It was just the three of us going for the first two weeks then Ken was joining us. Una said she might pop down for some day trips but she'd stay at home this time. I was really looking forward to being with the girls on my own.

I also stocked up on some books about psychology, as I wanted to be really prepared for when the course started. I still couldn't quite believe that I was going to do it. The doubts kept creeping up on me every now and then but I pushed the negative thoughts out of my head as much as I could.

Kate had wanted to bring her new best friend, Stacey, on the holiday and even told her that she could come. I didn't know anything about it until Stacey's mum rang to ask about it as Stacey had gone home and told her she was off on holiday with us. The tantrum that followed me telling her that Stacy wasn't coming lasted for a whole day. Then Jules talked Kate out of it and they went off into the garden making secret plans for the holiday adventures they could have together. It was a strange feeling watching them become more independent, needing me less. I couldn't imagine how I would feel if I didn't have something of my own to look forward to.

I'd passed my driving test at the start of July and Ken had given me the Austin Allegro to drive as he'd started cycling to work. So for the first time I was driving us on the holiday and I was really excited about being independent. The day we set off it was quite warm but overcast and I hoped that we'd get some nice weather while we were there. By the time we got to the caravan it was windy and raining, much colder than when we'd left home, and we all got soaked carrying the bags of food, clothes and games in.

We stood shivering in the front room after we'd finished bringing it all in, so we put our pyjamas on and had a cup of hot chocolate to warm up. Then we baked muffins. I'd been trying to think of healthier ways to eat without the girls feeling like they were going without sweet treats and my latest concoction was apple bran muffins, which they both loved and were always asking for. So to distract them from the rain and the fact that we couldn't go to the beach on the first day of our holiday I decided to teach them how to make them.

While the muffins were in the oven we did the unpacking and by the time they were done the sun had come out. I packed up a bag then we sat on the caravan steps eating our still warm muffins before heading to the beach.

•••

That was pretty much the only sunshine, and the only fun, we had before Ken joined us, and by the time he did I was almost out of my mind with having been stuck in the caravan for two weeks with Kate and Jules whining and fighting. I knew they couldn't help it – I was bored too – but I'd been stroppy with them and the tension in the caravan was rising day by day. We'd had a couple of days out, including a disastrous visit to the Laurel and Hardy Museum in Ulverston. I don't know what made me think the girls would be interested but I'd been desperate to find some way of entertaining them. It was just a poky little room stuffed with old pictures and other junk. They had a little cinema showing films so I took them in there but Jules ran around shouting and we were asked to leave.

That was on the day before Ken came to join us and we'd had a miserable evening after we got back. I'd sulked like a child, embarrassed about being kicked out of the museum and seeming like I couldn't control my children. I'd put them to bed early threatening them that if they got up even once we'd go home and there would be no holiday with Daddy. Then I'd sat and drank the whole bottle of nice red wine I'd brought for me and Ken to have with our dinner when he arrived.

So on the morning we had to meet him at the train station, which was sunny and warm as if to mock me, I had a terrible hangover, the girls were over-excited that Daddy was arriving to rescue them from me and my moods, and I'd had more than enough.

'I'm having a day by myself,' was the first thing I said to him.

'Well that's a nice welcome. Hello to you too,' Ken said over the top of the girls' heads. They were clinging to him like limpets and obviously had no intention of letting go.

A twinge of shame nearly made me change my mind but I knew I had to go or I would throw a childish tantrum to rival any that Kate and Jules had thrown so far throughout the holiday.

'Yes, well. You haven't been stuck in a caravan for two weeks looking at the rain.' I handed him the keys to the caravan and the car. 'I'm getting the next train and going to Arnside for the day.'

Ken could obviously tell it was best not to argue as he took the girls by the hand and walked off. 'OK, see you later.' He didn't look back. None of them did. I was all alone on the deserted platform. Now that they were gone I wanted them to come back. Tears welled up as I hurried after them. When I reached the end of the platform I heard Kate's voice.

'Where's Mummy going? She's been shouting at us lots, Daddy. Yesterday she made us go to bed as soon as we'd had our tea and it made me feel a bit sick.'

'And me,' Jules said. 'She said that if we got up we'd have to go home and have no more holiday. Kate weed in our beach bucket next to the bed as we weren't allowed to use the toilet.'

I stopped dead. God, I sounded like a terrible mother. What was wrong with me? I turned and walked back down the platform. They obviously needed a day without me too.

●●●

Things were much calmer for the rest of the week with Ken there to help. My day off had made me feel better and I'd come back determined to stop being moody and make the most of the rest of the holiday. But even so, many times I had to bite my lip, or blink back tears, as I found myself wanting to shout and scream at them. It was the sameness of it all. Why couldn't we go somewhere different on holiday for once? I was sick of Silverdale, the beach and the bloody caravan. I couldn't wait to get home and for the girls to be at school so I could have some time to myself. To start using my brain instead of just being a housewife. Maybe then I'd have things to talk about with Ken, too. I never seemed to have anything to say that wasn't about the housework, the shopping, the girls. I was boring myself.

I buried my head in a book most days while Ken took the girls out exploring. Even though I'd bought all those psychology books from the library with me I found I couldn't concentrate on them, which made me doubt my decision to do the course all over again. So I mainly read trashy novels – Danielle Steele, Sidney Sheldon, Jackie Collins – and stupidly found myself crying over them.

Two days before we were due to go home, Una turned up unexpectedly at lunchtime.

'Una, how lovely.' I gave her a big hug and as I squeezed her I could feel myself getting all choked up again. That's when I realised. My moods had been all over the place, I was crying at the drop of a hat, and I should have got my period just after we'd arrived at the caravan. But I hadn't. Oh God, surely not. Not just from that one careless night. I definitely didn't want another baby. Not now when I was just about to start having a life of my own for the first time ever.

Una must have felt me stiffen as she pulled away from my hug and her eyes searched my face. 'What's wrong, Laura? You seem very tense.'

'Oh it's nothing. Just been here for ages with lots of rain.'

I could see she doubted it was that but she decided not to press me.

'Where is everyone?' She asked.

'At the beach of course. They left after breakfast and will be back for lunch very soon.'

After a lunch that was filled with the girls chattering excitedly about the crabs they'd seen at the beach that morning, and the man that had been flying a kite and let them have a go, and the big brown dog that had licked Jules's face, and, and and...Una announced that she was going to stay over.

'So, you have a babysitter for the night. Why don't you take Laura off to a nice hotel, Ken?' She looked pointedly at him and I wondered what she'd guessed from my tears at her arrival and near silence all through lunch.

'Why would I do that when we have our own perfectly good caravan in a beautiful spot?'

God, sometimes he could be very dense for such a bright man.

'Because that's what a lovely husband does for his wife who has been in the caravan for weeks without a break.' Una smiled at me.

'Do you want to do that, Laura?' Ken said, in a tone that showed he seemed to find it very difficult to believe that I would. Did I? Just the two of us by ourselves would mean I'd have to make lots of conversation and I really didn't think I could manage it. But otherwise we'd have to stay here with Una, and she'd definitely notice something was wrong if we stayed.

'I'd love to. Thanks Una.'

KATE

I got a taxi from out the front of the station, even though the driver told me it was less than a ten-minute walk and seemed really annoyed that he'd waited in the rank to get me and my paltry fare. I told him I'd need picking back up in an hour to try and make up for it but he said he couldn't take pre-bookings. He'd sped off with a glare after I'd paid him. A real charmer.

I'd never done anything like this before and I was nervous. I had no idea what to expect but was strangely convinced that I would definitely find out what had happened to Jimmy. After I was buzzed in and told to come to the top floor I closed the door behind me and leant against it for a moment. Was I doing the right thing? The entrance hall smelt of chemical air fresheners and there was a row of letter boxes along one wall. How did the postman get in to put the letters in the boxes? Did he have a key? Or did he have to buzz to get in? What if there was no-one in any of the flats when he arrived? I shook my head – what did it matter – and pushed myself forward towards the stairs. They were deeply carpeted in dusky pink and there were flower arrangements on every window sill on every level as I climbed upwards. Carole the Psychic lived on the third floor and I heard her door open above me as I made my way up.

'Hello, dear,' she called. 'Sorry about the climb, no lifts here, but it keeps me fit.'

Her voice was friendly and warm, and very normal sounding. Not what I had been expecting. I realised then that my mind had been filled with clichés when I'd thought about what she'd be like. I'd thought her voice would be deep, smoky and she would talk in mystical rhythms. Instead it was chirrupy and she talked of everyday items like lifts. Even before I saw her I knew that my vision of how she would appear would be wrong too – she wouldn't look like a fairground gypsy, with long flowing hair and robes, smouldering eyes and gold hoop earrings. As I rounded the last corner of the staircase I could see her feet – swollen, fat ankles above slippers shaped like sheep. A long, shapeless, olive green dress with a zip up the front and an embroidered flower on the left breast covered a gargantuan body. She didn't look very fit to me. She was older than I'd expected too – her white thinning hair sprouting out in all directions around her heavily lined face. She just looked like the kind of granny you saw every day buying bread and humbugs in Marks and Spencer. Was she a fake?

She smiled at me as I walked towards her and her eyes disappeared completely then, swallowed by flab and creases. It made me think of those wrinkly dogs, I forget what they're called but they have rolls and rolls of fatty wrinkles just like this woman in front of me had.

'Hello,' I said as I reached her.

Her eyes reappeared as she stopped smiling to say hello again and ushered me in the front door. I felt edgy, which wasn't helped by being confronted by an elderly man in a vest and underpants, he was framed in the doorway to a bedroom off the hallway where we stood. It was dark in the room and I couldn't make out his features but I saw his eyes glinting as he pushed the door shut. I felt guilty, like I was prying, but he was the one that had been stood there like that when he knew I was coming in.

Carole led me towards a room to the right of the front door with a small push on my elbow. I wished I wasn't there, I'd made a mistake, I shouldn't have come. I felt like running straight back out the front door but she was ushering me into a seat at a round table covered in a crocheted tablecloth. The room was bright from the weak winter sunshine coming in through the floor to ceiling window and smelt of incense. At least one of my expectations about what it would be like had come true.

I looked around me. The walls were painted apple green and covered in pictures in garish frames. All of the pictures were religious but there seemed to be no affiliation to any one faith. There was Jesus and Buddha, the Christian cross, the Islam crescent moon and star, and the Jewish Star of David sitting alongside the Hindu's Aum and the Sikh's Khanda. My head was spinning but when Carole saw me looking she said: 'We're all the same, dear, when we pass to the spirit world. There are no religious differences then, we all become one.'

I smiled warily at her. Was she mad? I'd always thought that speaking to the dead was a lot of hocus pocus nonsense and I didn't really know what I'd been expecting to find here, but it wasn't this. I realised then that there was no way she could help me. It was as I'd always thought – you can't speak to the dead. I was about to tell her this when instead I heard myself asking for her help. She leant across the table and took my hands in hers as I poured it all out about Jimmy's disappearance. That the police hadn't really done anything, that I'd been working with the Missing People organisation but all they had done was send out notices, that his family had been convinced that he'd left me but even they were scared now as he hadn't contacted them either. That he'd left his phone, his passport, all of his belongings behind and had never been seen or heard from again after popping out to the shop one night nearly four months ago. That I wanted her to tell me if he was dead.

She looked sad when I finished and leant back in her chair. My hands were suddenly cold without hers encasing them so I tucked them under my legs.

'Well, my dear. That's a very sad story indeed and I'm very sorry for your troubles. But I have to be honest with you, I don't think I can help. What I do isn't so prescriptive I'm afraid. I can't just summon people from the spirit world on demand.'

'What do you mean? That's what you do isn't it, you talk to the dead.'

'I talk to the spirits dear, yes. But there's a popular misconception about how it all works. People come here expecting their loved ones to be sitting waiting to give them the messages they want to hear but it's just not like that.'

I didn't say anything, just stared down at my lap. I'd been so convinced that this was the answer, that I really would find out what had happened to Jimmy here.

When she saw my despondence she carried on, 'I'm sorry if you're disappointed but I don't want to mislead you. I'm happy to contact the spirits and see what they have to tell me but I just want you to be prepared. It could be someone you hardly know that comes through, or someone you don't know at all.'

'That's OK, I understand.' My voice was a shaky whisper. 'I want to try anyway.'

'Well, let's have a cup of tea first dear and I can talk you through what will happen and what you can expect.' She rang a little gold bell that I hadn't noticed and as soon as it tinkled the door opened immediately and the man from the bedroom, now fully clothed, brought in a tray with a teapot covered in a sheep cosy and two mugs on it. What was the sheep thing – did she just like sheep or do they have some spiritual significance? The man made me uneasy, he still had a funny glint in his eye and I avoided looking at him.

We drank fennel tea and Carole talked me through what would happen next. Despite what she was telling me I was convinced all over again that I would get a message from Jimmy. My legs were jittery and bouncing as I took off my wedding ring and handed it to her. She closed her eyes and just sat there holding it for a few moments. The silence was unnerving and I fidgeted on my seat wishing she would say something. I closed my eyes too and when she did finally speak it made me jump. 'I'm getting something, from Dotty, is it Dotty?'

I wanted to laugh and cry, the tension had been unbearable and then she said that. It felt like I was in a bad film.

'I don't know anyone called Dotty.' I said but she didn't open her eyes or answer me. 'Dotty says Jimmy likes ginger biscuits.'

Carole opened her eyes then and looked at me. 'Is that true?'

'What?'

'Does he like ginger biscuits?'

I couldn't believe what I was hearing. Ginger biscuits. I'd just sat and told this woman how my life had been shattered by my husband's disappearance and she was mocking me with talk of ginger biscuits. Did she think it was a joke? Furious, I stood up and grabbed my wedding ring back out of her hand; she flinched as my nails scratched her palm. I roughly pushed the ring back on my finger and picked my bag up off the floor. I didn't say a word just flung the door to the hallway open and marched past the weird man, who was loitering in the hall, to the front door. He grabbed my arm but I yanked it away and ran out the door and down the stairs. I could hear Carole calling me but I didn't slow down or look back. I burst through the door to the outside and carried on running down the road back the way the taxi came when it dropped me off. I was crying and panting and suddenly realised that I had no idea where I was going. I sat down on the kerb at the end of the road and started to cry. Why did she do that? A car came round the corner and the elderly man driving it was startled when he saw me slumped at the side of the road crying.

He slowed down and opened the window. 'Are you alright, love?' he called out to me.

'Not really,' I said as I stood up, 'Can you tell me the way to the station please?'

LAURA

A week or so after we got home from the holiday, I told Ken that I had to go to an introduction day for my course. He was surprised that I hadn't mentioned it before but I just put it down to being all caught up with the holiday and then back to school preparations. Two days later I drove all the way to Preston to get a pregnancy testing kit. Lancaster was still a very small town in many ways and I didn't want anyone to see me buying it. Even though I didn't really need a test, as I already knew. As soon as I'd realised that my period was late I started noticing the other signs. The cold, rushy feeling in my boobs and that horrible metallic taste in my mouth. If it was going to be like my other pregnancies the morning sickness would start in a couple of weeks.

After I'd bought the test I wandered around the shops for a bit killing time as I couldn't go home until late afternoon. I soon got bored though so I bought a picnic lunch and drove out to the Trough of Bowland. I'd always loved it there. It was one of the places Mum and Dad used to take me to on our Sunday drives. I parked in the same spot that Dad had always used to and wandered off through the woods, following the path of the stream. I saw the occasional walker but mostly it was deserted. After all the rain we'd had followed by a week of virtually unbroken sunshine everything was lush and bursting with life, even though the summer was nearly over. A squirrel ran across the path right in front of me and I stopped to watch it. I'd heard that in Hyde Park in London the squirrels were so used to people that they'd come and take food from your hand. I wanted to take the girls to see that one day.

When I came out of the woods I crossed the stream on the stone bridge that Dad and I used to drop sycamore seeds from. We had a tree in our garden and I used to gather them and take them with us as I was obsessed with them for a while. I used to imagine they were fairy wings. I climbed the hill on the other side of the bridge and sat looking out over the valley. I couldn't eat the picnic lunch I'd bought so I picked at the bread and threw bits of it for the birds. They were wary at first but soon there were sparrows and blackbirds swooping in to gorge on it.

There was no way I could have this baby. But I'd never thought I was the kind of person that would have an abortion. Why couldn't it just go away? Miscarry. Then the problem would be solved without me having to do anything about it. Ken would definitely want it. I could see him now, all excited and imagining that it would be a boy this time. But what about me? I'd been Mum and Dad's little girl, then Ken's wife and the girls' mum, never just me. I was finally getting a chance for some independence, of a sort, and then this had to happen.

I sat there for hours going over and over it in my head. Then I went home and did the test in the bathroom, which was incredibly complicated and involved vials and pipettes and test tubes and all sorts. It was positive, of course.

•••

Weeks went by before I told Ken. The girls were back at school, he was back at work and my course pack had arrived in the post. I'd sat looking through it and knew that there was no way that I could do it if I was having another baby. I rang Shelley at work. She'd become my only friend over the past few years as I never went anywhere to meet anyone else. We arranged to meet that night in the Water Witch at half past eight.

I hadn't realised that I looked so obviously upset but I must have as she took one look at me and said: 'God, Laur. What's up with you?'

I swallowed the lump in my throat down. 'I'm only bloody pregnant again,' I quickly swiped away the tear that had rolled down one cheek, 'and that is not a good thing.'

'Oh. Shit.' Shelley reached across the table and squeezed my hand before pointing at my beer. 'Should you be drinking that, then?'

'Probably not. But I don't really care. I don't want it.'

'What about Ken?' Her voice was high, and she blinked repeatedly.

'He doesn't know yet. You're the first person I've told.' I took a big gulp of the beer. 'He'll want it, of course he will.'

Shelley nodded and sipped her drink. 'Why don't you want it?'

'Because...I...God it sounds so selfish, but I want to have some time to be me. Now that the girls are at school I can have a life of my own during the day. Not just be a wife and mother. I've never done anything.' Even I could hear how forlorn I sounded.

'Of course you have. You've got two lovely little girls.'

Shelley and her husband, Adam, had been trying for a baby for ages with no luck and I suddenly felt really bad for telling her this. Not just a selfish wife and mother but a completely insensitive friend.

'Oh Shelley, I'm sorry. I didn't think.'

She shook her head. 'Don't be silly. I'm your friend and no matter what you should be able to talk to me about things. Actually, I wasn't going to tell you yet, but I'm pregnant too!' She looked so thrilled. Why couldn't I feel like that?

'Shel! That's brilliant! I'm really happy for you.'

'Well, it's early days yet, just a few weeks, but fingers crossed it'll all be alright.' She held up both hands and shook her crossed fingers at me.

I knew then that I had to shut up about not wanting the baby. I couldn't spoil it for her.

'And you'll get used to the idea of another one, Laur. It's obviously come as a shock.'

I nodded and smiled. Who could I talk to now? It would have to be Ken.

UNA

Dear Kate,

This is the umpteenth letter to you that I've started and I'm determined that this one won't end up in the bin like the others. I have something very important to tell you but first I just want to say how very sorry I am about Jimmy. But even more so, I am heartbroken that you have felt unable to turn to me, or your father, for support. What does that say about us and how we brought you up if you don't feel like we can help you when you most need it?

I have done so many things in my life that I am sorry for. When you get to my age, you start to look back and spend more time in the past than you do in the present. I'm getting old and I've got to tell you the truth now before it's too late. The truth about me, but more importantly the truth about your mother.

She never wanted to leave you. She didn't leave you. It wasn't like that. Your father and I lied all along about where she'd gone, and we should have told you the truth a long time ago. We were trying to protect you. We thought it was the right thing to do. But more of the blame lies with me, as I've also lied to Ken. He still has no idea where Laura went but I've known exactly where she is all along...

KATE

Even though I was freezing and the lights shining out of the church windows looked warm and inviting, I loitered outside the gate thinking about what Gloria had said last night. She was dead against me coming here, said the visit to the medium's house should have been enough to put me off looking for answers from a bunch of crackpots. We were sat at her tiny kitchen table and I fiddled with her crocheted coaster while she made us dinner and wished she would hurry up. I didn't want her to make food; I wanted her to make joints. Since Christmas, I'd gone round more and more often to get stoned with her. It helped. It didn't make the constant racing in my mind go away completely but it held it at a distance, let me think of things other than Jimmy and relax a bit.

'You must be mad,' she'd said straight away and we both laughed. If the last few months were anything to go by then I was mad. The world was mad and everyone was mad to think it wasn't, mad to think that they had their life under control.

'I have to do something. I just walk the streets searching for him, the same things going over and over in my mind. And if I'm not thinking about that then I'm thinking about Laura and Jules, Granny, Ken. I'm going mad.'

'So going to see other people that are mad, who believe they can talk to dead people, how will that help? How can you believe anything they say? You don't believe in ghosts, Kate. You work for a science magazine.'

'I don't know what I believe anymore.'

'What makes you think they're going to be any different to the ginger biscuits faker? It's all nonsense, Kate.'

She turned back to the vegetables she was chopping, then as an afterthought added: 'And you don't even know that Jimmy is dead.'

'Well, maybe I'll find out.'

She looked back round again. 'That really is mad, Kate. For God's sake, don't be stupid.'

'Don't call me stupid. What do you know about it? Nothing. You don't know what they do or believe.' My voice was rising.

'I know they think they can talk to dead people. Just stop and think about that for a moment. How mad that sounds. You can't talk to dead people as they aren't alive anymore.'

I threw the doily down on the table and stood up.

'I'm sick of you and Jules thinking you can tell me what to do all the time. It's as if Jimmy's vanishing act turned me into a child, or a mental patient. That I can't be trusted to make my own decisions. Well I'm sick of it.'

I stormed off towards the front door with Gloria calling after me. 'Kate, stop shouting. Calm down and come back. Have some dinner.'

I slammed the door shut and went home.

'Excuse me.'

A voice right next to me on the pavement startled me. A small old man was standing next to me. He smiled through thin cracked lips.

'Sorry I didn't mean to make you jump but I'd like to get through the gate.'

I looked and I was standing right in front of it, gripping it. I stood aside so he could pass.

'Are you coming in?' He said.

'Um, maybe. I'm thinking about it.'

'Would you like to come in with me?' He offered his arm, like a proper old gent, and on first inspection he didn't seem completely crazy. I was there to go in so I may as well get on and do it. I didn't want to take his arm though.

'OK, I'll come in with you,' I said as I walked ahead of him through the gate that he was holding open and up the path to the door. It was darker and colder inside the grounds because of all the trees and bushes. I was glad he was with me, it was spooky.

Inside it didn't really seem like a church, more like a community hall. A stage at the other end of the room had rows of chairs facing it. A few people were dotted around but it was pretty empty and very bright. There seemed to be a hundred lights blazing down from the ceiling and it hurt my eyes to look up at it. My escort led me to a chair and then went off to speak to some friends.

'I hope you enjoy the service.' He said then he was gone.

There were stained glass windows at the back of the stage but not like the ones you see in churches. There were no religious scenes on them, no Jesus, sheep or fishes. Instead, bright sunflowers and hands clasped together around the globe. It all seemed pretty normal, no-one looked mad; maybe a little sad, a little odd, but not certifiable. There were no obvious signs of religion anywhere and I wondered if the churches were the same as Carol and had no affiliation. Perhaps they don't have time to tell religious stories as they're too busy talking to the dead. Perhaps it is true that they can.

We hadn't had any religion in our house when I was little and the first time I heard about God was from Granny. It was a big year – I got a Granny, I found out about God, I started school and played an angel in the nativity play. The day I found out about God, Jules and I stayed at Granny's as Ken and Laura had a night out. It was a massive adventure, we'd never stayed away from home before and we loved having Granny all to ourselves. We stayed up and watched a TV programme about a lady police woman with curly back hair, and ate hot buttered crumpets. Jules and I didn't really understand the programme and she fell asleep on the sofa next to me with her heavy, hot head on my shoulder. When the programme finished Granny carried her upstairs and put her to bed then came back down and told me it was time for bed too. As she tucked me in she told me to say my prayers.

'My what?'

'Your prayers.'

'I don't know what that is.'

'It's when you thank God for the good things that happened today and ask him to keep safe all the people you love and the people that need his help.'

'Who is he?'

'What do you mean who is he? You know who God is.'

'I don't. I don't know.'

She sat down heavily on the bed muttering under her breath, then told me this fantastic tale about God making the world and everything in it. It was great, nearly as good as the bedtime stories we usually had and that's how I always thought about religion, a fairy tale. And like all fairy tales it's got a sting in it. I said the same to Jimmy years later when he confessed his belief in an all-seeing almighty. I laughed first as I didn't believe that he meant it. But he did. I told him he was mad then and yet here I am now, so who's right and who's wrong? That was his argument, that there was no proof, as far as he could see, to say there was no God. Until then he'd believe in him. Is Jimmy with him now? Maybe these spiritualist people would tell me.

Only about another six or seven people arrived and it was fairly empty still when the lights dimmed and a hush fell over the room. A middle-aged woman came onto the stage from the right. Her greying hair was long and unkempt and she had on a matching blouse and skirt set with garish red and yellow patterns on it. She looked like a nice person; there was an aura of calm about her and her eyes twinkled. She went to the left of the stage and lit a candle and an incense stick then looked round at her congregation, all twelve of us.

'Good evening everyone. Thanks for coming to our service this evening. I see a couple of regular faces and also some new ones so welcome to all of you.'

She then spoke about the service she was about to take but my mind drifted off and I studied the other members of the congregation from my seat near the back. Were they all there because something had knocked their lives off course as well? Or had they always believed in communing with the spirits? The solace seekers were split almost evenly between men and women but I was the youngest, by a good fifteen years, I reckon. Is it something that people come to when the end of life is nearer than the beginning and it hasn't been exactly what you wished for? Does a relationship with the dead through a medium seem preferable to those amongst the living? Maybe it was safer to maintain that distance. Maybe real life relationships hurt too much. Mine certainly did.

A woman down near the front in a green jumper and jeans was talking to the medium and I tried to concentrate. I couldn't believe in it though. Gloria was right. I wouldn't find out what had happened to Jimmy in a spiritualist church, no matter how nice the woman on the stage looked.

'Yes, he did,' the woman in the green jumper said and I watched again.

The medium was standing in front of her on the stage, her head cocked as if listening, her eyes half closed. Then she looked back at the woman and said:

'Dave says you should go to Whitstable again. Did you have a holiday there?'

The woman stifled a sob and nodded. Was this woman hearing voices, or could she just sense things? But of all the holiday places in England, I'd say that Whitstable is probably a lesser known one. I'd never even heard of it, had no idea where it was. If you were just guessing, wouldn't you go for somewhere more common, like Bournemouth, or Brighton? I mean, everyone's been there.

'Dave says he was happy on that holiday. You should go again and remember the happy times.'

Her head cocked to the other side then and I really wanted to believe, I wanted this woman in her polyester twin set to have the answers I needed. I wanted her to look at me and tell me she had a message from Jimmy, but she didn't. She turned to a woman on the other side of the room instead. Were they regulars? Were they getting messages as their dead knew where to come, knew they could find them there? Why would Jimmy think to come to a spiritualist church in Ealing when I've never believed in anything? Or maybe spirits can see everything at once. Or would that make them God? My mind was still racing when I'd thought this would help. Instead it was creating more questions that I had no hope of finding the answers to. I wanted to leave but felt like it would be rude to stand up and walk out in the middle of it. So I sat there half listening to what the medium was saying and wondering how I was ever going to move on from what had happened.

The service ended after another forty minutes or so with everyone standing and singing along to a CD that the medium switched on. It was a surreal experience as the quavering voices of the small congregation got lost in the large room, competing with Whitney Houston's beautiful voice at top volume. It felt like a dream and that any moment I would wake up in my bed and it would be Thursday morning still and I wouldn't have gone there yet. The applause rippled around the room as the song ended and the medium thanked everyone for coming.

'If you didn't get a message today, please do come again as it can take time.' She bowed then left the stage.

Stunned by the whole thing I sat in my seat as nearly everyone else started to file out of the room. The old man that had taken me to my seat was talking with the woman in the green jumper down by the stage and she seemed inconsolable. I knew how she felt.

The journey home passed in a daze and I went straight to Gloria's but she wasn't in. She'd been going out more and more often. I poured myself a large glass of red and called her mobile but it went to voicemail straight away. She must have it switched off. Where could she be? There were three missed calls from Jules. She was back in Japan and we hadn't seen each other since she left after our row at Christmas. We'd only spoken a couple of times and it wasn't great, both of us still angry and resentful but trying to pretend we weren't. I took long swallows of the wine as I listened to her message.

'I'm coming back to England as Granny isn't well. Dad said she's been getting confused and has a cold that won't go away and now it's turned into a chest infection. I'm going to stay with her and it would be good if you could come and see her Kate. She was really worried about you over Christmas.'

I dropped the phone down on the table. If she hadn't got better in a week or so I'd go up there.

•••

The next day I didn't get out of bed at all. I sat under the duvet with Cheddar next to me and drank myself back into oblivion as soon as I woke up. The next time I woke it was dark, my head and my heart were pounding. I'd dreamt of Jimmy again. I was in the spiritualist church but it wasn't the same as the one I had just visited, but I knew that's where I was. The man that I shouted at in the pub about Elton John was up on the stage and he was levitating. Not really high but you could see a few inches gap between his feet and the floor. Jimmy's voice was coming out of his mouth and he was saying 'I told you, I told you, I told you.' I kept asking what he had told me but he didn't answer, just kept saying 'I told you' over and over.

The door swung open behind me and the man from the medium's house was standing there in his pants and vest again with his glinting eye. As the door swung shut behind him the man on the stage started singing Elton John's *I Can't Stand It* in Jimmy's voice and I screamed and turned to run. I tripped and the man by the door put his right foot on my left leg to stop me from getting up. Then I woke up. I couldn't move my left leg, something was pinning me down. I screamed and then it was gone. It was Cheddar. Cheddar was lying on my leg.

I fell straight back to sleep and the next time I woke it was because the doorbell was ringing and Gloria was shouting through the letter box. I stumbled to the door, my toe stinging from stubbing it on the empty wine bottle at my bedside. I'd obviously polished off the remaining half bottle before going back to sleep.

'Kate, you look awful,' Gloria said as I opened the door.

The sunlight in my eyes and the fresh air made me dizzy and I staggered to the kitchen and sat down at the table. Gloria made tea and toast.

'Oh, Kate. What have you been doing? You can't go on like this you know.'

I didn't say anything just lifted my mug to my lips with a trembling hand, sipped at the tea hoping it would stay down. I could barely think straight my head ached so much.

A glass of water and two tablets appeared on the table in front of me and Gloria sat down with a sigh.

'I've got the day off today. Maybe we should do something, go out for the day into town. Be tourists.'

'I don't think I can, Glor. I feel dreadful.'

'Well, those tablets will work soon. Drink your tea, eat a bit of toast and have a shower and you'll be surprised by what you can do, I reckon. We're doing it anyway, Kate, so you can either come along willingly or I will drag you along.'

She smiled to soften the words but I knew she meant them. It was funny, I'd thought when we first met that I'd be the one to help Gloria get back on her feet after what had happened to her. It's the unfulfilled social worker side of me, always feeling the need to help people even when they don't want it. But instead I was always crying on her, relying on her, being the one in need of help. She'd sorted her life out while mine had gone down the pan. If only I could have a hair of the dog to help me get ready to go out, face the world, but I knew she wouldn't let me.

It was a beautiful spring day, one of the first of the year that was bright and crisp but with that faint tinge of real warmth from the sun. We walked up to Battersea Park, sat on a bench in the sun and drank cups of steaming tea as we watched the ducks on the pond. I sensed that Gloria had got something on her mind and then I realised that she'd got me out to have a 'talk' with me, again. I told her about the night at the spiritualist church as we walked to the park and told her she was right. She didn't gloat. She told me I needed to think about what I was doing, that, as hard as it was, I had to move on from what had happened. It had been four and a bit months since Jimmy vanished, which doesn't sound long, but in many ways it felt like a lifetime. A letter from Lionel had arrived the day before telling me that the end of my sabbatical was coming up and he wanted me to go in and talk to him. After he'd come to the flat that day when I ran away from the office, he granted me a sabbatical until the end of March, just three days away now. I'd been angry when I received it, felt like I'd been told how long it was acceptable for me to be sad for, and that I'd never want to go there again, but I was thankful for the small percentage of my salary that I'd been paid while I'd been off. Mine and Jimmy's savings were dwindling and Gloria was right, I needed to make some decisions.

With the weak sun warming my face and everything in the park around me coming back to life it felt easy to be more positive. My hangover had retreated and it was good to be sitting outside relaxing instead of frantically searching the thousands and thousands of faces you see each day in London for just one; Jimmy's.

'I got a letter from work,' I said.

Gloria looked round at me, a question on her face.

'My time's up. I have to go in and talk to Lionel about what I'm going to do.'

'And?'

'I'll go in and talk to him. See how I feel then.'

'Good. You have to stop drinking so much, Kate. It really doesn't help.'

'It does though. You don't know what it's like, my mind never stops. Questions racing around all the time.'

'I do know. I was like that when I got away from Stuart. He was mad, he didn't care about injunctions, just kept coming for me. Even though he was locked up I kept thinking he was coming anyway. That there was nowhere he wouldn't find me.'

'And ever since I've known you, you've drunk loads and got stoned every night.' I gave her arm a little shove.

'Well, that's different,' she said.

'Why?'

'Because I've always drank and smoked. You haven't and starting because you've got all this craziness going on in your life is not a good idea.'

'If I promise to try and drink less will you promise to stop telling me what to do? I am a grown woman, Gloria.' I watched a squirrel leap from one tree to another and wished I could do the same, but from one life to another. I didn't want this one anymore. So maybe I should do what everyone wanted me to, kept telling me to do. Move on. Get on with making a new life without Jimmy.

'OK, deal. I won't tell you what to do all day today and you won't have a drink until we get home this evening, when I shall make you dinner to go with it.' She elbowed my arm and we laughed as we hugged each other close.

Gloria made pasta for dinner and we shared a bottle of red, just the one. I wanted more but knew Gloria would get upset so drank slowly and implored her to make a joint. She looked like she was about to start with another lecture but I held up my wine glass and mimed zipping my mouth, so she shut up and made one. I think she quite liked having someone to smoke with rather than sitting indoors doing it by herself. We smoked two then I went home and drank more wine until I could feel my eyes drooping, then I collapsed into bed in a dreamless sleep.

The next day I walked again. The steady beat of my feet along the pavement was soothing. I'd rung Lionel before I left the flat and arranged to go in and see him the next day. As if it'd been magicked into action by my thoughts of a phone call, my mobile rang. It was Jules. Granny was dead.

LAURA

The day after I'd completed the pregnancy test, once the girls had gone to bed and we were sat in the front room watching TV, I told Ken about the baby. As I'd known he would be, he was happy and excited.

'But what about my course, Ken? What about me having some time to myself now that the girls are growing up a bit?'

He looked as if I'd just ruined a party by announcing in the middle of it that I was dying of a terminal disease.

'What do you mean? That was something for you to do so you wouldn't be bored now the girls are at school all day. But now you won't be.'

I wanted to hit him. Surely he couldn't mean that?

'No, it wasn't just about that', I shouted. 'It was for me to have something for me. Be something other than a housewife. Do something. I've never done anything.' I heard myself repeating the exact same words I'd said to Shelley and knew that, despite loving Kate and Jules, I did feel like I hadn't done anything apart from play nursemaid, cook and cleaner for six long years.

'You could still do the course as well.'

'Don't be stupid. Of course I couldn't. How would I fit in all the work with a baby and two little girls to look after?'

'But we could get you some help. A cleaner, a nanny, whatever you wanted, so you could do both.'

'No. I don't want it, Ken. I don't want to have another baby.'

'Well, that's not an option Laura as you are having one.' As soon as he said it realisation dawned on his face. He rushed over to me and gripped me by the arms. 'Don't even think about that, Laura. There's no way.'

'Don't tell me what to do Ken. This isn't just your decision. It's my body. My life too.'

He started shaking me then. 'But it's my baby. It's not just up to you either.'

The shock I was feeling at being shaken by Ken, gentle Ken who'd never behaved like that before, was pierced by Kate's scream from the doorway.

'What are you doing to Mummy?' She ran at Ken and started hitting him. 'Get off her.'

I grabbed Kate and pulled her away from him. 'It's OK, Kitty Kat, I'm OK.' She was sobbing in my arms now. 'Mummy and Daddy got a bit angry with each other. We're silly. We're stopping now. No more shouting.'

I took her back up to bed and while I was soothing her back to sleep I heard the front door slam and Ken stomp off down the road.

•••

He didn't come to bed that night. I heard him get home about midnight but he stayed downstairs. When I got up in the morning he was asleep on the sofa with a coat over him. He stank of stale beer and cigarette smoke. I had to run to the kitchen, where I was sick in the washing up bowl.

Back in the front room I gently pushed his shoulder. 'Ken. Please go upstairs before the girls get up. I don't want them to see you here like this.'

He groaned and rolled over, turning his back to me.

'Ken, please.'

While I was in the kitchen filling the kettle I heard him get up and go upstairs. I sat at the kitchen table with a cup of tea wondering where we went from here, then the girls were up and I had to get on with the day. When I got back from dropping them at school I expected Ken to have left for work but he was still in bed, sleeping. I left him there.

At lunchtime I was in the garden enjoying the sunshine when he finally got up and came out to see me.

'I'm sorry.' He stood in front of me in his t-shirt and boxers looking like a repentant school boy. 'I'm sorry.'

'Me too.' I reached up and held his hand before resting my forehead on his stomach. 'What are we going to do?'

He sat down next to me on the bench seat cut into the wall and shrugged. 'Well, stop fighting for a start.'

I took his hand again. 'I really don't want to fight. But I don't want to have this baby either.'

'But you can't get rid of it, Laura. It's our baby. It's Jules and Kate's brother or sister. You have to have it.'

I dropped his hand. 'I don't have to do anything, Ken. Why can't we even discuss the options? You can't just tell me that I have to have it.'

'And you can't just tell me that you're not having it.'

And on and on it went like that for days, weeks. Until all of a sudden I was two months pregnant and knew that we had to make a decision one way or the other.

KATE

The front door pushed inward as I reached the bottom of the stairs and then Ken was right there in front of me, looking old and sad. We both stopped and stared – it had been a very long time. He recovered first.

'How are you, Kate?' he asked.

I'd managed to avoid him at the crematorium and I couldn't deal with him then so I shook my head and walked away from him into the kitchen. How are you Kate? How are you Kate? What a fucking nerve. The anger made me feel even better than the gin but I poured another one from the bottle on the side anyway. The condensation on it cooled my fingers.

I stared out of the window into the sun-drenched garden, the gin glass clenched so tightly in my hand I wondered if it would break. On the way there, I couldn't believe that the sun was shining so happily and the sky was such a big blue expanse of goodwill. It should have been grey, rainy, when my lovely Granny was lowered into the ground. How could I have been so selfish as to shut her out of my life over the past few months? As the funeral car drove us slowly back towards the house I stared down at Jules's hand holding mine on my lap but I couldn't feel it. I pressed her hand to test it. Nothing. Nothing seemed real.

She thought I was trying to comfort her though and gave me a wan little smile. I looked down again and saw her hand squeeze mine back. Nothing. All I could think was that I didn't want to go to the wake; didn't want to be in Granny's house without her there. I didn't want to think about how long it had been since I last saw or spoke to her. I definitely didn't want to speak to Ken.

I was shocked when we arrived at the house. Granny had always been so proud of her garden. Expending much more effort on the front than the back, so that everyone could share in the loveliness, she always said. I wondered now though if it was so she could talk to people as they went past. She'd lived alone for so many years. Her husband, Frank, died long before Jules and I were born and she'd been alone ever since. Then Laura left, then I did, then Jules did. Till all she was left with was Ken. And who'd want him around? Anyway, the roses, camellias, rhododendrons, and God knows what else, were all buried under a shroud of weeds.

Jules and I walked slowly through the wreckage up to the front door. For me, the sad state of the garden hammered home the fact that she was gone so much harder than the funeral had, and I needed to get inside, to shut the door on it.

Once inside I headed straight upstairs to the bathroom then leant against the door to make sure that no-one came in. Granny didn't have a lock. 'Why would I need it, when there's just me?'

I sat on the edge of the bath and drank from the hipflask I had in my bag. It was a present I'd got for Jimmy last Christmas. The warm and syrupy gin left a thick coating on my teeth, but it made me feel calmer; abler to face the mourners I could hear arriving downstairs. Lots of old women. I knew I'd have to vacate the bathroom, that there would be at least two old biddies heading straight for it. Bladders weak, pelvic muscles wasted away. I stared into the mirror. I wasn't looking too bad but I felt sure that the gin had helped, fuzzed the edges. I took another swig to make sure then opened the door. Three old ladies were heading my way. I smiled and nodded as I headed past them to the stairs, licking the coating of gin on my teeth.

I pulled my mind back to the kitchen and Ken was still there behind me. I squeezed my eyes shut, willing him to leave. He cleared his throat.

'Kate, please...' he started.

'Please what, Ken? Please can I get you a drink? That was always what you wanted wasn't it.' I spun round to face him. He was shocked by my anger. He really was clueless. I picked up a glass and grabbed the bottle of Bell's, sloshed some into a glass and thrust it at him.

'Just get stuck in Ken, it's what you do best after all. Talking was never high on your agenda was it? Why start now?'

He looked like he'd been slapped and my stomach lurched. Part of me wanted to stop but I pushed it away. I needed to be angry, needed to let it all out. It'd been boiling away inside for too long.

'Kate, please.'

But he stopped as an old man came into the kitchen. He stood aside to let him get past to the drinks so I sidled out the door and went into the front room. Safety in numbers. There was a sea of old ladies in there, dozens of blue rinses merging into one long, fluffy cloud that hovered round the living room. I laughed at this and swigged back some gin. Jules was watching me from across the room but I didn't meet her gaze.

The afternoon seemed to drone on and on. The blue rinses telling endless boring stories about Granny that no-one wanted to hear. Where were all the men that Granny knew? Surely she didn't have a life filled with just women. There were only two men there, apart from her devoted son. I'd been back to the kitchen and topped up twice already and as I headed back again I could see Ken moving to follow. He came into the kitchen and started again.

'Kate, look, can't we try and get past this. I know I made some mistakes. I want to try and make up for them.'

He gave me a tentative smile as if he thought his little speech could mend all those burnt bridges. Well it couldn't. They didn't just burn, they combusted.

I shook my head at him, 'It's not that easy Ken...' but he interrupted me.

'It can be, Kate. Jules and I have made a new start, and there's no reason we can't too.'

A new start, God he was a walking, talking cliché.

'It may have escaped your notice, Ken, but we are at Granny's wake. This is not about you today. Not everything is always about you.' I headed for the door, wanting to get away, to get into the living room again where the others were being civilised, eating triangle sandwiches and talking of safe things. I'd be protected by banality there; he wouldn't want to cause a scene in front of everyone. He moved into the doorway though so that I couldn't get past without pushing him out of the way. And there is absolutely no way I was going to touch him.

'Kate, I'm sorry. I'm sorry I've been such a bad father. I dealt with things badly when your mother left, I know. I couldn't cope. I'm not making excuses...'

It was as if a floodgate opened then. All the years of not speaking to him, of hating him, resenting him, wishing I had any other dad in the world but him. Suddenly I was glad he was there in front of me to hear why I don't talk to him. Won't talk to him.

'Yes, yes you are making excuses,' I screeched, 'and I'm not listening to them. You couldn't cope? You couldn't? Me and Jules were little girls. Little girls whose mother had walked out and you wouldn't tell us where she'd gone. You wouldn't deal with any of it. Left us to cope with it by ourselves. So we didn't just lose Laura, we lost you too Ken. And it is definitely too late for me to find you now.'

I figured this would finally shut him up but no, he had things to say too and he'd obviously decided that he was going to say them no matter what. I retreated back to the other side of the kitchen to put some distance between us, and to top up my gin. No tonic this time.

'But you were always so self-sufficient, Kate. So independent. You always made me feel like there was no need for me to be around.'

I snorted. I couldn't believe what I was hearing. 'Self-sufficient, Ken, at nine years old? That's a convenient way to remember it. The whiskey has obviously clouded your memory. So it's all my fault is it? It's my fault that my mother left and went god knows where never to be heard from again and that my father turned into a lush?'

'Yes, Kate. No, no, I don't mean it was your fault. But, yes, even at nine years' old you were independent. Then when you got older you couldn't wait to get away. You went to university and never came back. I haven't seen you since you were eighteen. It's not right, Kate. We need to sort this out.'

'No, we don't. There is nothing to sort out. I don't need you, I don't want you. I don't remember feeling self-sufficient, Ken. I remember feeling scared and lonely. Is that how you're feeling now? Is old age staring you in the face and you think you better get some plans in place now for your little girls to look after you?'

Jules rushed in, pushing past Ken in the doorway and shutting the door very firmly behind her.

'Will you two stop this? Everyone can hear you in there.'

I was sick of both of them. I knocked back the gin in the glass in my hand, took the bottle off the kitchen table and put it in my bag, then opened the kitchen door.

'Just fuck off. Both of you.' I said this very quietly then walked slowly down the hallway towards the front door.

There was a stunned silence in the front room and I could feel twenty pairs of watery old eyes staring at me as I went past the door, but I didn't look round.

...

I didn't know where I was. I was itchy and uncomfortable and something was digging in my back. My feet were cold; my mouth tasted of old sick. I opened my eyes. I was on the sofa. I lay watching the dust dance in a shaft of sunlight that had snuck through a chink in the curtains. I followed the sun beam to the coffee table where it spotlighted a dirty coffee cup and illuminated an array of other cups. One was laying on its side with a congealed puddle of dark liquid spilling out of it. Like a murder victim, shot in the street, bleeding life out onto the pavement. Is that what happened to Jimmy?

I rolled over onto my side so I didn't have to look at it. As I rolled whatever was digging into my back dug into my right hip instead so I pushed myself up and stuck my hand down between the cushions. It came out with a quarter bottle of gin in it and I dropped it on the floor next to a half empty, family bag of tortilla chips. As it landed I saw there was still a bit of gin sloshing around in the bottom of it so picked it back up again. I thought about going into the kitchen and putting it in a glass with some ice and some tonic but in the end just slugged it straight back from the bottle. There wasn't enough in there to make a proper drink anyway.

I scratched my left thigh, my back, under my right armpit. My skin was crawling. My Christmas pyjamas were covered in vomit, food, coffee, cat hair. Where was the cat? I looked around the dim room and saw Cheddar staring at me accusingly from across the room. He was sat on the floor just inside the doorway. Had I fed him recently?

My legs were rubbery when I stood, as if I hadn't used them in years. I pulled off my pyjama top and threw it on the chair so I didn't have to look at the rubbish. Take-away cartons and empty crisp packets littered the floor under the coffee table. I rolled the pyjama bottoms down and kicked them off. Left them in a heap on the floor and walked naked into the bedroom where there was another quarter gin bottle on the unmade bed, half full. I knocked back a few slugs then sat on the bed. My clothes were strewn all over the bed and the floor. Some of them were wet. Gin. I'd spilt gin all over the bed and my clothes. I tipped the bottle to my lips again, swallowed twice then that one was empty too. I threw it on the bed.

What was I going to wear? Where was my dressing gown? I started rummaging through the stuff on the bed, the gin smell became overpowering and my hands were wet so I gave up and went over to Jimmy's wardrobe. It was pristine in there. He was always so tidy. I ran my hands along the shirts, trousers and jumpers hanging there in their own sections. All the shirts together, then the jumpers, then the jeans and trousers.

I pulled out the shirts still on their hangers and took them into the spare room, which seemed to have escaped the maelstrom that had swept through the rest of the flat, and lay them all out on the bed. The dark blue one with the green and white check was my favourite. He'd had it for years, bought it just after we came back from our honeymoon. I slipped it off the hanger and over my head. It hung down almost to my knees and the sleeves covered my hands completely. I rolled them up then looked back at the shirts still on the bed. I picked up the white work shirts and threw them on the floor behind me. I wasn't interested in those; I was greedy for the ones he wore when he was with me. There's the grey cotton, so soft, and a close second to the checked one I was wearing. I picked it up and rubbed its softness on my cheek and it came away wet. Crying again.

The tears rolled silently down my cheeks as I continued with my inventory. The lilac monstrosity his mother gave him for Christmas a couple of years ago, worn only for parental visits; the horrendous puke yellow one he bought home from a shopping trip with Alan. Why did he always try to please them so much? It never worked; he could never do anything right in their eyes. I left the rest of the shirts lying on the bed and went into the kitchen. I sat at the table and sobbed as I looked around at the mess everywhere, the mess of me. How would I ever get a grip on my life again?

After a while I noticed that my legs were cold. I carried on sitting there though and got one of the joints out of the box, which sat amongst all sorts of debris on the table. I couldn't find a lighter anywhere among the wrappers, cups and food scraps so I lit it on the cooker then sat back down and stared at my feet.

My head was starting to spin out so I put the joint down on a plate I found on the table and went into the bedroom. If I was going to pass out again, which is what I was hoping, I wanted to be warm. I put a pair of Jimmy's jeans on and tripped back to the kitchen with the bottoms trailing on the floor and sat back down again and re-lit the joint. The doorbell went about five minutes later and it was then I realised that, blissfully, I hadn't been thinking about anything. Just staring at the floor. This is what I'd wanted for ages. No more thinking. The doorbell rang again then the knocker went and Gloria called my name.

'Kate, I know you're in there. Please open the door or just call out to let me know you're OK.'

I didn't answer though. I'd smoked all of the joint so I threw the butt down onto the plate and opened the box to get another one. All the while listening to Gloria getting increasingly frantic at the door. There were only five joints left in the box now. I must have been smoking a lot. As Gloria called out that she'd come back again later after work I got the last bottle of gin from the cupboard. I'd need to get more. I sloshed a healthy slug into a glass and decided to be civilised and have some tonic and ice in it. But there wasn't any so I drank it neat. Back at the table I puffed on the joint and sipped the gin waiting for the numbness that Gloria had shattered to return. If she'd gone to work I had over eight hours before she came to knock again, another gin and the rest of the joint should take care of how to fill that. My head was already spinning out a bit. Cheddar came into the kitchen but I couldn't meet his eye. He seemed very disapproving of me.

I knocked back the rest of the gin and smoked the last of the joint. Cheddar sat on the floor in front of me and stared directly at me. He made me uneasy. I had to go in the front room and lie on the sofa to get away from him. Everything went momentarily black as I stood up and it felt like the floor had been pulled out from under me, so I sat back down hard on the chair. The edges of my vision were still grey and hazy so I stood up more slowly, picked up the gin bottle and lurched towards the door, tripping on the jeans that were falling down around my hips.

As I headed for the sofa a flash of lucidity cut through the gin and the stoned haze. I could see the state of it all. I shook my head to get rid of it. I didn't want lucidity. I took another large swig of gin. The bottom of the jeans got all caught up in my feet. Then I was falling. Falling onto the table. The rubbish flew off as my arms slid along the glass top then my full weight slammed in behind them and the table smashed. The pain as I landed heavily on shards of glass that slashed my arms was obliterated as my head smashed through the gin bottle and everything disappeared.

LAURA

Sick to death of the rows with Ken and feeling like I couldn't talk to Shelley about it, I made the decision by myself in the end. I knew I couldn't have the baby. So I lied again and told Ken I was going to another course meeting. That I'd make the decision once I'd been there and seen how likely it was that I could do the course if he got me some help around the house. That I'd have to stay overnight in Manchester as it didn't finish until 6pm and I'd be tired and nervous of driving back in the dark.

So on a Wednesday morning in early October I drove to the Marie Stopes clinic in Manchester and had an abortion. All the way there I talked myself into it – told myself all the reasons why it was the right thing to do, even though it felt so wrong to have lied to Ken. But I knew he'd never accept my decision and the thought of being stuck in the house again with another baby was making my head spin. I felt trapped. Alone. Scared of what it might do to me.

Even as the anaesthetic was kicking in the thoughts that had been in my head all the way there fought their way through the wooziness. But others popped up too. Vivid images of the baby and what it would be like, who it would be. I hadn't allowed anything like that to enter my mind until then. But with my defences down I could see it. Feel it, smell it. I tried to speak, to say no, I've changed my mind.

But it was too late.

KATE

When I opened my eyes Jules was sitting next to me. She burst into tears as soon as she saw I was awake.

'Oh Kitty Kat I was so scared. I thought you were going to die.' Her hand touched me briefly, lightly on the shoulder. It made me think of those summer days when we were little girls and used to sit completely still in Granny's garden wearing flowery tops to see if we could get the butterflies to land on us. Sometimes they almost did, they skimmed over our arms and shoulders, and that's what her touch felt like, a butterfly fluttering very close by. She gave me a bleary-eyed smile.

My arms were stiff and when I looked down I saw that they were wrapped in bandages from my elbows to the knuckles at the bottom of my fingers. A tube came out of my left hand into a drip. I could sense that someone else was at the other side of the bed. I turned my head to look and it was Ken; he was grim, haggard, old. He nodded his head, as if I was an acquaintance he was passing in the street rather than his first-born daughter. I nodded back, too tired to hate him anymore. Jules put her hand on my shoulder again more firmly this time; it was icy cold.

'How are you feeling?'

I tried to smile. I couldn't do it though and tears were rolling down my cheeks instead. Jules rubbed my shoulder gently with her fist and we both cried.

'I wish you would...have...called me. I didn't know...I didn't know...that you felt so bad,' Jules said

Despite how tired and scared I felt, a little glimmer of anger ignited in me again but I tried not to let it show on my face, it wasn't the time or place for another row. But I couldn't believe she'd said it. How did she think I felt after everything that had happened?

'I know things have been bad for you, really bad, but you shouldn't have done this.' Jules blurted out when it became obvious that I wasn't going to say anything.

She started to sob then and Ken came round the bed and pulled her into his arms. My eyes darted between their faces. What was going on? Ken didn't hug us, comfort us.

'What? What have I done?' My voice was gravelly, dry, unused.

Jules pushed herself away from Ken's chest and I could see that she'd left a bit of snot behind on his shirt and despite the situation I'd woken to, I wanted to laugh. It was that slightly hysterical feeling though, inappropriate laughing when panic is nearby.

'What do you mean what have you done? The mess everywhere. Everything smashed up. This...' She gestured towards me.

I could see mine and Jimmy's bed then, covered in clothes and takeaway cartons, feel the wet again on my palms. I blinked and tried to concentrate on Jules.

Ken put his arm around Jules's shoulders. 'Jules, I think we should go and get a cup of tea. Kate is not long awake and the doctors said we mustn't tire her out too much.'

He sounded like he'd been watching too many hospital

dramas but Jules picked up her bag and they both smiled weakly before going off and leaving me all alone, with promises to return soon. While they were gone a nurse came to see me. Colin was his name according to the badge he was wearing.

'Hello Kate,' he said as he reached me.

He had a faint Scottish burr in his voice, a leftover from a life much further north, and when he smiled I could see that he had a nice face, was a nice person. He put the tray he was carrying down on the table next to my bed and brushed my hair back from my forehead with a gentle hand.

'I suppose you're wondering what's going on?'

Gloria had found me on the floor in my front room with my arms all slashed up. I'd lost a lot of blood and was lucky that she'd found me when she did. She'd phoned an ambulance, come in with me, waited while I had an emergency blood transfusion, had been there for days, waiting for me to wake up. He took my hand in his as he told me that she'd had to go to work but would be in again later; that I'd been unconscious in the hospital for three days. He left me then and I lay staring at the ceiling wondering how things had got so out of control that I'd ended up in hospital and I didn't know how.

When they came back Jules was calmer and Ken slightly less grim. But I couldn't deal with either of them just then. I knew they wanted some answers but I couldn't give them any. I couldn't remember what had happened. I wished a doctor would come. Were there even any in the hospital? Did they not care that I'd woken up? Maybe it was Sunday and they weren't there. Or maybe they'd been while I was asleep. My thoughts scattered like seeds thrown for the birds and I didn't know which ones to go after so I closed my eyes hoping to still them all by willing Jules and Ken to leave instead. It didn't work. I could feel them still standing there. I just wanted them to go so I told them to.

'Kate, we need to talk to you,' Jules said.

Again a hand on the shoulder from Ken silenced her. She nodded at him then looked back at me.

'OK, we'll leave now and we'll come back tomorrow. OK?'

...

The next time I woke it was still dark but very close to getting light. Everyone on the ward was sleeping and as I lay in the quiet I tried to remember what had happened. How I had ended up in hospital. The last thing I could remember clearly was rowing with Ken at Granny's funeral. I was so angry when I walked out of the wake and got the train back to London. I was drinking the bottle of gin I'd taken from the kitchen while I was on the train. In disjointed flashes I see a man with grey hair in a red jumper in the seat next to me but he moved to another seat. Did I say something to him?

Gloria. I went straight round to her flat as soon as I got back. She was getting ready to go out. She'd had her hair done. The straightened and bleached blonde was gone, in its place chocolate brown, glossy curls.

'You look lovely, Glor. Your hair really suits you. Where are you going?'

I slumped down on the sofa, hoping she might cancel her plans and stay with me.

'What are you doing here? You're supposed to be in Lancaster.'

'I was there but I left. Bloody Ken was talking to me and I didn't want to listen.'

'Maybe you should have. Everyone wants to help you, Kate. He's your dad, his mum just died; maybe you can help each other.'

'Oh don't you start. I'm sick of being told how everyone

wants to help me. Well no-one knows what it's like. And they just think I can move on, get on over it. Well I can't!'

Then I stormed out. She didn't try and stop me leaving like she usually did. I found her weed box in my coat pocket the next day. I must have picked it up off of her sofa. I'd started drinking as soon as I'd woken up but it wasn't enough anymore. It didn't obliterate the pain. It didn't stop the constant wondering, the turning over and over of the same thoughts in my mind that never actually produced any answers. I needed to get completely out of my mind. But I didn't have any tobacco or cigarette papers, so I went to Eddie's shop to get some. Jimmy's face smiled out at me from the poster in the window, watched me approach. It had been there for so long that it was starting to fade, just like his face was fading in my memory too. I couldn't instantly recall everything about him anymore.

In the shop Eddie raised his eyebrows when I asked for gin, tobacco and papers.

'Is everything OK, Kate?' He said.

'Fine, Eddie. Everything is completely fine.'

Outside the shop I stumbled. Acne-Face was walking towards me and he grabbed my arm.

'Whoa there. You alright?'

I pulled my arm away. 'I'm fine.'

He stepped back and looked at me. 'Well you don't seem it. You can hardly stand up.'

He insisted on walking me home. His puppy had got big and it jumped up at my legs sniffing excitedly at the cat smells on my clothes. When we got home I found myself asking him to come in, to roll me some joints as I didn't know how to do it.

The woman in the bed next to me coughed suddenly, harshly, and I jumped. The cough came again, deep in her rattling chest, awful. I couldn't see her as the curtains around my bed were pulled but I could hear her dragging herself up in the bed as the cough hacked away at her. I heard the doors open then soft soles scurrying quickly to my neighbour's bedside. Whispers, loud swallowing, a cough dying down, soft soles strolling back the way they came. Then silence again.

My bed was next to the window and I could see little bits of lighter blue sky appearing in the gaps at the side of the blinds. I watched them as I turned my mind back to that day again. Acne-Face, whose real name was Liam, came in and made a joint then we smoked it. Then we smoked some more and I made him roll all of the weed into joints for me. I stopped caring about the rows I'd had, that my husband had vanished into thin air, that my life was in tatters. Liam, who was just seventeen, had been surprisingly funny and easy to be with when I was completely stoned.

My head thrashes from side to side on the pillow as the realisation hits me.

Oh god, but then he tried it on with me. A teenage boy. He was embarrassed and angry when I said no. He was standing in the hallway shouting, 'You fucking prick teasing whore.' How did I end up in a situation like that? It could have been so much worse.

I sat up and pressed the buzzer to call the nurse, trying to shake the memories off. I wanted to go back to sleep and I wanted some pills that would make it happen. I pressed the buzzer again repeatedly. A nurse I hadn't seen before appeared and in a very pronounced whisper asked me what I want.

'I want sleeping pills. I need to go back to sleep.'

She frowned and checked my notes on the clipboard on the end of my bed. 'Well I'm sorry you can't have them. It's morning and we don't just give out pills on demand.'

Then she just left me there with my memories and I lay back

down and turned what had just come back to me over and over in my mind, feeling sicker and more ashamed of myself with each revolution.

•••

A little while later the whispering nurse returned and fed me stodgy, tasteless porridge from a blue plastic bowl then shortly after that Jules appeared. She'd obviously decided the forced cheery approach was the best one so I tried for the same and gave her as big a smile as I could manage.

'Hello Kitty Kat, you look a bit better this morning.'

Why was she using my childhood nickname? What did it say about her state of mind that she'd suddenly started using it again? She sat down in the chair beside me. There were dark smudges under her eyes and her hair was greasy. For a moment I felt guilty, but why shouldn't she be up worrying about me? I'd looked out for her all her life. I needed someone to worry about me for a change. I just couldn't seem to do it for myself anymore. The door at the end of the ward opened and Ken appeared.

'How are you feeling?' he said as he came to stand next to Jules.

'Oh you know. Not that great.'

Jules started crying again. 'Why didn't you tell me things were so bad?'

'I don't know. I'm not sure that I knew.'

She did a sobby little laugh at that.

'Really? What happened, Kate? What did you do to your arms?'

Do? What does she mean? I didn't do anything. I had an accident, didn't I?

'Well?'

Ken touched her shoulder as if to try and silence her again but this time it didn't work.

'Well?'

I couldn't answer. I didn't know what happened, so I said nothing, just stared at her.

'I'll tell you then shall I? Tell you what they've told us. They think that you…that you might…have done it yourself. Cut your arms.' She mimed slashing her arms as she said this and her voice was loud but broken all at once. 'They're saying you might have tried to kill yourself.'

This last statement was a sob again and even Ken looked like he might cry.

'What? Who does?' My brain was sluggish; it couldn't keep up. I couldn't make sense of what she was saying.

'The doctors. They're saying that you might have been attempting suicide.' Ken delivered this bombshell in a monotone, like he was telling me it about someone else.

I tried to sit up but my arms wouldn't hold me and I slumped back on the pillows again.

'I didn't try to kill myself. I wouldn't do that.'

But as I said it I realised that I didn't know if it was true. That's what crazy people do and I wasn't crazy. I'd always been the one who kept things under control, been the strong one. They were wrong. The sound of my whimpering penetrated the whirling in mind, I sounded like a small animal trapped and frightened.

'So what did happen then?' Jules said.

'I don't know. I can't remember,' I whispered.

They both stared at me and I knew that they thought I had tried to kill myself. They were going to say I was insane and lock me away. Panic erupted in me and I screamed and shouted. Not making any sense. They both looked really scared. Then a nurse

came. She held me down in the bed and gave me an injection.
Then everything was gone.

LAURA

The next day I arrived home at lunchtime. The house was too quiet. I couldn't believe what I'd done. How was I ever going to tell Ken? How could we ever be the same after this? I wanted my mum. She'd know what to do. But she was long gone. Had never been there to help me through anything when I needed her. It was so bloody unfair.

In desperation I called Granny. As soon as she answered the phone I started sobbing hysterically.

'Laura, Laura, calm down. Stop. Tell me what's wrong.'

I couldn't though. How could I tell anyone what I'd done? So I just wailed. I could tell I was frightening her but I couldn't stop.

'Is it Ken? The girls?' Her voice shook.

'No, no, it's me.' I managed to say.

'What? Are you sick?'

Sick in the head, that's what I was. What sort of woman did what I'd done? But I couldn't tell her.

I took a deep, shaky breath. 'It's nothing. I'm just being silly.' I wanted to get off the phone.

'What do you mean being silly? It doesn't sound like it's nothing.'

'It's just the girls. They played up all morning and I had a row with Ken. It all got on top of me.' Lying again. I was becoming a master at it.

'Well it sounds to me like you're over-reacting.' I could tell she thought that would help but it made me want to scream.

'I know. I told you I'm being silly. I better go anyway. Lots to do.'

'Oh, OK then. Might you come and see us soon?'

'Yes we will. Sorry, Gran. Are you OK? And Granddad?

'We're fine, love. Apart from your Granddad's feet. You know how he is with his ailments.'

There was no way I could listen to that so I said goodbye, see you soon.

...

At the school gates I knew all the other mums must be wondering why I looked so terrible. I'd pulled myself together enough to put some make-up on but it couldn't hide my red swollen eyes.

Kate ran up and hugged me hard, her little arms squeezing round my waist.

'Mummy, Mummy. You're back. I missed you.'

'I missed you too, Kitty Kat. Where's your sister?'

'She's coming. She couldn't find her gym bag.' Kate stood back. 'What's wrong with your face? You look funny.'

'I've got a bit of a cold.'

Jules arrived and we set off down the road.

'Let's go and see Granny shall we?' I called after them as they skipped in front of me holding hands and singing.

At Una's I told more lies. Ken and I were having a tough time, we needed some time to talk. Could she have the girls overnight? I'd already packed a bag for them.

'But Mummy we want to come home with you.' Jules whined when I told them they were staying at Una's.

'I know, but Daddy and I have got something to do this evening. You'll have a nice time with Granny and then I'll pick you up from school tomorrow and we'll have the whole weekend together.'

I shut the door on her cries and hurried off down the hill towards home.

I felt sick as I waited for Ken. My stomach was cramping with period-like pains as I tried to plan what I would say. I couldn't get it all straight in my head though. It was all mixed up with thoughts of the baby I'd just killed. What if he, I'd decided it would definitely have been a boy this time, was supposed to be someone special? Was going to make an important discovery that would change the world? Or was supposed to be born so he could meet someone one day and do something that would change their life? Maybe it was Kate or Jules, perhaps they'd get sick and need one of his organs. And now I'd ruined their chances as he wasn't allowed to be born, could never be there for them.

When I heard the front door open I was in the kitchen, gripping the sink as I stared out into the garden. I had no idea how long I'd been there but when I unpeeled my fingers they were stiff, hard to move.

'Hello?' Ken called.

I couldn't make my legs move. I couldn't go and tell him. I couldn't speak. It was as if the wait and the thoughts I'd been having ever since I'd done it had rubbed me out. I wasn't there anymore. There was nothing left in me that could say what needed to be said.

Then he was there behind me.

'Oh, there you are. Didn't you hear me?'

My throat clicked but no words would come out.

'Laura? What's wrong?' He grabbed me by the shoulders and turned me to face him.

I stared at the floor, scared to look at him, of what he would see. But even without seeing my face, somehow he knew. His hands dropped down.

'What have you done?'

'Ken, I'm sorry...' but I couldn't say any more. I finally looked up and tried to hug him, his face was blurred by my tears but I could still see the fury, the hurt. What had I done?

He pushed me away from him. His footsteps thundered up the stairs but seconds later he ran back down again and then he was gone.

He didn't come back that night. Nor the next. When I collected the girls from school I managed to find out without directly asking them that he hadn't gone to Una's. My mind was creating all sorts of horrible ideas about where he might have gone, what he might have done. But on Saturday morning he turned up.

Kate burst into tears as soon as she saw him. 'Daddy, where have you been? Why does everyone keep not being here?'

Ken hugged her and soothed her. 'I had to go away for work, Kitty Kat. But now I'm back. So no need for tears.' He didn't look at me.

All day long he avoided me. Then once the girls were in bed I cornered him in the kitchen where he was making a cheese sandwich.

'You can't ignore me forever, Ken.'

For the first time since he'd come back he looked straight at me. The contempt in his eyes shocked and scared me. 'I don't intend to. But I can't talk to you at the moment. Stay away from me as much as you can.'

He was so calm. I'd expected accusations and anger. Not this blankness.

'How am I supposed to do that? We have to talk.'

'What's the point? You made your decision. You went and did it without talking to me.'

'I did talk to you about it. But you wouldn't listen.'

'No, *you* wouldn't listen. It was all about what *you* wanted. Well you've got what you wanted now. I hope you're happy.'

'I'm not.' My voice broke and I was sobbing again. The grief I'd had to hide all day bursting out of me. 'I'm not happy. I made a mistake. I'm so sorry.'

Part of me hoped that would bring him back to me but it made it worse.

'You're sorry, you made a mistake. My God, Laura. What is the matter with you? Do you think your platitudes can make up for this? You lied. You went off and killed our baby in secret without a thought of how I might feel about that. I don't even know who you are anymore. The Laura I know...the Laura I knew...would not do that.'

Stupidly I tried to hug him but he shoved me away. 'Get off me. Go away.' Then he turned his back and stared out of the window into the darkness.

KATE

When I was released from the hospital Jules came to collect me.

'We're not going back to the flat,' she said as soon as she saw me, 'I think it would be best for you to have a change of scene.'

I still couldn't remember much between Liam leaving the flat and waking up in the hospital, just little flashes of things would appear but then fade again just as quickly and the counsellors I'd had to see during my stay in the hospital said this was my mind trying to protect me from the things I didn't want to remember.

But they'd also made me look at the fact that my problems went back way further than what had happened with Jimmy. We'd looked at my behaviours and relationships and they said that I'd always been messed up because Laura left us all. Jimmy's disappearance was the catalyst that brought everything I'd been hiding from since then to a head. Who'd have known it? I thought I was a normal woman living a normal life but it turned out I'd been emotionally bereft for most of it. And the thing is as soon as we started to talk about it all, I could see it. I could see how uptight I'd always been, always needing to be in charge, in control, and never really admitting to anyone, not even myself, how I really felt about things.

It was as if everything that had happened in the last few months, and everything that I'd learnt about myself, had completely wiped me out. I couldn't make any decisions so I just let Jules do what she wanted with me. She'd booked us into a hotel in Devon for two weeks – a recuperation holiday by the sea. Then we'd go back and empty the flat before we moved into Granny's house, which we'd inherited. Granny had also left a life insurance policy that had paid out twenty-five thousand pounds to each of us, and Ken, and about another twenty thousand in savings that had been split between the three of us. I couldn't believe it.

We didn't speak much on the journey and I stared out the window watching the grey concrete towers give way to green fields and big skies. We arrived at the hotel just before six o'clock. It was in a stunning spot in Exmoor National Park. We climbed out of the car and I stretched my arms over my head then down to my toes before looking around. The early evening sun lit up the top of the trees and the paths leading out along the cliffs, but the valley that the hotel sat in was so deep that the sun was long gone down at ground level.

The hotel was a pub too and the garden at the front was full and busy. As Jules saw all the people there laughing and drinking she clasped her hand across her mouth.

'Kate, God, I'm so sorry. I didn't think. We don't have to go in the pub. We can just sit in the hotel and our room, walk and go to the beach.'

'It's OK, Jules. There are going to be pubs everywhere. I'm alright, honestly. I don't want a drink.'

She smiled warily and I knew she was wondering if I was going to go on another massive bender. You couldn't blame her for thinking that but unless it's happened to you, you can't really grasp how waking up in hospital with no memory of how you got there really petrifies you. People say it all the time because it's really true – it's a wake-up call.

Once we'd checked into our luxurious room with its floor to ceiling windows we went for a walk. Almost five hours in a car had left us both feeling cooped up, and we've always loved the outdoors. Growing up on the edge of the Lake District means we had a love of walking instilled in us from a young age. Out the front of the hotel the garden was quieter and we headed off up the path that led back behind the hotel.

It was dry and still very warm despite the sun not reaching the path. The river was low and you could tell it had been a hot and dry few weeks. After ten minutes of following the river we came to a little wooden bridge and crossed to the other side. The path climbed then and when we came out of the trees, a sheer cliff covered in scree and scrub faced us. The path went along the base of it to where the river tumbled down the rocky beach and joined the sea. When we got there a couple and a dog were down near the water's edge so Jules and I walked in the opposite direction and sat down on a flat rock. As we watched the water, she linked her arm through mine and rested her head on my shoulder.

'This is nice isn't it?'

'It is. Thanks for bringing me here. For looking after me.'

'Oh Kate, you don't have to thank me. Everything that's happened has made me realise how much I've taken everything you did for me for granted. It must have been really hard for you having to look out for me all the time. I've realised that you were like a mum and you didn't have anyone to help you.'

'Well I had Granny. From the counselling sessions I've realised too that I took it upon myself to be the grown-up one, the one in control, so that I wouldn't have to think too much about things. Best to keep busy.'

We laughed together at that. Jules was always telling me to relax, stop bustling about. But I never did. Stillness brings thinking and I never wanted to think. It was only when Jimmy went that the thinking started. And look where that led. We stared out across the water to where Wales was a hazy shadow on the horizon. A sleek black seal popped its head up in the shallows so we walked down to the water to get a closer look. The couple with the dog had gone so it was just us, the seal and the sunshine. It was the first time I'd been to Devon and it sort of reminded me of the Lake District but a softer, gentler, brighter green version.

'I'm hungry, shall we walk back?' I said.

Jules clapped her hands. I hadn't really been hungry for ages and had lost a lot of weight. My arms had healed well though and there were just the fading pink lines of scars. None of the gashes were very deep luckily and the surgeon did a good job of sewing them up so in a few years he said I would barely notice them at all. I wasn't allowed to get them out in the sun for a couple of months though, so I had a long-sleeved top on to protect them. I was glad as I didn't want people looking at them.

At the hotel we ate dinner in the pub and listened to the band of local folk musicians. I drank cranberry juice and soda and so did Jules, which was a first for her. I told her that she could have a drink, that it wouldn't bother me, but she insisted she didn't want one. We were back in our room at half past ten and went straight to sleep after our day of travelling, walking and sea air. But I woke in a panic a few hours later, drenched in sweat. It was pitch black and I didn't know where I was for a moment. The wisps of a dream floated through my mind but I couldn't quite grasp them, then they were gone completely.

Jules moved and my eyes had adjusted to the dark by then and I remembered. The hotel. Devon. I lay back down but my t-shirt was drenched and sweat pooled between my breasts. I'd been getting a lot of night sweats as my body recovered from the abuse I'd put it through over the past six months. I got up quietly and went into the bathroom and closed the door. As I waited for the shower to warm up I sat on the toilet. Dark middle of the night thoughts started creeping into my mind. The counsellor said when I have racing thoughts I should do a visualisation exercise where I have them all in little envelopes and picture myself posting them into the post box, getting rid of them, sending them away. I'd thought it sounded really stupid but as I stood under the hot water I gave it a go. The steam and the heat made it easier I think, but I did manage to still my mind somewhat while I was in the shower, but then I was wide awake.

'Kate, what are you doing?' Jules called through the door as she knocked on it.

I pulled it open and she had the lights on. Her face was pinched and pale as she squinted at me.

'I was just having a shower. I woke up and I was having sweats again, I felt horrible.'

'Oh, right.'

I rummaged in my bag to get another t-shirt. Jules climbed back into her bed and I sat on the edge of mine, rubbing my hair with the towel.

'Are you really alright?' Jules said. She looked like a little girl again with her head poking out from the duvet and her hair all bed messy.

'I'm getting there I think. I won't pretend that everything is back to normal but I do know that I can't carry on like I have been. I can't get pissed all the time so that I don't have to think about things.'

She nodded but didn't look quite convinced.

'Although, with the example that Ken set for us, it's not

surprising that's how I tried to deal with things, is it? I can't blame him though either. My decisions – good or bad.'

'He really wants to sort things out with you, you know. He has for ages.'

'I know. I will. One thing at a time though, Jules.'

We lay down and tried to go back to sleep. Jules dropped off quickly, her breathing heavy and even, but I had to drop many envelopes into the red pillar box before I slept again.

•••

The two weeks passed quickly and at the end of them both of us were tanned, fitter and healthier. Not a drop of alcohol had passed either of our lips; we walked everyday on the paths from the hotel that led out along the edge of Exmoor, where it joins the sea. We discovered a secluded bay where a waterfall came tumbling onto the beach from the wooded cliff and a deep aquamarine rock pool sat surrounded by great sunbathing rocks. Jules basked while I leant against a rock with just my legs in the sun and read book after book after book. One of them was Maggie O'Farrell's *After You'd Gone*, which Gloria gave to me.

'It's sort of like what's happened to you, but not. I think you should read it anyway, see what you think,' she said.

I heard her and Jules talking about it later when they were sat by my hospital bed and thought I was sleeping. Jules didn't think it was a good idea for me to read about someone's husband getting killed, but Gloria insisted it was a hopeful story despite that and that's what I needed, some hope. It's not like my husband had been killed. I didn't know what had happened to him but that didn't mean that everyone had to walk on eggshells around me forever. Gloria was right, it was a desperately sad book that made me cry but it was hopeful in the end. As my life could be. I could still have hope, move on from what had happened if I chose to, or I could carry on drinking and getting stoned until I ended up back in hospital again, alienated from my family and everyone else that cared for me.

As we carried our stuff to the car and prepared to head back to London, I was heavy footed. The holiday had been even better for me than I could have imagined. Jules and I had talked in a way that we never had as adults before. In a way that sisters should, rather than me feeling like I had to mother her. That's what she kept telling me anyway but I knew a lifetime's habit would be hard to break and I would lapse into old ways now and then.

As the car neared the city, thoughts of Jimmy started crashing around in my mind again and I just wanted it all to be over with. Get the flat sorted as quickly as possible and get out of it. Thank God it was just rented and I didn't have to worry about selling it.

When Jules parked up outside it was grey, hot and sticky. I knew the flat had been tidied as Jules got professional cleaners in, but I was dreading going back in there. Even though I wanted to get it over with, I also couldn't quite face it so went round to Gloria's instead. She'd been looking after Cheddar and I really wanted to see him.

'Hello?' Gloria's voice called through the intercom.

'Hello Glor, it's Kate. And Jules.'

'Hey, hello. Come up.'

Her voice was happy and excited. She'd turned out to be the best type of friend you could hope for in life. Without her it was unlikely I'd be around. She hugged me hard at her door and then stepped back to look at me.

'You look so much better.'

'I feel it. How are you?'

'I'm fine. Hello Jules.'

She leaned in and gave Jules a hug too and I put my arms around them both, swallowing over the burning lump in my throat.

While Jules made tea I looked through the pile of post she'd got for me. Among all the junk and bills there was a letter from Granny.

UNA

Dearest Kate,

I've started this letter to you too many times now. I have to talk to you. The reason I can't finish the letter is that it would be wrong to tell you like that. I have to tell you the truth to your face. Both you and Jules together.

Please come to see me as soon as you can. I've not been too well and I'm worried that time is running out for me to sort this out. I should have told you a long time ago what really happened with Laura. It's not what you think. She didn't go off with another man. I'm so sorry that I lied to you but your father and I thought it for the best at the time. But I should have told you the truth a long time ago.

I hope that you can forgive me when I finally do.

All my love,

Granny
xxx

KATE

When I'd finished reading the letter out, Jules looked at me with wide eyes.

'What on earth is she talking about?' Gloria said.

'Did she say anything about this to you, Jules?' I said.

'No, not a word.' Jules picked the envelope up from the table and looked at the date on it. 'She sent this just a few days before she died. I was there with her then.'

So that meant it had been in the flat all along, before I'd gone to the funeral. But I hadn't been opening my post, there were piles of it by the front door and I'd kept looking at it all and thinking I'd deal with it.

'How did she post it?' Jules said. 'She didn't go out.'

This seemed like a minor detail to me. 'What can she mean? Was she still with it when she was sick?'

'She wasn't her usual self, obviously, but she didn't seem like she'd lost her mind.' Jules scanned the letter then put it back down on the table.

'We'll have to talk to Ken about it.' I said.

Jules and Gloria's eyes met briefly.

'Call him, Jules, find out what Granny's on about.'

'He's away. He's gone on a research trip. He won't be back

until the end of the month.'

Something snapped in me then. Just when I'd started to get myself back together, there was something else to deal with. 'For fuck's sake, I'm so sick of all of this.' I shouted then ripped up the letter and threw the pieces in the bin.

Neither of them said anything. Gloria had sympathy in her eyes but Jules looked frightened.

I grabbed my bag and walked out. I didn't know where I was going but I just had to get away. There was no way I could sit around wondering what it could mean, I'd drive myself mad again. As Gloria's flat door closed behind me I could hear Jules calling my name so I hurried down the stairs and out of the front door then ran to the end of the road and turned the corner so she wouldn't be able to see me when she came outside.

I slowed to a walk, my head filled with questions again but this time about Laura. Where had she gone then? Why did they lie? Was she dead? I was so distracted I hadn't noticed that I was nearing the shops until a voice broke through the turmoil.

'Look who it is. The crazy bitch.'

Liam. Just what I needed. 'Leave me alone.' I said, not slowing down at all.

'Don't flatter yourself. I wouldn't fuck you. It was just a wind-up. Why would I want to fuck a skanky old hag like you?'

His words were vicious but I could see I'd wounded his pride that day. For a moment I thought about trying to explain but in the end I ignored him and just carried on walking. On Battersea Park Road I slowed down when I realised where I was. Without even thinking about it, I'd headed for the pub. I stopped outside and looked through the windows but made myself walk on. I crossed the road and cut down Parkgate Road and went into the park instead.

I found a shady bench by the Ladies Pond. I'd only been there a few minutes when someone sat on the other end. It was the homeless man that had knocked on the door all those months ago the night after Jimmy had vanished.

'Hello.' I said.

He startled. Only crazy people spoke to strangers, especially homeless ones.

'You knocked on my door late at night and I gave you some money for the bus. It was last winter when we had all that rain.' I wasn't sure why I said that, I didn't think he'd remember he probably knocked on lots of doors.

He looked me in the eye. 'You gave me ten pounds.'

'Yes, that's right. You remember then.'

'Course I do. Always remember the kind people.' He tensed as a crowd of teenagers, boys and girls, approached us. 'You look sad,' he said after they just walked straight past without taking any notice of us.

My breath caught in my throat. This man whose life was obviously a lot harder than mine, no matter what had happened recently, could still have enough empathy to see I was upset.

'I am sad.' I smiled and he returned it. 'I've not had a great time of it lately. But I'm sure it's nothing compared to what you have to deal with.'

He shook his head. 'I'm alright. Been getting help. Got a place in a project. Not sleeping rough no more.'

'That's great.' Now that he'd said that I could see his clothes were clean, still old but not dirty like they'd been before.

'Why are you sad?'

I shook my head. 'You don't want to hear all about my problems.'

'Yeah I do. That's what they been teaching us at the project. You has to talk about things or you ends up in trouble. Like I did.'

So I found myself telling him all about it. Starting with Jimmy disappearing that night and ending with Granny's letter, and a potted version of everything in between.

'I seen the posters around about your fella. I seen 'im too.'

I nodded. 'Yes, well we'd been living round here for a while before he went missing.'

'No. I see 'im that night. Before I knocked your door. He was walking down the road by the park and I asked him for some money. He wouldn't give me none but he stopped and turned around after I asked 'im. Walked back the way he just come.'

'You must be mistaken. If he'd been walking there then he'd have come home.'

He shook his head. 'I ain't mistaken. And I seen 'is picture on the posters just after that. It was 'im.'

'But-,' I couldn't think straight, 'but...well where did he go? Why didn't he come home?'

The man shrugged, there was only one person who could answer that.

I hurried back to Gloria's. I burst through the door as soon as she opened it.

'Oh my God, Jimmy was here, he was here the night after he went missing. Someone saw him. He was coming home then turned around and went the other way. Why did he do that? Where did he go?'

Jules rushed through to the hallway from the kitchen. 'What are you talking about? Calm down. Speak slowly.'

They both looked at me like I was mad when I told them what had happened. 'I think you really have to take that with a pinch of salt, Kate.' Gloria said.

'Kate, you've been doing so well. You can't start up with all this again now.' Jules added.

It was as if all the air rushed out of me. They were right.

And even if that man had seen Jimmy, then that would mean he had left me deliberately and hadn't told me. How could he be so cruel?

'Sorry. It's being back here I think and Granny's letter.'

'Well, let's get everything sorted as quickly as we can so we can get out of here and go to Granny's. Maybe we'll be able to find out what she was talking about there.'

But I didn't know if I was ready for any more revelations.

...

A week later, Jules flew to Japan to sort out her stuff there and get it all shipped back and I drove up to Granny's with my car full of boxes. The morning after I arrived I sat in the lounge enjoying the late summer sun streaming through the windows. It warmed my face and illuminated the blanket on the back of the sofa so that it glowed like embers in a winter fire. I drank a cup of Granny's favourite rooibos tea, remembering when she first made us some the day that Laura took us to her house. Laura's nose had wrinkled up at the smell.

'I like it,' she said.

Granny had been away since a few months after Jules was born and had just returned after four years working with a charity in Africa. I'd been to her house before she'd gone but couldn't remember it, or her. When we went inside on this day she seemed so big, and loud, and exotic. The African clothing she was wearing had such bright colours and bold patterns, not like anything anyone else in Lancaster was wearing at the time; or now probably. When she enveloped us all in a hug as big as the patterns on her loose flowing dress, she smelt of other continents too – something earthy and spicy. I fell in love on the spot and became her shadow for years to come, while Jules was mine. I can see us now trailing around after Granny, hanging on her every word as she told us tales of her African adventures, but also sad stories about the women and children she worked with there. She tried hard to instil in us a sense of obligation to the other people we shared the world with, and it worked for a while. But then everything changed after Laura left and I found it hard to care about the plight of people on a continent far away when my own life had fallen apart. Where had she gone? Jules and I had talked of little else as we'd packed up the flat. Surely Granny couldn't have done anything really bad. She was probably confused in those last days.

Laura and Granny had always seemed so close, as if Granny was Laura's mum not Ken's. I wished I could remember exactly what Laura looked like but I couldn't – just impressions. Wavy brown hair, green eyes, long thin hands that always felt cold. When we were little she had always been laughing.

I was beginning to feel melancholy so went out into the garden. The sun was really warm and I decided to distract myself by making a start sorting out the garden. I changed into old gym shorts and a t-shirt, slipped some flip-flops on, then dug out the key to the shed from the drawer in the kitchen.

It was dark and hot in the shed, the air stale and undisturbed. It was crammed full – spades, trowels, organic fertilisers, bags of soil, packets of seeds and empty plant pots jostling for position on the laden shelves. Old fashioned deck chairs, their thick red stripes faded to a dusky pink, were propped up against the back wall, lost and abandoned as if days in the sun were a thing of the past. The spiders had been busy and there were dusty cobwebs connecting all areas of the shed – an arachnid super highway, with flies dotted around for sustenance like service stations on a motorway. I said sorry under my breath as I brushed them aside.

I worked in the front garden for a couple of hours before it got too hot. The plants and bushes lining the pathway were neater, smaller. You could walk up the path without getting snagged or having to push them out the way. Everything was still very brown and thirsty but one thing I did remember Granny telling me was not to water the plants or the grass in the heat of the day as the sun would scorch everything. I dropped the secateurs on the pile of cuttings and pushed my hands into my lower back. Hot, achy and sticky but it had been a good morning. I hadn't thought about Jimmy or Laura the whole time I'd been working.

•••

After a shower, I went into town to get some shopping. Apart from Granny's funeral, it was the first time I'd been to Lancaster for years but when you've grown up somewhere, it never takes long for it to feel like home again. I got an egg roll, a bottle of water and a banana from a sandwich shop and then walked up to the castle. It was as lovely as I remembered. It exuded a sense of peace and tranquillity, perched high on the hill watching over the town. I sat under a tree in the grounds with the castle behind me and looked out over the town to the river, which was still a murky, muddy brown despite the sunshine, like a sullen child that wouldn't be cheered with a sweet. It was quiet, peaceful. The familiarity and beauty of the town outweighing all the sad memories I'd always associated with it. Or maybe what'd happened in my life had helped me to put it all into perspective.

'Kate?'

I looked round and there was a man standing a couple of feet away. The sun was behind him and I couldn't make out his face.

'Yes?'

He moved closer and as he came into the shade under the tree his face appeared. He was familiar but I couldn't quite place him.

'I thought it was you. You've hardly changed!' He said as he sat down opposite me.

'Hi,' I said, hoping I'd remember who he was before he noticed. He was wearing work clothes – shorts, a t-shirt, sturdy boots.

'It's Mark Gosling, from school. We were in the same year.'

As soon as he said it, I could see that it was him. My cheeks burned as the night of the school disco in our sixth year came to mind. Kissing him for hours on the dance floor. All his friends laughing at us. He grinned as he saw my blush and I knew he remembered it too.

'How are you? It's been years.'

He was familiar but also different to the boy I remembered. He was comfortable in his skin now but back then he'd been too tall and hadn't known where to put those lanky arms and legs.

'It was in our last year at school,' I smiled back at him.

'It was; the leaving disco I believe.'

Our eyes met, we both laughed and any residual embarrassment left over from that seventeen-year-old drunken snog drifted away on the summer breeze. The counsellor said that being in Lancaster could be the best thing for me, that getting in touch with old friends who didn't know about Jimmy could really help me to move on. That I could just be me without having to be 'the woman whose husband went missing'. But those school friendships were so long ago, and I didn't keep in touch with anyone after I went away to university, so it would have been weird to just turn up out of the blue and expect to be friends again. Perhaps just bumping into people could be a way of doing it naturally.

'So, what are you doing here? I thought you moved away years ago,' he said.

'I did. I went to uni in Bath then moved to London. I've been there ever since. Well, until now. My Granny died so I've just moved back.'

'Oh, I'm sorry to hear that. I liked your Granny. She always seemed so exotic.'

I wondered how he knew her but then I remembered that his dad owned the hardware shop and he used to work in there after school. Granny would have been a regular customer with the many projects she always had on the go in the house and garden.

'She was exotic,' I smiled as I pictured her in my mind, 'What about you, have you always stayed in Lancaster?'

'On and off. I've lived away but I came back when my dad was taken ill and decided to stick around when he got better. It was nice being near the family again.'

'And do you have a family of your own?'

'No. Not yet. What about you?'

There was absolutely no way I was going to tell him about Jimmy so I just said that I'd been married but it had broken up, and that's why I decided to move back. I felt conscious of my wedding ring still on my finger and wondered if he'd noticed and thought that I couldn't let go of things.

'So what do you do for a living then? Have you got yourself a job here yet?'

'No, I haven't. I worked on a magazine before but I'm not sure what I'm going to do now. What about you – do you run your dad's shop?'

He shakes his head. 'No, it's long gone. That's what made him so ill. The business struggled after they opened up the big Homebase. He didn't want to tell anyone, or even admit it to himself, and the stress of it all got to be too much and he had a heart attack.'

'Oh, Mark, that's awful. Is he OK now?'

'Yeah, he's fine. But the doctors said no more stress and when he was in hospital and Mum and I saw the state of things in the shop, we closed it down and he hasn't worked since.'

'So what do you do then?'

'I'm a boat builder.'

'Really? Do you get to build a lot of boats around here?'

He laughed. 'Yes a few. I've got my own boatyard out Halton way.' He stood up then. 'Well, it's been lovely to see you, Kate. I've got to get off though – work calls.'

I stood up too and there was a moment of awkwardness – should we shake hands, kiss? Mark leant in and kissed me on the cheek – his rough hands warm on my forearms.

'You too, Mark. Take care.'

'I'm sure we'll see each other around, Lancaster's a small town.'

He waved back over his shoulder as he walked off. I sat back down again, surprised by the smile on my face. Remembering how full of excitement I'd been the last time I'd seen him, when I was just about to set off for my life as an adult on my own. And now I was back where I started but doing the same thing again. Starting a new life on my own.

•••

Back at the house I made a start clearing Granny's room. It still smelt of her. Rose oil. I wished she was there so I could tell her how sorry I was for how things turned out, for only coming to visit a handful of times since I went to university. Why did I shut her out too? She was always there for me. What had I been trying to prove by being so closed off and independent? For the life of me I couldn't see it now. All I'd achieved was loneliness. Even though I was married I could see now how lonely I'd been. Jimmy and I had never really connected deep down as I hadn't ever let my guard down properly.

When I opened Granny's wardrobe I gasped at the mess. Clothes crammed together so tightly that I could barely move them along the rail. A jumble of shoes at the bottom, the shelf at the top a muddle of boxes with scarves, gloves and hats stuffed in all around them. I moved the dressing table stool over to the wardrobe and climbed up on it. The shelf was crammed with boxes right to the back. I took a pile from the front then climbed down and placed them on the bed. I did this again and again until all the boxes were on the bed and the floor in front of the wardrobe had disappeared under a rainbow mountain of accessories. I was hoping that I'd find some old photos so I could see Laura, fill in the memory blanks again.

I opened a heart-shaped box that seemed familiar and inside, nestled on faded red tissue paper, was the Valentine's gift Jules and I made for Granny that first February after she'd come home from Africa. We'd found a smooth grey stone shaped like a love heart on the beach and Laura had helped us decorate it. There were still bits of glitter glinting on it but the painted patterns were not quite so bright. I turned it over and there just about still visible, written in the gold pen that we had so adored, was the little poem we'd composed:

We're glad you are our Granny
We're happy you came home
We'll never call you Nanny
No matter where you roam

Smiling over the burning lump in my throat I could see Jules opposite me at the kitchen table, glitter in her hair and paint all over her hands as we'd tried to think up rhymes to express our love for our newly discovered Granny; Laura telling us something about A and B rhythms. I put the box to one side to show Jules. The next three boxes were filled with more scarves – how many did one woman need? They all had exotic prints on and looked like they came from Oxfam or Traidcraft, and then I realised that Granny must have kept buying them to support the women who made them.

Cheddar meowed and came padding into the room. He'd been out of sorts since we moved here. He jumped up on the bed and knocked a pile of boxes onto the floor then scampered from the room, hissing, his tail fluffed up like a fox's brush.

'Oh, Cheddar, look what you've done,' I called after him.

Necklaces and bracelets of brightly coloured beads and glass had spilled onto the rug. I scooped them up and dumped them back in a box. The one next to it was full of letters and another, notepads. When I looked inside they were diaries. I'd had no idea Granny kept a diary. I picked up a handful of the letters and sifted through them – many were postmarked from different places in Africa, some from Eriskay, which would be from Granny's brother. He lived up there counting waves, or something like that. Although he'd be retired now. If he was even still alive. Had he been at the funeral? I couldn't remember.

There was a bundle of letters all kept together with an elastic band. The writing on them was the same and they'd come from New Zealand. I opened the top one.

Dear Una,
I know it's been some time since I've written and I hope this letter finds you, Ken and the girls well.

The girls? Me and Jules? I turned over to see who it was from and it was signed:

with love always, Laura

I read through it. It was our Laura. I threw it down on the rug as if it was scalding my fingers but my whole body had frozen from the inside. Then I was hot, clammy and nauseous. I ran to the bathroom, the rest of the letters spilled to the floor and Laura's writing stared up at me from them all.

I sat on the bathroom floor, my skin clammy, shivering despite the sticky August heat but the waves of nausea passed. At the sink I splashed my face with cold water. When I looked at myself in the mirror, my eyes were sunken and dark, skin pale. The improvements I'd seen in the past weeks wiped out in an instant. I sat down on the edge of the bath, shaking and scared.

Back in the bedroom I bent down and scooped the letters up. I would not let this set me back. I took them and sat in the armchair by the window, there were twenty-eight. I opened them all. They went back to nineteen-eighty-nine, three years after Laura had left us. I put them in a pile on Granny's bedside table and went into my room and lay on the bed. I couldn't face dealing with them and what they might reveal. Tears soaked into the pillow as I lay there for a long time before sleep finally came.

LAURA

Afew days later, Una turned up. I was sitting on the sofa staring into space. I'd been there for hours. Ken had told her and for the first time ever I knew what it was to be on the wrong side of Una. It was a scary place to be.

'How could you?' Her voice was tight, controlled, but her eyes were flashing warning signals and she was gripping her hands in her lap as if she was holding herself back from hitting me. Or wringing my neck.

'I don't know. I wasn't thinking straight.' My voice was papery. I seemed to have cried myself dry.

'It's a despicable thing to do. Ken is destroyed.'

'So am I.' I knew I had no right to be. That it was me that had done this, so it was me who had to deal with it. But even so, I was driving myself mad. Terrible thoughts constantly chasing themselves around in my head. Nothing I did, or told myself, made any difference. Somehow I was dealing with the girls but it was as if I was looking through a kaleidoscope and everything around me, the wonderful family life I'd had before I ruined it, was broken into jagged bits.

'Don't you love Ken? Is that why you did it?'

'Of course I do. I don't know...I can't explain it.' My fingers were drumming on my leg, which was bouncing up and down. I pushed my hand down hard on my thigh to stop it.

'You have to explain it. You can't do something like that and then just expect us to accept it. Oh never mind, Laura, you sneaked off and had a secret abortion because you weren't thinking straight, but that's OK.' By the end of the sentence she was looming over me.

I wanted her to hit me. I deserved it.

'I'm not judging you for having the abortion, I'm pro-choice as you know, but the lies…'

'I didn't mean to lie. But Ken wouldn't listen to me. I was trapped. I wanted to not just be stuck in the house with another baby.' I looked up at her, surely of all people Una would be able to understand that?

'Well what about what Ken wanted? It wasn't just your decision to make.'

'I know. I don't know what you want me to say.' I pushed myself up off the sofa so I was standing right in front of her, hoping she might hug me. I really needed someone to. The last person who'd touched me voluntarily, other than the girls, was the abortionist. I needed someone's embrace to try and cancel that out. But she moved away from me and picked up her bag.

'I don't want to dictate to you what you have to say. I just want…we just want…an explanation. We think you should see someone. What you have done is not the behaviour of a person in their right mind.'

'I don't feel like I'm in my right mind. I haven't been for a long time.'

She softened slightly then. She still didn't touch me but the anger in her eyes dimmed a little. 'Well, let's get you an appointment at the doctor's then. You can tell him all about it, how you're feeling, what you've done, and see what he says.'

'No! I don't want to tell anyone.' Especially Dr Spencer who had been my doctor forever and was ancient and old fashioned, and would definitely not understand why I'd done what I had.

But she wouldn't take no for an answer. She rang and made the appointment for the next afternoon and delivered me to the surgery to make sure that I definitely went ahead with it. When I was called in and sat across the desk from Dr Spencer I couldn't say anything.

'Come on Laura, chop-chop. What's the problem? I have lots of patients to see after you this afternoon.'

I definitely wasn't going to tell him what I'd done. 'I feel sad all the time.' I expected him to scoff at me, tell me to pull myself together and get on with things.

'Well, that's not good is it? What are you sad about?'

He really looked like he cared and for a second I thought maybe I could tell him. But then he'd look at me like Ken and Una did. I didn't want him to do that, I wanted him to still care.

'Everything. Mum and Dad being gone. My girls growing up.' Tears were streaming down my face now for the first time in days. It felt good to cry again. Like the tears were washing away the numbness.

'And how long has this been going on?' He scribbled something down in his notepad.

'I don't know. It's as if after the accident I didn't ever really stop to think. The world moved so quickly after that and now everything's hit me.' As I said it I realised that it was true. It was like the abortion had brought it all to a head. I wasn't just ashamed and guilty about that; I was really bloody sad about lots of things. I didn't really know who I was as I'd never had a chance to find out.

'Well, let's start you off with some antidepressants and see how you go with them. I think I should give you a referral to a therapist as well. Do you think talking to someone about how you feel would help?'

I had no idea but I really wanted to. A stranger who wouldn't judge me. Who didn't know my family. Someone I could tell everything to. 'Yes, probably,' I sniffed.

Dr Spencer handed me a tissue and a prescription. 'Well, these should help. There's a month's supply there. Talk to Wendy when you leave and book an appointment to see me in a month's time. We'll be in touch soon with the details of the therapist appointment.'

Una took me to get the prescription on the way home. I stayed in the car. I was so embarrassed. Mrs Oliver in the chemist would see what I had been prescribed and would be telling everyone all about it. At home Una stood and watched as I swallowed the first of that day's pills. Three a day and apparently I would start to feel better in a couple of weeks, which seemed a very long time to wait.

•••

Over the next two weeks I took the pills everyday but they didn't make me feel any better. My mouth was always dry no matter how much I drank. I couldn't sit still or sleep properly and my hands started to shake. My head ached all the time. Una was always around. Taking the girls to school and then picking them up again. Making meals while I paced around. Ken was going out all the time in the evenings after work and sleeping on the sofa. Getting up early every morning so he could be up and dressed before the girls woke up so they wouldn't know there was anything wrong. Although they noticed I wasn't my normal self.

Whenever they spoke to me it was if their voices were muffled and filtered. I couldn't seem to get all the way through a sentence when I tried to answer them.

'Why do you keep doing that, Mummy?'

'Doing what Kitty Kat?'

'Stopping talking all the time. You're not making sense.'

'Mummy's just tired, Kate. She hasn't been well and now she's starting to get better.' Una was always butting in and I'd started to resent her. I could tell my own daughter myself. But I couldn't. Then I felt bad for wanting Una to leave. She was only trying to help. And she'd been very patient with me. She wasn't angry with me anymore, although we still hadn't really talked about what I'd done. It had all started to seem like a dream. As if it was a horrible story I'd been told about someone else and was watching from somewhere outside myself.

Then one day I woke up feeling frantic. I couldn't remember what Mum and Dad looked like. The house was silent. Everyone out. I needed sound so I put the stereo on really loud, hoping the music would drown out the panic in my head. When Una came back from the school I was in my dressing gown on the front room floor surrounded by picture albums. I started crying as soon as I saw her.

'Why did they have to die, Una?' I wailed.

She sighed. 'Oh, Laura. This really isn't doing you any good you know.' She turned the stereo off and sat on the sofa, her look of pity making me cry all the more. 'I don't understand why you're bringing all this up now. It's as if you're using it as an excuse to not think about what you've done.'

'No, it isn't! I can't stop thinking about them. About what my life would have been like if they hadn't died.' I clutched the photo album of our last family holiday to my chest.

'But they did die, Laura. And you need to face up to things

that are happening now, not keep harking back to the past.'

She was so cold. She didn't know what it was like. I threw the album at her and it hit her in the arm. 'Don't tell me what I should be feeling. You don't know. You don't know.' I picked up the other albums that were lying on the floor all around me and started throwing them too.

She sprang up from the sofa and knelt down next to me, grabbing my arms and pinning them to my side. 'Laura, stop this. Stop it!'

I struggled against her but she was strong and I couldn't get away. I screamed and wailed. She slapped me in the face. The silence was instant. I went completely still and so did she. We just stared at each other.

'I'm sorry, Laura. But you have to stop this. Look at yourself. Listen to yourself. We can't go on like this.'

My head dropped onto her shoulder and I sobbed. For the first time since she'd found out what I'd done her arms went around me and she held me tight. We stayed like that for what seemed like ages then she took me upstairs and put me to bed. I could hear her downstairs on the phone then later Dr Spencer was there.

'Laura, what's going on?' His faced loomed over mine.

'I don't know.' I turned away, pressing my face into the pillow so he couldn't see me.

'How have the pills been making you feel?'

'I don't know. I can't sleep.'

'Well, I want you to come back into the surgery tomorrow so we can talk properly. I'll give you some sleeping pills. Take one now and one again tonight so you get some rest then we'll see what we can do to sort this out.'

Then Una was there again with a pill and water.

'Take this. I'm going to bring the girls home to my house

after school tonight. Then after I've dropped them at school in the morning I'll be back to take you to the doctor.'

When I woke up it was starting to get dark. In the bathroom mirror my face was pasty and puffy. I didn't look like me. I stretched my hand out and touched my reflection. I don't know how long I stood like that but suddenly Ken was behind me.

'What are you doing?' His eyes met mine in the mirror. I couldn't remember the last time he'd really looked at me straight in the face.

'Nothing.' My arm dropped down and I turned to him. 'Are we going to be OK, Ken?'

'I don't know, Laura. What is going on with you?' His voice was small, tired.

He didn't seem angry for the first time since I'd done it. I thought he still loved me. I stepped forwards and put my arms around him but he stiffened.

His arms stayed by his side. 'Don't,' he said.

'Please, Ken...' I really needed him to love me again.

'I can't. Not yet. You need to sort yourself out.'

Then he left me standing there and a few minutes later I heard the front door slam. What had I done? I'd ruined everything, forever it seemed. He was never going to forgive me. And I couldn't forgive myself.

KATE

I woke from a dream where I was with Jimmy and Laura in the caravan we used to go to when I was a little girl. We were all sitting at the kitchen table, both of them opposite me, but I couldn't see their faces properly. They were wearing snood type things that looked like they were made of spider webs and were longer than normal, covering their shoulders and going down their arms almost as far as their elbows. The rain was lashing against the windows behind the frilly net curtains.

'Where are you?' I kept asking.

But neither of them answered. Just shook their hidden heads, backwards and forwards, in time to my repeated questioning. There was a strange sound coming from outside, a distant drumming which was almost blocked out by a closer keening. There was a bowl of ravioli in tomato sauce on the table in front of me and I was pushing it around with a fork.

I sat up brushing the thoughts of the dream aside. What did it matter anyway? Dreams are just dreams. As I pushed myself up from the bed I remembered the letters. My legs gave way and I sat back down, wishing I could go back to that moment when I was still blissful in my ignorance.

I went downstairs to make tea, taking the letters with me, and saw that it was quarter to three in the morning. While I waited for the kettle I stared at the letters, lying on the kitchen table looking so innocent, as if they didn't really have the power to push my self-destruct button again. Although I know from all the things the counsellor had told me that it was me that controlled the button, it was me that pushed it, nobody else.

The thought of blotting it all out by getting out of my head was very appealing. But I sipped herbal tea instead and read through the letters. I couldn't believe it. How could Granny have done this, how could she have told so many lies? I didn't care that it was almost four o'clock in the morning, I had to know whether Ken was in on this. Jules and I had decided we'd ask him about what Granny had said in her letter together when Jules was back from Japan, but I couldn't wait.

I got my mobile from my bag and called him for the first time in years. It rang and rang and I thought he wasn't going to answer. But then his groggy voice croaked a hello at me.

'Ken. It's Kate. I found Laura's letters in Granny's wardrobe. Did you know about this? Did you?'

I wanted to sound calm and in control but there was so much heat, hurt and anger in my voice that, for a moment, I felt sorry for Ken, wrenched from his sleep to have angry questions fired at him by the daughter who'd just returned to his life with a bagful of issues.

'What? What time is it?'

'It doesn't matter what the time is. Did you know about this or not?'

'Know about what?'

'Laura's letters. I found a bundle of letters from her to Granny. She's been writing to her for years.'

Silence.

'Well?'

'No. No I didn't.' Even though he's fully awake now Ken's voice has got smaller.

'Honestly?'

'Honestly Kate. What do they say?'

I started crying and I couldn't tell him. I pushed the letters around on the table with my fingertips then found myself telling Ken that he should come over later for breakfast and he could read them himself.

...

The sun arrived with Ken, and I wondered if it was a sign that he was bringing joy. But as I watched him walking up the garden path I realised again how old he looked, how broken. I know I hadn't seen him for years so you notice it more, but he was only in his mid-sixties and he looked like an old man. I wished we could all be happy and learn to start making the most of life. I'm like Ken. Jules is freer and more able to keep things in perspective. Ken turned into a morose alcoholic when things went wrong for him, while I went for the raging version. Both of us running away, though.

When I opened the front door I realised that all the anger I'd felt towards him previously was gone. It looked like the discovery of the letters had crushed him more than me, and he hadn't even seen what was in them yet. He was ashen, as if the grey from the day had disappeared because he'd sucked it all up inside him. I wanted to hug him, but we're not like that so I just put my hand on his back as he walked past me to come in. He held up a paper bag.

'I stopped by the baker and got some pastries.'

I smiled and went through to the kitchen. The letters were still there on the table and I had thought that we would get straight into talking about them but instead we both seemed happy to postpone it.

'How are you? You're looking much better.'

'I'm much better than I was. Why don't you go and sit out in the garden and I'll make tea and put these on a plate?'

He shuffled off without another word and I busied myself preparing the breakfast. Wishing we could just be a father and daughter having a nice breakfast together; that there wouldn't be one drama after another to deal with. Life didn't used to be like this. It's calmer, quieter when you just go along in a little bubble not getting too emotionally involved in people's lives, even your own. The realisation hammered into me then like a physical blow. Granny knew, she knew that if she told us about Laura it would mean more upset, more pain. I think she knew all along that I was a mess. That my rigid self-control was all a front and that it would be so easy to shatter, so she didn't want to give Laura the chance to upset me. I knew she must have done this out of love but I couldn't believe how misguided it was.

When I had all the breakfast things on the tray I tucked the letters in between the teapot and the mugs and joined Ken in the back garden. We sat at the picnic bench under the apple tree and I poured the tea.

'So these are the letters then?' Ken gestured towards the tray.

I nodded and took a bite of my pain au raisin before picking them up and passing them to him.

'I think it's best if you read them all.'

We sat there in the dappled sunlight listening to the late summer sounds of the garden, busy bumble bees and fat flies droning by, Ken reading and me thinking about my dream from earlier. The caravan. We used to go there all the time when I was little, before Laura left. It was at Silverdale, just half an hour from home but a different world. One filled with rock pools, games and lazy mornings reading in the top bunk bed instead of early rising for long, boring days at school. Me, Jules and Laura would go for three weeks and Ken would come down too for the last one. We loved it there. It's where Laura taught us to bake her signature apple bran muffins, on the days that it rained. Of which there were many. Where she also taught us about her love of books and read us story after story. I loved The Magic Faraway Tree the best. It's stuck in my mind to this day with the Saucepan Man, Dame Washalot and all of the amazing lands that appeared at the top. That love of books that had filtered down into my genes but not Jules's.

A strange sound from Ken pulled me back to the garden. The letter he was reading had fallen on the floor under the table and he was crying. Properly sobbing. I felt terrible then. Always worrying about myself and how I felt about things, never stopping to think how Ken might be affected by it. I went round to his side of the bench and sat next to him, put my arm round his shoulders.

'I thought you knew. I thought it would be in the letters but it's not. You still don't know,' he said.

'What. What's not in the letters? Why do you think they wrote all those years back and forth and Granny never told us?'

Ken's sobs had subsided and he wiped his eyes with his knuckles until I handed him one of the paper napkins from the tray. After he'd mopped his face he looked me straight in the eye.

'I'm not sure this is the right time to go into all this.'

I was just about to protest when he added, 'I didn't know about the letters, but we lied. We lied about where she had gone. That's what I thought you knew.'

His face crumpled and he dropped his head before he started to cry in earnest again.

'What do you mean? Why did you lie? Where did she go?'

He sobbed into his lap.

'Ken, what are you talking about? Tell me what's going on.'

My voice rose. The anger returning. He always did this. Avoided the issue. Went silent.

'Ken, tell me!' I shouted.

He continued to sob though and I could see I wasn't going to get much sense out of him so I left him to cry it out and went into the kitchen to make more tea. I was weary to the bone with it. All the lies. Why did everyone tell so many lies? When the tea was ready I went back into the garden expecting Ken to have pulled himself together, but he'd gone.

'Ken?' I called out.

Silence. I put the teapot on the kitchen table then rushed back out into the garden. Where had he gone? I ran around the house into the front garden and I could see him then, down near the bottom of the road. He'd run away again. I contemplated running after him but knew there was no point, and I didn't want to talk to him about it in the street.

Back at the garden table I pick up the dropped letter from the floor and put it back with the others before taking them all inside.

•••

There were voices coming through the door, muffled so I couldn't make out what they were saying. It sounded like there were a few people in there. I didn't want to go in. I'd been seeing a new counsellor since I moved to Lancaster, Jane, and she found this group for me. Reckoned it would really help me to meet other people who'd beeh through the same thing. I wasn't so sure. I've never been good at talking about how I feel and it had taken me a few sessions to even start to open up to her.

I took a deep breath and pushed the door open. The room was small and stuffy with a few plastic chairs like we used to have at school arranged in a haphazard circle. Grimy windows high up in the wall let in a dim light. Two people were sat next to each other talking in low voices, a man and a woman. They both looked up as I come through the door and the man stood up and came towards me with his hand held out for a shake.

'Hi, hello. I'm Clive.'

I felt panicked, like I wanted to run but made myself accept his handshake. His hands were hot and clammy and he squeezed really hard. I wanted to wipe my hand on my jeans but felt rude so it just hung stiffly by my side after we'd introduced ourselves.

'Come and sit down, Kate.'

He led me over to sit with the other woman and smiled encouragingly at me. For the first time I noticed he had a nice face, soft with gentle eyes. There was a dimple in his left cheek when he smiled and I suddenly felt a bit better about being there.

'This is Abena, and this is Kate.' He waved his arm back and forward between us.

Abena was wearing loud and colourful African clothing, just like Granny when I first saw her. Unlike Granny, this woman looked like she actually might have come from Africa. Her nut brown skin gleamed against the bright patterns in her robe. I smiled at her and she smiled back.

'So do you know what these meetings are all about, Kate?' Clive asked.

As he sat down next to me I noticed he had cat hairs all over his clothes, and a small crumb of food in his curly black and grey beard. A slight mildew smell hinted at clothes that might have not dried quickly enough, or lived in damp cupboards.

'Um, well people that have gone missing, I thought.'

He gave a fake little laugh at that, as if it was a mistake he was often correcting, then glanced behind him as the door swung open again. Clive waved at the man who had just come in and then turned back to me.

'Yes, sorry didn't really make myself clear. Do you know what we do, rather than what they are about?'

I stared stupidly at him for a moment. I had envisaged something like an Alcoholics Anonymous meeting. 'Hello, I'm Kate, and I am a missing person...survivor?' What was the name for the person, or people, that are left behind? So I told him that's what I imagined. He smiled and patted my knee. I was glad I had jeans on so couldn't feel the clamminess of his hand on my leg and wished I was brave enough to tell him not to touch me like that. I could see he meant it to be reassuring though, he wasn't a letch, but I'm not good with strangers touching me.

'Well I suppose it is like that in a way, but just in that we share our stories. We don't stand up, we have nothing to confess – we, you, haven't done anything wrong. We just talk about the feelings that we have about the situation that led to us being here. Everyone here has had someone go missing and has had to come to terms with a difficult situation and hopefully by talking about it together we can help make that easier.'

I smiled at him and nodded as if I agreed but the thought of telling these people about what happened with Jimmy, let alone how I felt about it, terrified me. Clive went off to speak to the other man who'd arrived, as he'd sat down right on the other side of the room as far away as he could get. I turned to Abena and said hello again.

'Hello. It's nice to meet you, Kate.' She had an accent that I couldn't place.

'Have you been here before?' I asked.

'Yes, I have been coming for a while now. I think almost eight months.'

The other man that came in started shouting and stood up so suddenly that his chair clattered to the floor. Clive reared back from him, as if he was afraid he was going to end up on the floor next.

My heart pounded. What was going on? Abena didn't look remotely ruffled though.

'Martin. He always does this, he's very angry still about his daughter and he turns up here drunk most times.'

I glanced over at her when she said this. Did she know about me? Would Jane have told Clive and Clive told her? I thought not, she was just telling me the situation.

Martin shouted loudly, incoherently, spittle flying out from his red face. Clive tried to calm him, speaking to him softly, slowly, constantly, like I'd seen people do to horses that were all het up. He managed to get him back into his seat and it was as if when his bum hit the uncomfortable plastic it punctured the balloon of his anger. His face and shoulders slumped and he cried. I wanted the ground to open up and swallow me, or him, I didn't think I could deal with it.

'Sorry, sorry everyone.' Martin said when he'd got himself back under control.

'That's OK, Martin. We understand, don't we?' Clive said as he looked round at me and Abena.

I didn't understand though. I didn't think it was alright to behave like that. Then I remembered the American man in the pub. The way I'd shouted at him then run out. No difference. I shouldn't judge, so I smiled at Martin and nodded. We were all distracted by the door opening to let another man in and Clive went off to greet him. My shoulders were hunched up round my ears and I forced them down. No need to get stressed.

While Clive was talking to the newest arrival another woman arrived and then everyone sat down on the chairs in the circle and Clive officially started the meeting.

'Welcome everyone. Thanks for coming. We have some new

visitors today so if everyone could introduce themselves and say a bit about what has brought them here. Just whatever you feel comfortable telling us.'

Martin started talking straight away. His face was blotchy and red from crying and his eyes had virtually disappeared but he didn't sound drunk.

'My daughter, Abbie, she went missing two and a half years ago after we argued. She never came back and I haven't heard from her since.' He looked around at us all as he said it.

Two and a half years. I stared back at him in horror. Had he been like this for that long? Raging and drinking. My God.

Next the woman who came in last told her story. Joanne. She was about twenty-five and was wearing what looked like men's clothes. A lumberjack shirt and combat trousers. Anyway, her brother had gone missing. He moved to Manchester about a year before and had started taking heroin when he got there. Now she hadn't heard from him in nearly six months and none of the people that knew him seemed to have any idea where he'd gone. I wondered then if she was wearing his clothes.

The man next to me, Tommy, had lost his wife. He came home from work one day three months ago and she was just gone. No note, left the kids behind, packed a bag and gone. Like Laura. Well, what I had always assumed about Laura. Turns out I was wrong. Or lied to. Ken still hadn't talked to me about it despite my threats, tears and anger. Said he wanted to talk to me and Jules about it together when she got back from Japan. In the meantime, I planned to read Granny's diaries and see what I could find out.

I'd looked through all the boxes from the wardrobe that morning and there were hundreds of diaries, going back to when Granny was a teenager. If I hadn't been so angry with her it would have felt like a gift. As it was, part of me was scared to look in them as I had no idea what I might find out.

Everyone looked round, waiting for me to speak and my mouth dried up as all the moisture in my body seemed to be forcing itself out through the pores on my palms, lower back and armpits. I cleared my throat.

'Hi. I'm Kate. My husband went missing ten months ago and I've never found out what happened. He just went to the shop and didn't come back.'

They all gave me sympathetic smiles and for the first time it seemed to sink into my head that the world was full of people with problems, that people went missing every day. My story was not unique. Then it was Abena's turn and her story stunned me.

She'd lost her husband, her two sons, a daughter, a sister, brother-in-law, a nephew and her parents. Her village in Rwanda was ransacked by rebels and in the confusion and rush to escape she became separated from them. Ended up in a Red Cross refugee camp but had never been able to find any of her family again. This happened four years ago and she'd lived in the camp for more than two years before being granted refugee status to come to the UK.

'But I have never stopped looking and never given up hope that one day I will either be reunited with or get answers about what happened to my family.' She smiled at us as if she felt she had to try and make us feel better about what happened.

The silence in the room was a palpable living thing when she finished telling us. When you have facts like that presented to you in person by someone who has lived through it, rather than by some fakely sympathetic newsreader, it certainly has a different impact.

'Thanks everyone for sharing their stories today. Kate, Joanne or Tommy, as you're joining us for the first time today would you like to talk to us a bit more about your situation?

I didn't want to and we all looked around at each other before Joanne offered to share some more. I couldn't really listen though; my mind was whirling. I had been so self-absorbed, acting like I was the only person that anything bad had ever happened to. If waking up in hospital hadn't been enough of a wake-up call, then that first day at the help group definitely showed me that I needed to make the right choices now about how I dealt with this. I could end up like Martin – in fact had already been there – or I could try to be more like Abena. I was determined that I would sort myself out, move on.

LAURA

After Ken had gone I went downstairs and sat on the sofa. He'd left the TV on and Eastenders was just finishing. Den and Angie screaming at each other. I turned it off then stared at the blank screen. Sometime later the phone rang but I didn't answer it. There was nobody I wanted to speak to apart from Ken and I knew it wouldn't be him.

The photo albums had all been cleared away and piled on the table in the corner. Everything was tidy and normal looking but it felt like nothing would ever be normal again. It had all gone so wrong so quickly. Why did I do it? Why didn't I listen to Ken? We could have had a baby boy on the way and been happy. I could have tried doing the course and seen how it turned out. Why was I so selfish?

The headache that had been dully throbbing behind my forehead started pounding. I went into the kitchen and filled a glass with water then took it back to bed with me. I took two paracetamols and lay flat on my back staring at the ceiling. I knew there was no going back. Ken hated me. Una hated me. Kate and Jules soon would when they realised what an awful person I was. They'd all be better off without me.

So I sat up and took two more paracetamols, then two more.

But then there were no more. So I took all of the antidepressants I had left. I gagged as I tried to swallow them all. My throat closing as if my body knew it shouldn't be doing it. But I forced them down. Then I took the sleeping pill that Dr Spencer had left for me. I'd expected it to work straight away like the one I'd taken earlier but I lay there for ages and didn't sleep. So I went and got the bottle of whiskey from the drinks cabinet and filled a tumbler with it.

My vision was all wavy as I took the tumbler and the bottle back to bed. I bounced against the walls going up the stairs, then collapsed onto the bed. I sat crossed legged in the crumpled mess of the sheets and blankets swigging back large gulps. The whisky burned my throat and chest and I could feel it travelling all the way down inside my body. I gagged but took deep breaths to stop myself. I couldn't let the pills come up as I didn't have any more. My head started to spin, I couldn't see the glass properly and spilled the whiskey down my chin when I took the next swig. It ran down my chest and between my boobs so that it was burning me on the outside then too.

I poured more whiskey into the glass, sloshing it in so it spilt on my lap. There was whiskey everywhere. The second glass was half drunk when I heard the front door open. Ken. He came back.

'Ken...' I said it so quietly I could barely hear myself but I really wanted to see him again before I died. 'Ken! Please come here, quickly!' I shouted. Panic making my voice shrill.

I heard his footsteps on the stairs but before he came in the room I passed out.

•••

I woke up in hospital. My nose and throat felt like they'd been burned. My arms were strapped down and I couldn't really move. I couldn't believe I was still alive. I couldn't even do that right. The curtain was around my bed and I had no idea what was on the other side of it.

After what seemed like hours a nurse appeared. When she saw I was awake she left again straight away and returned with a bearded man, who had a clipboard and a very caring look on his face.

'Hello, Laura. I'm Dr Daniels.'

I stared at him.

He didn't seem put off by my lack of response. 'Do you know why you're here?'

I shut my eyes.

'Laura, if you don't speak to me, answer my questions, then we're not going to be able to help you.'

After a couple of minutes' silence, I heard him leave.

He kept coming back and trying to talk to me but I never answered. I wanted to but I couldn't. There were all these thoughts going round in my head that I wanted to say but whenever I opened my mouth to speak, I couldn't say any of them. Una and Ken appeared at one point but it was if the muteness was catching and they looked at me without saying anything then left again.

I don't know how long I was there for. The drugs they gave me meant time had no meaning. Then one day they got me up, put me into a wheelchair and took me to another part of the hospital. They left me there and I was put in a new bed. Given some more pills. Then I don't really remember anything that happened after that, until much, much later.

I was catatonic they told me later. Said that I was like it for weeks and weeks before they started with the electric shocks. Then I slowly started to come around.

I was kept in an acute psychiatric ward and filled with drugs;

my mind was fuddled and muddled for a very long time. I wasn't even sad anymore about what had happened because I couldn't really feel anything. I kept saying I wanted to go home but they said I wasn't well enough, that if I stopped taking the drugs and being watched over I'd be a danger to myself and others. That statistically as I'd tried to kill myself once, I'd do it again. I didn't really believe that but what could I do? I tried to talk to Una about it when she visited but she said the doctors knew best. Ken didn't even come to visit after a while. They left me there for a very long time and I didn't think I was ever going to be allowed to leave.

KATE

After the help group session I went home and sorted out Una's diaries. They went back to 1951 when Una was seventeen and continued up until 1994. A whole lifetime. Even though I knew all I had to do was go to 1984 and I would find out where Laura went, I put it off. I didn't know if I was strong enough to face it on my own. I only had to wait a few more days and Jules would be home and we could find out from Ken what had really happened. Then when we knew why Laura had left, together we could read Granny's diaries to find out why she kept her away when she wanted to get back in touch with us.

But before that, I wanted to find out who Granny really was. I still couldn't believe that the woman who had brought us up could have done what she did. So I figured that maybe I never really knew her. But having forty-five years of her diaries meant I could find out.

UNA

19th May 1951

Today is my seventeenth birthday and Ruthy gave me this lovely notebook, she said it was to keep all my hopes and dreams in so that I could make sure that they happen. I have so many hopes and dreams for this life that I don't really know where to start. I hope we will never have another war. My Uncles Jack and Harry were both killed by the Germans and even though he's gone back to work managing his business, and it would seem like everything is just like before, Daddy has never been quite the same since he came home. War is cruel and barbaric and I thought that we were too intelligent and civilised for things like that to happen anymore.

I dream that one day Ruthy and I will live in a flat together in London so we can go to dances and museums and restaurants and galleries and exciting things will happen to us. Nothing ever happens in Lancaster and everybody knows everybody else. I'd like to be anonymous. Ruthy's brother, Gerry, has told us about a place called Soho where they have Jazz clubs. He goes to them all the time when he's in London. I want to go too.

I also want to go abroad and travel. There is so much to see out there. I have an atlas of the world that I look at all the time and even the names of the countries and towns sound exotic so I'd imagine that actually being in them would be amazing. How different it must be from here. Ruthy says she'd be scared but that if we went together she'd be brave enough. I never want to go anywhere if Ruthy isn't coming with me. We are both going to apply to study at Hughes Hall in Cambridge, so that we can get away from home and get a qualification that will mean we can get jobs in London.

Those are the things I do want – what I don't want is to get married and have children, which is what Mummy says I have to do. Boring!

3rd August 1951

This is the last summer holidays that I'll have as a schoolgirl. When we go back in September it will be the final year before we take our exams. So I'm making the most of it. It feels like this is the last summer I'll have before life will change forever, as by next summer I'll be getting ready to go off to Cambridge. Mummy and I are staying at Silverdale in our new caravan, well there's two of them actually. Daddy bought some land and he's planning to build us a house on it but for now we're having holidays here in the caravans. I hope the house never gets built as caravanning is such fun. We have to cook outside on a little gas ring so it's lucky that the weather has been fine. Although we do have a little tent shelter that goes over the kitchen area but it doesn't have any walls so won't be much good in the rain. I'm not sure that Mummy likes caravanning that much though, she has Mrs. Sheldon at home who does the cooking, but when she'd started to say something to Daddy he'd just laughed and said it would be an adventure.

The land that Daddy has bought is absolutely gorgeous and you can see the sea from the caravan window. It's a large flat meadow surrounded by trees and there's a path that leads through a little woodland, down the cliff, directly to the beach. Mummy and I have been lazing around in the sun reading since we arrived a few days ago and going for walks out on the cliffs and to the beach. It's just been us here as Daddy has had to stay behind and work and even though Michael was supposed to be coming home from university for the whole of the holidays he popped back just for a couple of days then left again. He's met a girl there, Rose, and he's spending the summer at her parents' house in Hertfordshire. But Ruthy is arriving today and staying with us for the week. We're collecting her from the train station this afternoon. Daddy's coming down on Friday evening for the weekend.

· 6th August 1951

The most extraordinary thing has happened. Ruthy and I are in love. Obviously I've always loved her as we've been best friends our whole lives but being here together this week, things between us have changed.

It all started when we met her at the station.

Mummy waited in the car and I went to the platform to collect Ruthy. I was feeling excited that she was arriving but when she stepped down from the train it was as if something grabbed hold of my heart and squeezed it. It had been over three weeks since I'd seen her as she'd been away visiting her grandparents who live in Northumberland.

I ran down the platform and she dropped her suitcase to the floor and we hugged. My tummy was all fluttery at the feel of her arms around me and she must have felt the same as we pulled back to look at each other and in that instant something between us changed.

'I missed you' I said.

'And I missed you.' She replied then kissed me on the lips before laughing and we walked to the car arm in arm.

Then when Daddy arrived last night, Ruthy and I had to move all our stuff into the other caravan so that he and Mummy could sleep together. He allowed us to have some wine with our dinner and it was the perfect evening, the sun was still warm until late and the sky didn't get dark until well past midnight.

When we all went off to bed, Ruthy and I were lying on top of the covers of the double bed we were sharing as it was so hot. We were facing each other and she reached out and pushed my hair back from my face then leaned forward and kissed me on the lips again. My entire body was trembling. We kissed and stroked each other for ages then talked for hours before falling asleep in each other's arms.

I am so happy but also very scared. What would our

parents and friends think? I don't think they'd like it at all. So we have decided to keep it our secret.

28th August 1951

I have had the most dreadful few weeks. Mummy and I aren't speaking and I've been told I'm never allowed to see Ruthy again.

After Daddy went home from Silverdale at the end of the weekend, Ruthy and I didn't move back into the other caravan with Mummy as we were enjoying discovering our new feelings for each other. After a few nights of just kissing and stroking, Ruthy took my nightie off completely and started kissing my breasts. It was the most intense experience I've ever had, my whole body was flooded with heat and covered in goose bumps at the same time. I pulled her nightie off too and we pressed our bodies hard against each other, as if we wanted to feel and touch every single part of each other.

Ruthy was on top of me, kissing my neck, and my body was arching up to meet hers when Mummy opened the door and came in. We all froze, then Ruthy gave a strangled little laugh, grabbed the sheet and pulled it over us to hide our nakedness. Mummy gasped and put her hand to her mouth then just walked out.

I scrambled from the bed and started pulling my clothes on. 'Oh my God. Oh god, oh god.' I kept muttering but Ruthy was strangely calm.

'It will be OK', she said, 'We'll be gone soon and then

we'll be able to live how we want. There's nothing they can do.'

She couldn't have been more wrong. We left the next morning, Mummy wouldn't really look at either of us and when she told Daddy what had happened she insisted that something drastic had to be done as I was out of control. So I'm not going back to school, I won't be able to apply to Cambridge and I'm being kept in the house like a prisoner while they try to find a suitable husband for me. I am seriously considering running away.

10th November 1951

Tomorrow is my wedding day. I can't quite believe this is happening. I'm being married off to an old man. Frank is thirty and has been married before but his wife ran off with an American GI after the war. He's the accountant at Daddy's office and although he doesn't seem like a bad person, I don't want to marry him. I don't want to marry anyone but I was too scared to run away and now I'm stuck with it. Ruthy's parents visited and tried to convince Mummy and Daddy that we were just young and curious and that they shouldn't overreact. But Mummy told them to mind their own business, that it was up to her and Daddy how they dealt with me. So, that's that. All of those dreams for me and Ruthy to study, see the world and share a flat in Soho are over. I tried to appeal to Daddy but even though I could see that he was not one hundred per cent sure about what they were doing, Mummy made him go through with it. I hate her.

14th January 1953

I haven't written for such a long time. What was the point? This was a book for hopes and dreams and all of mine had been ruined. Being married to Frank has not turned out so bad as I'd been imagining, he is kind enough but very dull, as is being a housewife. I cannot begin to describe the tedium of doing nothing but cooking, shopping and cleaning. Mrs Sheldon had to teach me how to do it all, and I'm not sure I'm very good at any of it but especially the cooking. Frank never says anything but sometimes he seems to find it hard to swallow the dinners I make.

Even though Daddy bought Frank and I our own house when we married, it turns out that his business was not doing so well and he had to close it down. Frank had to get a new job, which he did with no problem, so we have been fine. Mummy left Daddy and he lives in the caravans now. I think he's gone a bit mad. I haven't seen or heard from Mummy since last summer when it all happened. Nor do I want to. She is living with a man that Daddy used to do business with; Michael says he's sure that she was already having an affair with him.

So as you can see, life has been a bit depressing. But here I am writing in my book of hopes and dreams again. A new year, new dreams? No, a new year, old dreams. Over Christmas I saw Ruthy again. For the first time since we left the caravans that summer. She was home from Cambridge for her Christmas holiday. I bumped into her in town when we were both doing our Christmas shopping. I thought my feelings for her may have faded but as soon as I saw her I knew nothing had changed. For me anyway. I had no idea how she might feel.

'Ruthy.' I whispered as I stopped in front of her, my voice cracking. My heart was pounding so hard I could hear it in my ears. She looked so lovely but also so different. Her dark curly hair was cut into her neck and she was wearing black trousers under a coat that swung around her hips. I felt so dowdy and old-fashioned in comparison.

But her face lit up as soon as she saw me. She dropped her shopping bags and pulled me into a tight hug. I could feel her heart beating as fast as mine. Neither of us said anything for ages. Just clung to each other. I was feeling things that I thought I never would again, that I never felt when Frank touched me. I knew then that I couldn't let her go again. Frank was at work and wouldn't be home for hours so we came back here and spent the whole afternoon together. We started out just talking but we soon couldn't keep our hands off of each other. We made a plan. When Ruthy finishes university we will move to Soho together. We won't let what other people think stop us this time. She'll work while I get my degree. From now on I'm going to put a bit of the housekeeping money aside every week so by the time we go I should have a good amount.

Before she went back to Cambridge yesterday we spent as much time together as we could. My mind and my body feel alive again.

30th March 1953

I'm pregnant.

1st May 1953

Frank is very excited at the thought of being a father but I don't want this baby. How can I take a baby to Soho with me for my new life with Ruthy. A baby was never part of the plan. It's due on 16th September. I already look fat. Michael was here last week and I wanted to ask him to help me but I couldn't think what to say, where to start. Now he's gone. Off to London to do a doctorate. He's to be a marine biologist. It seems like everyone is doing the things they want with their lives apart from me. I wrote to tell Ruthy today.

19th May 1953

My last birthday in my teenage years. I received a parcel in the post from Ruthy. A beautiful shawl. The message in the card said: Happy birthday and many congratulations darling, I can't wait to meet your little one. R x

What does she mean by that? Can we still have our Soho life – is she saying this changes nothing?

14th August 1953

I am so large now I feel like a tank as I try to manoeuvre myself around. Even though I didn't want this baby, I am looking forward to meeting her now. Ruthy has been home for the summer and we did the ring on a string test. It's a girl. We'll be all girls together in our Soho flat. Ruthy still wants me – she says that we'll find a way to make this work. She has just one more year to complete at Cambridge then we can go. I feel bad about Frank if I think about it too much but I have to be able to have the life I want. I didn't want to marry him so it's not really my fault.

11th September 1953

I have a baby boy. Kenneth. Not a girl after all. He is gorgeous though. His eyes are blue at the moment but they told me that would change, and he has very fair soft downy hair all over his head. He was born on 1st September – so a little early – and we came home from the hospital a couple of days ago. My feelings for little Ken are fierce, as if I could eat him all up. As soon as they put him in my arms the love I had for him took my breath away. Frank is smitten and can't stop looking at him. It's very sweet. But I hope he doesn't get too attached.

28th December 1953

It's happened again. Ruthy and I have been caught in bed together. She was home for Christmas and came round on Christmas Eve to see me, and meet Ken. Frank was at work still and we had lunch then I put Ken down for his sleep. As soon as we came out of the nursery she took my hand and led me into mine and Frank's bedroom. The months of being apart made us both more eager. We didn't hear Frank come in, he'd been allowed to leave early for the festive season, and then all of a sudden he was there in the bedroom. Looking down at our naked bodies with such a look of disgust on his face that, for a moment, I felt ashamed.

Ruthy told him though. She told him we love each other and will be together as soon as she was done with the university. He was so controlled. Cold. He told her to get out and never come back. He's been the same with me ever since. Said there is no way that I will ever take his son away from him. That I can do what I like but Ken stays. And he will go to the authorities to make sure of that. Apparently what Ruthy and I feel for each other is not just disgusting, but illegal. So I'll have to stay. I can't leave Ken behind.

KATE

To say that it was a bit of a shock to read all of that in Granny's diaries would be something of an understatement. I remember Ruth, she was Granny's best friend and always around when Jules and I were growing up. Were they still lovers then? Ruth had a daughter, Virginia; she was much younger than Ken and used to babysit for us sometimes. Maybe it really had just been a passing phase, although I don't recall there ever being a husband on the scene. They do say though that some women have lesbian experiences in their teens. Not that I did. But then I didn't have any sexual experiences until I was twenty when I lost my virginity to Christopher Granger, who was on my course at university. I couldn't wait to tell Jules what I'd discovered. Poor Granny.

•••

The doors opened and the first passengers spilled out. I scanned the faces for Jules. When I saw her she was pale and tired as if the holiday in Devon and how well we were when we left was a figment of our imaginations.

'Hi,' she said as she stopped in front of me.

We hugged then walked to the car in silence, Jules pulling her suitcase behind her with one hand the other linked through my arm. We didn't really say much of anything until we were on the motorway heading north.

'What do you think's going on?' Jules said without looking at me.

'God, I don't know. Ken won't say a thing until you're here too and the letters didn't really say much beyond her wanting to get in touch with us. From the early ones I get the impression she might have been sick. They're in my bag. Read them.'

I concentrated on driving while Jules sat quietly and read through all the letters.

'How could Granny have done this?'

'I'm sure she thought she was doing the best thing for us, Jules. Despite how we might feel about it now.'

'Maybe when we were little. But not now, she could have told us when we grew up. She should have told us years ago. We're in our thirties for fuck's sake.'

There wasn't much I could say to that. We both stayed lost in our own thoughts until we were turning off at Junction 33. Nearly home.

While Jules was in the shower I made toasted cheese, ham and tomato sandwiches. We munched on them and drank apple juice while I wondered how to tell her what I'd found out about Granny.

'What do you think he's going to tell us?' She said.

'I don't know. All he said was they lied about where she'd gone. Well, that's the bit that Ken lied about, Granny lied about a lot more. Ken says he didn't know about the letters and Laura being in touch with Granny and I think I believe him.'

'Why would they lie? And why would they make up such an awful lie that she left us to go off with another man? There's no man in her letters for ages after she starts writing.'

'Jules, there's no point in sitting in here speculating. Ken knows what lies they told and why they told them so he's the only one that can answer these questions.'

'I suppose so.'

'But I've found hundreds of Granny's diaries. Going back to when she was seventeen. I haven't looked yet to find out about Laura, I wanted to wait for you, but I've found out all sorts about Granny.'

•••

As we pulled up outside Ken's, Jules turned to me.

'I can't quite get my head around all of this. Are you going to be alright Kate? This isn't going to set you off again is it?'

Despite everything I laughed. 'No, I don't think it's going to set me off again. I've managed to get through the last few days finding out all of this without going off on a bender so I think I'm going to be OK.'

I hadn't had time to tell her about the meeting, and Abena, and how it'd made me see things with even more clarity than the accident did. It was if the rigid self-control that I'd always thought of as strength was being replaced by the real thing, drip by drip. But she didn't know that yet.

'Come on, let's go find out what Ken's been hiding all these years.'

My determination to remain positive took a hammering though when he opened the door. He looked dreadful. He'd aged ten years since he'd left the garden. Jules looked at me with wide eyes as we followed him in.

'Dad, are you alright?' Jules asked his back as he walked away from us into the living room.

Although it was a lovely warm day outside, he had all the curtains pulled and the doors and windows shut. It was stifling and my breath caught in my throat. I'd not been there before so I didn't feel like I could do anything but Jules yanked the curtains open and then pushed the windows as wide as they would go. Then she opened the doors into the back garden. Ken sat on the sofa without saying a word. I looked round for signs that he'd been drinking but couldn't see anything. And it was clean and tidy, just very hot. I sat down on the chair behind me, facing him on the sofa, and Jules sat next to him.

'Dad, are you OK? Have you been eating?'

He nodded. 'Yes, I've eaten. I haven't been drinking. I've been thinking, remembering.'

I was scared then and I didn't want to hear what he was going to say so I went into the kitchen to make tea. I didn't know how to behave. It'd been so long since I was a part of this family that I didn't know how to be in it any more. When I took the tea in they were sat in silence but Jules had hold of Ken's hand in between them on the sofa. I raised my eyebrows at Jules as I put the tray down on the table in front of them and she answered with a shrug. Ken had reverted to type – sitting on the sofa saying nothing. Different sofa, different house, different Kate and Jules come to that, but here we were again needing something from Ken that he seemed incapable of giving. I clenched my fists and took a deep breath, I wanted to shout at him but I swallowed my words. I knew that wouldn't help any of us so I took my mug of tea and sat down.

'I know I need to tell you,' Ken finally said, 'I just don't know how. I don't know where to start and it was all such a long time ago.'

'Well why don't you start by telling us where she went?' Jules said.

He looked like he was going to talk, then faltered, then started, then faltered again. I bit my lip.

'She was sick.'

I met Jules's eyes. I was right, I'd sensed from the early letters that she'd been sick.

'Well, why couldn't we be told she was sick? And why did that mean she had to go away and never come back?' I said.

'It's complicated.'

'I'm sure it is. But we have a right to know the truth. Especially after all this time.'

Ken dropped his head down into his hands, his elbows resting on his knees, and staring at the floor the whole time, told us the truth at last.

We were all crying by the end. I couldn't see Ken's face but I could see the teardrops falling from it onto the carpet.

'But why didn't you tell us she was sick?'

'Because then you would have wanted to see her. She was in a bad way; it wouldn't have been good for you to see her like that.'

'But she must have got better?' I looked at Jules for support but she was staring out the window.

'She didn't. Not for a very long time. They told me I should stop going. That I agitated her. Your Granny went though. For two years she was in there. They had her doped up for a lot of it as she just cried and cried when she wasn't. They gave her electric shock treatments.'

'So how did she end up in New Zealand?' My voice shook.

'I don't know. She was slowly getting better apparently, returning to her old self. They were giving her more talking therapy and fewer drugs. I was thinking that soon I would be able to start visiting her again when she was released and she just didn't come back.'

'But Granny knew all along where she was, and you didn't?'

Ken finally looked up at me then. 'It seems that way doesn't it?'

Jules had been silent throughout the whole revelation. Her face was even whiter and more drawn, she wouldn't meet my eye or look at Ken. She just stared out into the sunny garden, it felt like she wasn't really in the room with us anymore.

Why did that have to be the story? Why did it have to be more misery? Why couldn't something in our family just be good for a change? I was supposed to be coming here to get over Jimmy and start afresh but instead there was more shit to deal with. A dead sibling, a mad mother, suicide attempts, and a whole fucking lifetime of lies.

My whole body was shaking as I tried to control the rage that coursed through me but I couldn't, it burst out. 'I am so sick of this. All of this. I knew I was right to keep away from you all these years. How could you treat us like this and lie to us about everything our whole lives? What the fuck is the matter with you?'

Jules held her hand out towards me. 'Kate! This is not just about you. Think what Dad's had to go through too.'

I sat back down, deflated. Ken had a dead child, a disappearing wife, a lying, lesbian mother (did he even know about that?), and two little girls to bring up. Did other families have lives like this? Lives that just veered off in different directions with no warning? Get up, think it's a normal day, but no, everything you thought about your life is going to be blown out of the water today. After today you've got a different life. Just like that.

'Sorry.' I said. 'I have to go. Get some air. I'm going for a walk.'

Jules was alarmed. 'I'll come with you. Dad will too, we'll all go.'

'No, I want to be on my own.'

'But Kate-'

I talked over her. 'I won't drink. I won't go off the rails. I just need some time by myself. I promise I'll be alright.'

...

I walked down onto the canal path and out past the old mill buildings that were now offices and cafes, under the bridge past the narrow boat docking station where holiday sailors stocked up on water and enjoyed lunch at the Water Witch. I didn't stop in the pub, I walked straight past and followed the path out of town. It didn't take long before there were just fields and trees and the canal. The walking calmed me.

After about forty minutes of walking along the canal path out towards Halton, I sat down on the grass and watched the water. I hadn't expected that from Ken. I don't know what I'd expected, but not that. I came to the conclusion that we were a weak-minded family. Laura, Ken and me all unable to cope with the things that life threw at us. Just Jules to go when something happened in her life that she couldn't control. Because it would. I'd learnt that. Would finding this out about Laura and Granny be the thing that ignited the family weakness in her mind? I lay back down on the grass and stared at the sky wishing for a normal life, if there was such a thing. I lay in the sun for a while mulling everything over. I wasn't going to start ranting and raving. There was no changing the things that already happened but I could make sure that the future was better. Make my own life, without Jimmy, let the past go and concentrate on being happy instead of wallowing in self-pity.

I walked back to Ken's. 'I bought lunch. Come on, let's go eat it in the garden.'

There was a tone in my voice that hadn't been there for a long while, if ever. We sat at the garden table and ate the hummus and carrot sandwiches I bought back with me and no-one really said anything. But it was alright. We were alright.

•••

Jules and I read through Laura's letters again, trying to discover hidden meanings between the lines, see if there was any sign of the madness Ken had told us about. There wasn't. There was no clue as to why she'd just accepted Granny's reasons for not getting in touch and didn't insist. They also didn't say why she was in New Zealand, but why would they? It seems that Granny knew all along that Laura was out of hospital and why she'd gone to New Zealand.

'Why has she stopped writing do you think?' Jules said.

'I don't know. Maybe she thought there was no point anymore. We don't know her.'

'Do you think Granny ever intended to tell us?'

'Well yes, that must be what the letter she sent me before she died was about.'

We both went quiet then. Thinking. Thinking. Always thinking. No wonder I'd been going mad.

'I'm going out anyway.' I said, standing up. 'There's a group counselling session again today. I went last week. It was good, I think it can help.'

'That's great, Kate. Will you come straight back after?'

'You could come with me. Your – our – mum disappeared too.'

'No, I don't think so. I could meet you after though.'

'I'll call you.'

•••

When I got to the meeting it was just Abena and Clive there again. I sat down with them. There was something about Abena that made me feel calmer. If she could cope with what happened to her then I could cope with what'd happened to me.

'Hello Kate. I'm so pleased you came again.' Clive said.

Martin didn't turn up and nor did anyone else so about ten minutes later, Clive said as it was just the three of us why didn't we go somewhere nicer to talk. We ended up sitting on a sunny bench by the canal and I told them about Jimmy and how I hadn't been able to deal with it all. Went into meltdown. Granny dying, waking up in the hospital, moving home to Lancaster again.

'I'm so sorry for your troubles, Kate.' Abena said and I knew she really meant it. I blinked hard so the tears welling up wouldn't spill over.

'There's more.' I said.

I told them, voicing it for the first time, really admitting it to myself for the first time instead of pushing the thoughts away every time they came into my head, that I was sort of glad about Jimmy. Not about what happened and the not knowing but that being without him had made me realise a lot about myself, about him and about our relationship. That I could see now that I'd married him as I didn't want to be alone, that he was the first man to show any real interest in me so I just…settled.

I sobbed loudly once I'd confessed this and Clive put his arm around my shoulders while Abena leant across him and held my hand. Neither of them said anything, they just let me cry myself out.

'Unbelievably, there's more again,' I said, once I'd got control of myself enough to speak again.

My nose was blocked and my voice cracked and broken as I told the final instalment about Laura, and Ken, and Granny, and lies, lies, lies. There didn't seem to be any tears left though and I just sat there feeling numb once I'd finished.

'My goodness Kate. What an awful lot you have had to deal with in the last year,' Clive said and squeezed my shoulders where his arm was still draped around me. 'I'm so glad that you have found the strength to come to our group. You can get past all of this you know.'

He told me his story then. His daughter was fourteen when she ran away after an argument and she was never seen again. That was eight years before and her body had been found in a woods outside Manchester three years ago. The police said it had been there since she'd left, that her killer must have got her straight away and dumped her body there within a matter of days of her running away. He blamed himself for being too strict with her, forcing her to run away. She was fourteen. She wanted to dance and wear makeup and gossip with her friends, she didn't want to go to church with him. He should have let her; he knows that now. Then he would still have her.

Instead he has nothing. He lost his faith, his wife and all hope. Then he started coming to the group about a year after Nicola's body was found. His wife had been gone four years, his daughter six and he just needed somebody to talk to. The group was being run by a young woman called Lena then. Her little sister had gone missing in Australia, hadn't been heard from in three years. She was only in her late twenties but so strong the way she dealt with life. When she moved away, Clive took over running the group so he could help others to come to terms with people they love going missing.

'So what are you going to do now?' Abena asked me.

'I don't know. I feel overwhelmed and confused. Go home and think about it I suppose.'

I said goodbye and set off to walk home, my head buzzing with it all, but I felt lighter, freer.

•••

When I walked in the front door Jules came running into the hallway. She was semi-hysterical and babbling at me.

'Calm down Jules. What's happened?'

She'd looked online and Laura's name was still registered at the address on the last letter. She'd got a phone number, we should ring her. The shock winded me and my legs weakened, my knees started to buckle. I held on to the door frame.

'Don't be stupid Jules. We can't just ring up.'

'Why not?'

I walked into the kitchen and sat down at the table. Jules followed me.

'Why not?'

'I can't do it. Could you really just pick up the phone and call her?'

'Don't you want to talk to her?'

'Yes. No. I don't know. Definitely not yet.'

'Why not? When then?'

'God Jules. I don't know. Give me time to think will you.'

I needed to get away from her so I went back out again. Walked round to the Greggy, it was quiet in there on a weekday afternoon and I got a cup of peppermint tea and sat in the corner by the window where the sun was shining in. Jules needed to stop and think about this properly. We couldn't ring Laura up out of the blue like that. What would we say? Just blurt it out over the phone that although it happened nearly twenty-five years ago we just found out that she aborted our little brother or sister then went mad.

While I was thinking about what we should do, my phone rang. When I saw that it was Baz my heart missed a beat. We hadn't spoken in months. My mouth was dry as I answered.

'Kate, I've spoken to Jimmy,' he said.

My breath was catching in my throat. I stood up to go outside. I couldn't get any air. The darkness whooshed in.

When I came round, the barmaid had put me in the recovery position. I was on the floor in front of the table I'd been sat at. She was talking on my phone.

'Alright, love?' she asked when she saw I'd opened my eyes. 'She's coming round,' she said into the phone. 'OK, see you in a bit.'

I sat up. The memory of what Baz had said hitting me instantly. 'That was your sister, she'll be here soon,' the barmaid said as she helped me up and sat me back down on the chair. 'You gave me a fright you did. Made ever such a loud bang when you hit the floor.'

'Baz. I was talking to Baz.'

'Yes, I spoke to him. He told me to ring your sister. You'll be alright, you just fainted. Only out for a couple of minutes, you were. Let me get you a drink.'

She came back with a brandy. I drank it down in one and the warmth flooded through me. The first drink I'd had since before I was in hospital. It was so good, the familiar glow as it spread through my veins. Jimmy was alive.

I picked up my phone and called Baz back.

When I got off the phone I ordered another double brandy. I was half way through it when Jules came rushing through the door.

'Kate, what's happened. Are you OK?' She stopped dead when she saw the glass in my hand. 'Oh my God, you're drinking. What are you doing?'

'Jimmy's alive. Baz has seen him. He did leave me.' My voice broke at the end.

Jules looked like she might faint this time. 'What?' She

screeched. 'Where is he? Where's he been all this time?'

The barmaid was eyeing us warily. Fainting, screeching, crying, we were the kid of customers a bar could do without. Jules sat down opposite me, shaking her head, her eyes wide.

'He's in Wales. He's got a baby. He'd been having an affair all along.' I gulped back the rest of the brandy. I thought Jules would tell me to stop but she went and got two more.

'The complete fucking bastard,' she said as she sat down. 'Who with?'

'What's the matter with me, Jules? Why would he treat me like so badly after all that time?'

'Oh Kate, it's not your fault. He's a coward, obviously.'

'Baz said that Jimmy had asked him to tell me, that he still couldn't do it himself but that he wanted me to know so that I could move on. How considerate of him.'

All this time, while I'd been going mad, he'd been playing happy families with his new baby on a farm in Wales. I couldn't quite get my head round it. It was surreal.

'She was the barmaid in a pub near his work. Bronwyn.' The one they'd said had left the week before when I went looking for Jimmy in the city. How close I'd been to finding out the truth all those months ago. 'They're living on her parent's farm in Wales. Jimmy doesn't even like the countryside.'

But even as I said that I realised that I didn't really know who Jimmy was. The man I thought I knew wouldn't have left all of the people who loved him in limbo for so long, always wondering what had happened to him. Jules and I stayed in the Greggy all evening and she listened to me weep and wail over more brandies as I tried to understand why he had done that to me.

Over the next few weeks I seemed to operate on auto-pilot. It didn't even seem important anymore to find out why Granny had lied or why Laura had given up trying to contact us. I slept a lot, walked a lot and got drunk. When I came stumbling in at three o'clock one afternoon pissed out of my face and raging at Jules, she finally lost it with me.

'Enough Kate. You can't do this again. You can't just give up again. Yes, it's a fucking terrible thing to have happened but you know what, you just have to think so what in the end. So fucking what. We'll all die one day and none of it will matter so get a fucking grip will you.'

I cried myself to sleep then got up the next day and rang Clive, told him what had happened. I went to the group session the day after that and Abena just held my hand while I cried again. Martin turned up drunk and I looked at him and knew that would be me if I didn't try to keep focused on the positives. Didn't learnt to say 'so what' but just carried on saying 'why me'. Was being able to get in touch with Laura again after all this time a positive? I couldn't decide, so kept making excuses when Jules tried to talk to me about getting in touch with her.

Then one day it was if I had thawed. I was home alone and suddenly I really wanted to know what had happened with Granny and Laura. So I went upstairs and started reading Granny's diaries again.

LAURA

The journey took forever and Una barely said a word to me all the way. My mind was still fuzzy from the drugs they'd given me that morning. There was going to be no more of that as far as I was concerned. I didn't know if Una wasn't talking because she didn't know what to say to me after everything that had happened or because she felt bad about what she was making me do. Because she did make me. I didn't want to leave. I wanted to go home and be with my little girls. With Ken. I still loved him then and a part of me has never stopped. I wish I'd been stronger, stood my ground. What would life have been like if I'd insisted? But I was scared and confused, so I didn't.

When the car came to a stop outside the terminal and I looked at Una's stony face I couldn't believe it. We'd always been so close. She was the only one that carried on visiting me.

'I don't want to go, Una.' My voice was tiny, which was how I felt. I'd not been out of the hospital grounds for two years. Surely making me do this as soon as I'd left was not the right thing?

Something in Una broke then and she pulled me roughly into her arms and hugged me tight.

'I know you don't but it really is for the best. For now. We'll sort something out soon when the girls are a little older and you're more like your old self.'

I wasn't sure who my old self was anymore. I figured I'd probably be finding a new me. 'But it's so far away.'

Una looked as sad as I felt when I said that but she shook me briskly by the shoulders.

'It'll be good for you, Laura. You'll see. A fresh start. An adventure!'

A sob that I'd been trying to suppress burst out of me. 'But I don't want an adventure. I want my babies back.'

Una dropped her arms from around me. 'They're not your babies anymore, Laura. It's been two years and they've grown up. They're getting over it, putting it behind them. We can't do this to them now. It was so hard at the beginning and they've had to come to terms with so much.'

'But-'

Una held up her hand. 'No. No buts. Believe me this is the right thing. You will see them again, of course you will, but we have to think about what is best for them.'

'I could live nearby and we tell them when you think it's right. It doesn't have to be now.'

'How would you live? You're still not right, Laura, and this way you can get back on your feet properly. Kathy and Rob are good people; they'll look after you. It's wonderful where they live. You'll see. It's for the best. Then when you're completely better you can come back and the girls will be older and able to cope with you reappearing in their lives and understand why you've been gone.'

After so long of not thinking for myself and just doing what I was told, I did what I was told again and got on the plane to New Zealand. And I never went back to England again.

Every time I tried to get back in touch with Kate and Jules,

Una always had convincing reasons for why it wasn't the right time. Why it would do more harm than good. And I let her talk me out of it every time. I should have been stronger but a part of me was scared that she was right, and the last thing that I wanted to do was cause more problems for my girls.

UNA

18th February 1989

While I'm so relieved that she got on that plane and went, I've been questioning myself all day about whether I've done the right thing. Part of me thinks that I should have given her a chance to get back on her feet and then see how things went but a much bigger part knows that it's better to protect the girls, keep them safe.

She didn't see what they were like. The nightmares, the bed wetting, the tantrums and tears. They've been so much better this past six months. How could we disrupt them again? And what if Laura were to relapse? Go mad again? How could they cope with that if she reappeared in their life just to vanish again? No, this way is definitely for the best.

It's much better for them to be with me. I can give them the security they need. I've seen what having an unreliable and often absent mother has done to Ken. Oh, he loves me and we're close but I know he resents me for it. This is my chance to put it right, make sure that Kate and Jules don't have the same. Be there, finally, for Ken.

Ruthy says I'm wrong though. That I'm playing God in their lives the way people did in ours. But even though Ruthy and I never did get that life in a Soho flat we've still had our time together. Still loved each other and been happy together on our many trips and holidays, when we could pretend for a while that we were a proper couple. And Frank and Ken got to be happy too. So yes, I'm definitely doing the right thing.

KATE

When Jules came home I gave her the diary to read. Neither of us could be angry with Granny anymore. She really had thought she was doing the right thing for us. Jules insisted that we write to Laura. If I didn't do it with her she would write on her own.

'It's been weeks since you said give you time to think. Well, I have. I'm going to write to her.'

'OK, let's write to her.'

She clapped her hands together like an excited child. Why didn't she feel any of the worry I did? We had no idea what she might be like. We didn't know her, our memories of her were sketchy and old. Why couldn't Jules see how many things could go wrong? We wrote the letter though, told her of Granny's death, my discovery of the letters, that if she would like to write back then she could reach us at Granny's address.

Then it sat on the kitchen table for two days while we tried to pretend we didn't know it was still there. It was different talking about sending her a letter and actually doing it, even for Pollyanna Jules. Then, on day three, we sent it. From that moment on it was like we had taken in a giant breath and were unable to let it out again properly until we had a response.

It took ten days and then the postman delivered a letter that looked exactly like all the ones Granny had in the box. Jules found it and came into my room holding it in front of her calling me to wake up. Then we sat and stared at it lying between us on the kitchen table.

'Are we going to leave it there for a few days?' Jules asked.

I shook my head. 'No. We're going to open it.'

I picked it up and handed it to her. 'Read it out.'

Jules slit the envelope open with a knife and cleared her throat. I watched her face intently as she started to read.

'Dear Kate and Julia,

I can't believe it's really you after all these years. I am so happy to hear from you and sorry to hear of Una's death. She was a good woman. I'm sad that she didn't speak to you of our contact before she died but I do know that she only ever wanted what was best for you both.

How is Ken? I hope he is well and that you are all happy. I never believed I would ever hear from you again and I can't begin to describe what I felt when I received your letter. Please write to me again soon to tell me more about yourselves and your lives. Do you have families of your own now?

I have been living in New Zealand for twenty years, and it seems quite incredible to me that so much time has passed so quickly. Although I have a partner, as I believe you call them now, Barry, I have not had any more children and you have never been far from my mind.

I'm so glad that you got in touch and I really hope to hear from you again soon. I'm sure you are both feeling as overwhelmed as I am though so please don't feel any pressure. Whenever you are ready to write again I will enjoy hearing your news after so many years. You can email me at laura@thebakehouse.co.nz – I don't know if you remember but I always loved baking. I now have my own bakery and cafe, which has been very hard work but a lot of fun over the years.

As you have read my letters to Una you will know that I never wanted all this time to pass without contact between us. I should have been stronger and insisted that I be allowed to see you but I thought that maybe Una was right and you would be better off without the disruption that my return to your lives would have been. But we cannot change what has happened and I hope that instead we can start to make up for these lost years now.

With love always,

Laura xx

Jules put the letter down on the table and I picked it straight up and read through it again quickly. It was a lovely letter. Open and friendly. She said no pressure. It was exactly the response you'd want, which made me suspicious.

'It's too perfect. If she's so loving and balanced why did Granny keep her away from us all those years?'

'Why do you have to be so negative all the time, Kate? It's like Mum said in the letter, Granny had her reasons. We know from her diaries she thought she was doing the right thing. She wouldn't have done anything to hurt us deliberately.'

'Why are you so sure that it's all going to turn out to be a happy ending? We don't know her, she's been gone from our lives for so long. She was mad. Maybe she still is.'

'Well, she doesn't seem it in that letter.'

We argued back and forth for a while but it was half-hearted. I knew that Jules was going to carry on this correspondence with Laura even if I didn't and I also knew that there was no way I'd let her do it on her own. No matter how scared I was that it might end badly, I did want to see her again too. After everything that had happened, and all that I'd learnt about myself, I knew that to move on to whatever was going to come next, I had to. And that no matter how much things might hurt, it was better to do them and feel the pain than live a life with no strong emotions.

•••

The plane began its final descent into Auckland Airport and I gazed out the window. It wasn't what I'd been expecting – the height of summer in a sub-tropical climate, sunshine is what I was expecting. Instead the gloomy clouds seemed barely able to lift themselves from the ground and rain slid down the plane window. A choppy grey sea crashed into little brown cliffs covered in scrubby green grass. Jules pushed me backwards in the seat so she could get her first glimpse of New Zealand too. I still couldn't quite believe we were there. After a flurry of emails back and forth we were suddenly arranging to visit. Then we were getting on a plane.

I felt strangely detached from it all. I'd felt this way since we'd left Kuala Lumpur – the nearer we got, the further I retreated until now I felt as if I was watching everything that Jules and I were doing rather than actually being a part of it. We didn't even leave the airport in Auckland, though after sitting in a cold and half empty lounge for almost two hours, the detachment had gone and I was tired and getting grumpy. We were eventually herded on to a small plane to take us to Christchurch in the South Island. From there we'd drive in our rented camper van to the little town where Laura lived, Akaroa. After visiting Laura we'd go touring. Jules's idea, she'd always wanted to do it apparently. She also thought it would help us to understand Laura better to see some of the land she'd lived in for the past two decades. Jules can be very hippy. But you already know that. Despite the trepidation I felt about meeting Laura, I was starting to feel that sense of freedom that Jules had always gone on about when she talked about travelling.

We collected the camper van and Jules drove first. We stopped at a mini-mart for provisions then headed out on the motorway, which was just a two lane road with occasional passing lanes and hardly any other cars. It was all so empty.

'Hit the road Jack, don't you come back, hit the road Jack and don't you come back no more,' Jules sang.

She bounced on her seat and it was infectious. I started to feel excited too. My first ever big road trip. I was so glad to be doing it with Jules and I loved that she was still excited about life when most people lose that when they get older. I don't think I'd ever been like that

'I read about a lovely campsite about half way between here and Akaroa. We'll stay there tonight and then drive the rest of the way tomorrow, stay a night in the campsite there, then we'll go to Laura's.'

The excitement dimmed a bit. Laura. Was it going to be traumatic and upsetting like everything else with our family? But I pushed that thought away. Maybe Jules was right, maybe we did deserve something to go right for once. Maybe it would be positive. I tried not to dwell on it anyway, instead focusing on the incredible scenery. Craggy, purple mountains at the end of the vast flat plain, so much blue sky filled with big billowy clouds. Space all around. I tried to stay awake to take it all in and keep Jules company but it'd been such a long journey and before I knew it my head had fallen backwards and I was sleeping.

When I woke up it was dark. The camper had been parked and Jules had gone. I opened the window and called her and she appeared almost instantly.

'Where are we?'

'I'm not sure. I think I might have taken a wrong turn. I've been looking for the campsite for ages and I can't find it. This is a car park at the side of the road, a viewing point it said. I think we should just stay here and then we can find our way tomorrow when it's light.'

'OK. You should have woken me though.'

'That's OK. Now I get to rest while you make us something to eat.'

I made beans on toast and a cup of tea while Jules lay on the seats at the table and read the Lonely Planet; planning an itinerary to make sure we saw as much as possible. Apparently the things we definitely couldn't miss were the glaciers, the pancake rocks and whale watching in Kaikoura. She also wanted to climb a mountain.

'Don't worry, not a big one – we can walk up and down in about eight hours. And we should go to Golden Bay, it's supposed to be amazing there – the Abel Tasman National Park. There's a chocolate shop in a tiny place called Collingwood where you can get the most delicious handmade chocolates.'

There were a whole host of other things too but she didn't have time to tell me as the beans were ready.

After we'd eaten we sat in the camp chairs outside wrapped in sleeping bags and stared at the sky. I'd never seen stars like it, it quite took my breath away and I felt small and insignificant, a tiny speck of flesh and bone in something much vaster. It made me realise once again that everything I'd been through didn't really mean much in the grand scheme of things. We were both quiet and sat there for ages looking at the stars before going in and curling up in the bed and sleeping like the dead.

When I woke the next morning the van was filled with sunshine. The spot where Jules parked in the dark was on top of a hill with views out across the peninsula that stretched for miles. There was a glinting blue sea in the distance, a winding river far down below and a million shades of green from the rolling hills and woodlands. It was so incredibly beautiful. I woke Jules and after breakfast we set off again, me driving this time.

'I don't want to wait any longer. Let's go and see her today,' Jules said without looking at me as she watched the scenery go by out of the window.

'But she thinks we're coming tomorrow.'

'What difference will it make?'

'I don't know. She might not like it.'

'I think we should.'

I neither agreed nor disagreed, just kept driving. We stopped in a small town and had lunch in a cafe, it was surprisingly good. Savoury muffins filled with gooey melted cheese and roasted peppers. We did some more shopping at the grocers then browsed around an art gallery and jewellery shop. Everything seemed to me made of a blue and silver shell. 'It's called Paua,' the woman in the shop told me. I bought a necklace and Jules a bracelet and we put them straight on then headed off again, Jules behind the wheel this time.

'Kate, wake up. Kate, Kate.'

My eyes opened slowly and I was slumped in the seat of the camper, which was parked next to the sea.

'Come on sleepy head. Wake up. We're here.'

'Where? How long have I been asleep?'

'Akaroa. About an hour.'

'Come on, let's go stretch our legs then we'll get a cup of tea.'

We walked around the small town, sticking to the water's edge. I shivered. A biting wind and billowy clouds that blocked out the sun for minutes at a time meant it was pretty chilly.

'It doesn't feel like summer,' I said.

'Well we're near the Antarctic. There's nothing really between New Zealand and all that ice so it gets really cold down here in the South.' She sounded like a tour guide.

After a cup of tea to warm up we went back to the van and although we hadn't said anything more I knew we were going to Laura's. Jules looked at her map and the address and then set off. We were both silent, nervous.

The little town was so pretty. All of the houses were wooden clapboard with verandas and surrounded by flowers and trees. They looked like the kind of houses where only good things went on. Tall, spindly trees lined the streets and their silvery green leaves glinted in the sun. Their bark was hanging off in long strips as if they'd been sunburnt and were peeling. It all seemed so foreign and I wondered how Laura fitted in, why she came and stayed for twenty years. I didn't feel prepared for meeting her. Our emails steered clear of any big revelations or discussions of the issues. We all agreed – some things need to be talked about in person.

'This is it.'

Jules had parked the van outside one of the pretty wooden houses. It was painted white with olive green shutters, window frames and doors. Green is my favourite colour. A riot of other colours came from the garden; reds, yellows, purples, and more, from the exotic looking flowers that were everywhere and a creeping vine that covered the railings lining the veranda. A swing seat sat just behind the vine. It looked so welcoming, so homely. But neither of us moved. We sat there and stared.

'Are you alright?' I asked.

'Yes, I think so. You?

I nodded. 'Are we going in?'

Before she could answer me, from behind her I saw the olive

green front door swing open and a woman stepped forward from the shadows. A woman that looked like me and Jules, but also like neither of us. The wavy hair was short now and lighter than I remembered. Jules looked round too and the woman ... Laura ... Mum ... lifted her hand in a wave, and her face broke into a smile. I wondered if her hands were still cold all the time.

My hand was on the door opening it and before I knew what was happening I was walking up the path towards her. There was only one way to find out.

Amanda is a nomad who writes for magazines when she's not writing stories. Many of her articles are about engineering and technology developments for helping with climate change and sustainability. At the moment she's house sitting with her husband but in the past fifteen years or so she's lived in a tiny village on Exmoor, in London, the Lake District, Brighton and Lancaster, and also spent three years in New Zealand. She roamed up and down England on a canal narrowboat for several months too and travelled around the South Pacific coconut islands, Australia and Asia.

When Amanda is not writing, she runs writing retreats and competitions through her tiny business, Retreat West, and walks about in wild places. She studied Creative Writing and Literature with the Open University and her short stories have appeared on the Fish Flash Fiction prize longlist, in the best-selling Stories for Homes charity anthology, and in various literary magazines. Her next novel is in progress and she's also working on a short story collection of interconnected stories.

ACKNOWLEDGEMENTS

There are many people that deserve many thanks for helping me get this novel all the way from my initial idea to being published. I can't fit them all in here but the ones that definitely have to have a mention are those that played the biggest part. So first, always, is John: thank you for believing in me unconditionally and making me believe in myself. I could not have done it otherwise.

A big thank you to Shaun Levin and Maggie Hamand for being there at the birth when I wrote the very first scenes in your Advanced Creative Writing class and for the invaluable skills you taught me. But also for your class being the place where I met Jen Squire and Michelle Scorziello, who both played a huge part in helping me develop the story and the characters. Thanks just doesn't quite cover it, Jen and Michelle, for the countless hours of feedback and editorial advice you've given, the countless drafts you've read, and the countless number of times you've spurred me on and told me not to give up. You've listened to me wail and cry, fed me alcohol and cake, made me laugh a lot, and become my good friends in the process.

To Shelley Harris for her invaluable advice about the structure at the very early stages when she book doctored me at the Festival of Writing in York. Isabel Costello for reading my very rough first draft and being so encouraging despite how awful I now see it was! Debi Alper for introducing me to the wonder of psychic distance, giving me confidence in my writing style and teaching me how to self-edit.

Deb and Bob (and Rosie), the wondrous thing you have created at Retreats for You has been such a big part of this and I can't thank you enough for looking after me so well; for freeing my mind to do nothing but write; for your friendship; the great food, drink and conversation; and for all the other lovely writing folk I've met and befriended there.

Sophie Duffy, thank you so much for your insightful and very encouraging edit in the later stages – Una would not be here telling her side of the story without you. Jackie Buxton – how can I ever repay you for introducing me to Matthew Smith, founder and owner of Urbane Publications? Thank you for believing in this book enough to take a chance on it, Matthew. I'm beyond chuffed to be a part of your exciting new publishing house.

RETREAT WEST

LEARN, DEVELOP, GET PUBLISHED

CREATIVE WRITING COURSES, RETREATS & COMPETITIONS

http://www.retreatwest.co.uk

The
Huntingfield
Paintress

by PAMELA HOLMES

£8.99, Paperback
ISBN 978-1-910692-66-0

'A genuinely original, utterly enchanting story' – A.N.WILSON

'A slice of Suffolk history brought beautifully to life' – ESTHER FREUD

'an atmospheric and enjoyable story of a singular and free-thinking woman' – DEBORAH MOGGACH

Plucky and headstrong Mildred Holland revelled in the eight years she and her husband, the vicar William Holland, spent travelling 1840s Europe, finding inspiration in recording beautiful artistic treasures and collecting exotic artifacts. But William's new posting in a tiny Suffolk village is a world apart and Mildred finds a life of tea and sympathy dull and stifling in comparison.

When a longed-for baby does not arrive, she sinks into despondency and despair. What options exist for a clever, creative woman in such a cossetted environment? A sudden chance encounter fires Mildred's creative imagination and she embarks on a herculean task that demands courage and passion. Defying her loving but exasperated husband, and mistrustful locals who suspect her of supernatural powers, Mildred rediscovers her passion and lives again through her dreams of beauty...

Inspired by the true story of the real Mildred Holland and the parish church of Huntingfield in Suffolk, "*The Huntingfield Paintress*" is unique, emotive and beautifully crafted, just like the history that inspired it.

Urbane Publications is dedicated to
developing new author voices, and publishing
fiction and non-fiction that challenges, thrills and
fascinates.

From page-turning novels to innovative
reference books, our goal is to publish what
YOU want to read.

Find out more at
urbanepublications.com